UNDER THIS RED ROCK

ALSO BY MINDY MCGINNIS

The Initial Insult

The Last Laugh

Be Not Far from Me

Heroine

The Female of the Species

This Darkness Mine

A Madness So Discreet

Not a Drop to Drink

In a Handful of Dust

Given to the Sea

Given to the Earth

UNDER THIS RED ROCK

MINDY McGINNIS

KATHERINE TEGEN BOOKS
An Imprint of HarperCollins Publishers

Katherine Tegen Books is an imprint of HarperCollins Publishers.

Under This Red Rock
Copyright © 2024 by Mindy McGinnis
All rights reserved. Printed in the United States of America.
No part of this book may be used or reproduced in any manner whatsoever with-
out written permission except in the case of brief quotations embodied in critical
articles and reviews. For information, address HarperCollins Children's Books, a
division of HarperCollins Publishers, 195 Broadway, New York, NY 10007.
Library of Congress Control Number: 2023937011
ISBN 978-0-06-323041-5

Typography by David Curtis
24 25 26 27 28 LBC 5 4 3 2 1

FIRST EDITION

This one's for me.

This book contains depictions of suicide and suicidal ideation. Readers who struggle with these topics should proceed with caution.

ONE

From the beginning, I have made rules for my monsters.

That they are not real is the first rule, and the one that we all tacitly agree is only occasionally true. I informed them they were not real as a young child, but they became louder; more frantic, fingernails within my brain scratching for purchase, desiring acknowledgment, gray matter shredding as I ignored the plaintive voice that came from under my bed, asking for water. And so the rule was amended—my monsters are real, but only when I cannot ignore them any longer, when the desire for contact has superseded my need to remain sane.

In this way, I have negotiated with them.

Also, it would be helpful to have more friends.

Or at least one.

"Neely? We're going."

This voice is real. This voice is Grandma. This voice also refuses to be ignored and is gratingly nonspecific. Grandma will not say the destination or the function—namely, to put flowers on the grave of my mother and brother for Memorial Day.

"Are you leaving?" asks the girl under my bed, and I give a small kick to the mattress. It's light and chiding, not aggressive, a simple reminder to her that she is not real.

"Neely?"

Grandma is here now, in the doorway, watching me.

"I'm ready," I tell Grandma, yanking my hand away from my neck when she spots it twisting there, furtively pinching.

"You're not," she says. "When's the last time you took a shower?"

There's a snicker from the closet.

My hand goes back up to my neck, fingertips brushing over the line of small bruises and tiny half-moon marks, the topography of invasive thoughts.

"Neely?" Grandma asks again, this time coming into the room. She stands directly in front of me, which is a good move on her part. The more something can fill my five senses, the more chance it has of proving that it is a real thing, in the real world, attempting to interact with me.

I can hear Grandma, see her, smell her. The scent of the lilies that she puts on Mom's grave every year have stuck to her, a trail of bright yellow pollen smears her wrist. They are the flower of resurrection, a promise of everlasting life, a symbol of purity. They belong on the grave of a young mother who was killed by a drunk driver, calmly asking her children to recite their full names and addresses before she died so that we could identify ourselves when the first responders arrived.

Mom gets lilies. Lance gets a plastic display that sticks into the ground, bought on sale, with very little attention paid to the message or the meaning. Last year, Grandpa had grabbed a blue wreath that assured Lance he might be gone but not forgotten, then thanked him for his service. He was never in the armed forces, but it was only one of the lies—he was definitely gone, and the forgetting part was being actively engaged. Grandma and Grandpa practically chase it.

Dead single moms get lilies.

Suicides get half-off, factually inaccurate statements.

Someone grabs my hand, yanks it from my neck.

"Neely, shower!" Grandma says. "We can't take you out looking like . . ." She trails off, trying to find a word that won't break me, won't make me start crying, curl into a ball, or declare the absolute impossibility of personal hygiene today.

"Looking like this," she says. She grabs my wrist, gives it a light squeeze. Unlike my kick to the girl under my bed to remind her she is not real, this is Grandma telling me I am.

I am real, and she is real. The world is real, and something is being asked of me; I must shower and then go say important words to dead bodies that are six feet underground, whose tympanic membranes rotted away years ago and most certainly cannot hear me. Somehow, that is considered sane. But if I answer the girl under my bed, or the man in my closet, that is a problem.

"Okay," I tell Grandma. It's all I've got, the most I can offer right now. I will clean myself and go to a location where we gather all the dead bodies and do what is expected of me. I know these things make Grandma and Grandpa if not happy, then at least a little less worried. And if pretending to be sane can alleviate some of the burden I bring to their lives, I will do it, every day, for as long as I can.

"Sorry," I tell her, digging deep, finding words, working to make my tongue move. "I haven't been sleeping."

"I know, honey," Grandma says, her fingers clenching my wrist. Whether she is saying that she can hear me moving around the house at night or if she's aware that lately I have been answering the monsters, I can't say. Maybe she is simply saying she knows, as if she understands.

Because Grandma doesn't sleep, either.

And she can sympathize with me to a point. Her only daughter married a man that left her with no money and two children that carried a seed of instability growing inside their minds, small root systems developing, tree trunks of madness thickening, making rings, crowding out normality until we wore leaves like crowns.

"Neely!"

Grandma's back, standing in front of me, arms crossed. I've been drawing, ink-stained fingers creating a tree boy and girl, heads intertwined, laced together. His half has died.

I never showered.

"Sorry," I say again. "Sorry." If my mouth makes twenty words today, this will be at least eight of them. I jump to my feet, grab some clothes from the clean laundry basket, and head for the bathroom.

I need to do better. Grandma sees a lot and guesses more. And while she might understand sleeplessness and grief, while she might be familiar with the long night and despair, she can't ever know about the depths, the monsters, and the voices.

Or the fact that sometimes, they have really good ideas.

TWO

I'm greeted by a wave of applause when I step outside.

It's true I have showered, but that's not the reason for the sudden onslaught of joy at my presence; no one has ever been that glad to see me. When I was little, I would take a bow at the cinder block steps of our trailer, acknowledging my fans. Mom loved my confidence and what she dubbed my imagination. Dad frowned, pulled me aside, the first of the very rare moments when we spoke of the seed of madness from which our family tree sprouts.

"Don't react to them," he said, pushing my hair out of my eyes.

"The people?" I asked.

Dad put his hands on my shoulders and turned me in a slow circle, letting me survey the yard. The foxtails reached my elbows, ticks traveling their long stems. A rusted-out red Ford Escort stood on blocks, a tree growing through the windshield.

"Do you see people?" Dad asked.

It had never occurred to me that the sounds needed a source, and I locked eyes with Lance, who was waiting by the truck.

"Other than your brother," Dad clarified, and I shook my head.

"No people," I confirmed.

"Well, that's something at least," Dad said.

Sitting in the truck bed, the hot metal burning the backs of my legs, Lance had turned to me.

"Like this," he said, pointing to his face, which was perfectly blank. "You keep your face like this until you know Mom can hear them. Then it's real."

"Not Dad?" I asked, pushing up onto my knees and glancing through the back windshield, watching Dad sneak a cigarette.

"No." Lance shook his head. "Not Dad."

This is how I learned, early on, that Mom was the litmus test for reality, the only one of us who didn't have to filter the world. I slid down next to Lance, our arms touching in the summer heat, his freckles starting to pop.

"Am I doing it right?" I asked, holding my face perfectly still.

My name came from the tall grass, and I flinched.

"No." Lance smiled. "But you'll get better. What's hard is when they say the bad things."

"Bad things?"

But Dad started the truck then, the engine roaring to life, shaking the chassis, black exhaust fumes pouring out around us. Lance didn't tell me the bad things then, or ever. I don't know how long he fought it, just that he lost.

So far, my only bad thing is the Shitbird Man.

I don't name my monsters, as a general rule. But the Shitbird Man is persistent, and mostly harmless. All he wants to do is tack *shitbird* onto the end of other people's statements. He pops up right away as I get into the back seat of the car.

"How are we doing today?" Grandpa asks, meeting my eyes in the rearview mirror.

"How are we doing today, shitbird?"

I sigh, both because Grandpa has no idea how terrible it is to refer to someone who has auditory hallucinations in the plural, and because the Shitbird Man usually doesn't show up first thing in the day.

On the other hand, Grandpa doesn't know about the voices, so I can't blame him for referring to me as the royal *we*, but also, part of my negotiations with the Shitbird Man is that he gets only three uses of *shitbird* a day, and he just spent one. The downside is that I have to repeat it, or it doesn't count.

I cover my mouth, and whisper quietly, "How are we doing today, shitbird?"

"What, dear?" Grandma turns in her seat, eyebrows drawn together.

"I'm fine," I say, dropping my hand.

My childhood playmates resurface when we arrive at the cemetery, bubbling laughter, unintelligibly shouting. I used to join them, running through the tall grass, loving the invisible friends who also delighted in the tickling touch of the foxtails, answering when they called my name. I learned in kindergarten not to laugh with them, or push them on the swings, not to offer them part of my lunch or introduce them to my classmates. I learned the hard way, Fiona Fugate's brow wrinkling as I explained that the swing wasn't empty and she couldn't have it.

It didn't help that the Shitbird Man showed up right then.

I laugh, and Grandpa meets my eyes in the mirror again. I can't explain that it's actually okay. I'm not having an outburst without stimuli. I'm reacting to a funny memory, like a normal person would. I suppose it's debatable, though, since the memory involves imaginary friends and my suspension from kindergarten for inflammatory language prompted by a disembodied voice.

There are other people at the cemetery, all of us remembering our dead. We did not go to the parade in town, or listen to the mayor give a speech about the patriots of East Independence who gave their lives for their country. The recently departed in the Hawtrey family gave their lives for nothing quite so easily packaged, or explained. Grandma and Grandpa raise their hands in greeting to a few people, who respond in kind but don't approach. The smell of charcoal rises from a nearby house, and two little girls zip past us on their bikes, the gravel path crunching under their wheels. Red, white, and blue streamers fly from their handlebars, and one of them sports a handmade sign that declares, "Yay! A Prade!"

Grandma and Grandpa walk in front of me, and he reaches for her hand as we pass into the shade of a weeping willow, its long fingers brushing against Mom's tombstone.

"Hey, honey," Grandma says, reaching down to yank at some crabgrass that has sprouted at the base. "We brought someone to see you today."

I come forward, as if being nearer makes a difference. Grandpa reaches for my hand, too, but I pull away. It's hot, my palms are sweaty, and feeling someone else's pulse against my own will not help me speak.

Grandma does not have this problem. She talks to Mom like she's still here, telling her that she brought lilies again, that I have finished my sophomore year in school—although she doesn't share my GPA. She tells Mom that they finally recarpeted the living room and that Grandpa's test came back negative.

I glance at him, but he's staring at Grandma's hands while she pulls weeds. I want to ask *What test?* I want to ask why I wasn't told, and I want to say that the reason why I stare blankly is not because I don't care but because I am first determining what has and has not actually happened before I react. I do this so they won't worry. I do this so they won't look at me and see Lance—a burden that may no longer be present but is still heavily felt.

"Neely? Do you want to say something?"

It's Grandma, wanting me to speak, to interact, to talk to my dead mother. But my jaw has hardened, every word she's said counteracting any sounds I might try to make, soldering my teeth together, making speech impossible. The things she says are right and correct, the way that a person is supposed to behave in a cemetery—a place where it's socially acceptable to talk to someone who isn't there. I fight so hard not to do this that when I am asked to, I cannot.

"Do you want to try?" Grandma asks. She puts her hand on my back, like a little pressure on my spine might cause spiritual healing. "Just say whatever is inside. Something you think your mom would want to hear."

But what Mom wanted to hear was our address, full names, and social security numbers, her last duty as a parent to make sure that we could identify ourselves when we were found. That took a while, and the flies had begun to circle Mom's open mouth, the temperature rising in the car as Lance and I sat, securely strapped into our car seats, baking with a corpse in the ditch.

I know that I'm supposed to say things for Grandma right now, not for Mom, or myself, the Shitbird Man, or anyone else. I'm supposed to make Grandma feel better, let her know that I'm okay. But that's not true, and I don't want to get anyone's hopes up. We made that mistake with Mom, the three of us—Dad, Lance, and me—a pact I'm the only one left to maintain.

"I'm going over there," I say abruptly, walking toward Lance's grave.

I don't pull the weeds or place any flowers. I don't participate in the rituals that everyone else does. My rituals happen in private, with witnesses that don't actually exist.

"Well, I fucked that up," I tell Lance.

But he doesn't show up, doesn't add to the conversation or join me at his graveside. Mom never has, either. I don't get the consolation of departed loved ones whispering in my ear; I get a perpetually dehydrated toddler and a hovering foulmouthed dude.

Grandpa walks over, hands me this year's memorial for Lance—a cross of red carnations. They are plastic and will have to be removed once they start to fade, prompting a return trip to the cemetery, one that I will not be invited to, the trip where my brother's flowers are tossed in the community recycling bin at the end.

But they are trying, I remind myself.

Grandma and Grandpa have been trying for a very long time, bringing Lance and me into their home, swelling their household from two to four. The subtraction came after that, and now we are a trio.

I should be nicer, try harder, stop hearing voices.

All these things are important and probably listed in the wrong order.

Beyond Lance's grave is another, older, nearly swallowed by a fast-growing honeysuckle. It's tilted, moss growing along the shaded side, a tuft of rabbit hair stuck to the curve in the top where a hawk had perched, eating its prey.

I wander over, pushing branches aside.

Mary is buried here, but her last name is gone, washed away by rain and years. I don't know when she was born, or when she died. Soon, no one will even know she was Mary.

"How long does it take?" I ask as Grandpa comes up behind me.

"This is sandstone," he says. "It's very soft, so it wears away easily. When I worked at the quarry . . ."

He goes on, but pretty much any story that starts with *When I worked at the quarry* is one that I excuse myself from. And besides, that's not what I meant, and the question wasn't for him.

I was asking Mary how long it takes to be forgotten.

THREE

"I've been thinking maybe it's time for me to get a job," I say, concentrating on my cheeseburger, trying hard not to notice Maddie Sayers behind the counter of the Grill & Chill, dripping caramel over a scoop of vanilla ice cream. I cut my eyes away, focus on Grandma's face. I'm asking for a lot, asking to leave the snow globe of their protection, asking to go out and move through the world like a normal human.

"Why do you want a job?" Grandpa asks.

"Why do you want a job, shitbird?"

Dammit. Of course, in public, and when there's a hot girl a few feet away. I pretend that I'm wiping my mouth, and hurriedly whisper the sentence back into my own palm. "Why do you want a job, shitbird?"

I've got to be absolutely positive that one isn't overheard. Grandpa does have a job, so does Grandma, and I guarantee neither one of them wants it. They were pulled out of retirement when the care and keeping of their grandchildren was foisted upon them. Walmart took them in, and now residents of East Independence can be welcomed by Betsy Holt when they enter and be encouraged to have a good day by Ed Holt as they leave.

Grandma definitely means it; Grandpa, probably not so much.

"Why do I want a job?" I repeat, my stomach tumbling the french fries I just ate, as if examining them for a possible exit strategy back the way they came. I can be honest and tell them that I want to alleviate the financial responsibility that I am the cause of, or that I am becoming aware, as I grow older, that the girl under the bed, the man in the closet, and the Shitbird Man will likely be with me forever. That is approximately *not* the amount of time I want to live in their house, a parasite that drains and returns nothing. If I start now, I can ease myself into normality, depending on the safety they provide less and less, until one day, I can be a real human, in the real world, with a job and a place of my own.

And maybe, just maybe, the man in the closet and the girl under the bed won't make the trip with me.

That's the real answer, the one I can't give. Unfortunately, Maddie drops a can of whipped cream and bends over to get it, right when I'm trying to come up with an alternate, and my mind goes blank, so I choose to skip over the *why* and go straight for the *where*.

"I was thinking I could work at the caverns."

"I used to work with the owner," Grandpa says, inspecting a bit of fried egg that hangs off the end of his fork. "I could probably get you in there, at least get you a leg up on the other kids looking for summer work."

"Well . . ." Grandma glances at Grandpa, the concerned divot above her nose deepening. Grandma never looked her age until Mom died and Lance and I moved in. "I know how much you like it there," she finally says.

They might believe they know this, have watched their granddaughter exploring nature and enjoying history, feeling a connection with the earth and the passing eons. This could be what they think when they see me there, underground, the tension gone from my shoulders, my teeth no longer meeting in a forced, continual grind. They don't know, can't understand, that my monsters don't follow me there.

It was not a rule that I made, for those seem to be permeable and ever fluid, broken at the whim of whoever is strongest in the moment; them or me. But I'd made the discovery early, after Dad left and Mom died, when Grandma and Grandpa did everything they could to make sure Lance and I were normal kids, leading average summertime lives. The pool, the park, picnics—and the caverns, a tourist attraction that brings in outside money. When it gets hot here, people go underground to cool off.

I go there to not be crazy.

"Could be real good for you," Grandpa goes on. "Honest work makes everyone feel better."

"And lots of kids work there," Grandma adds, that Walmart smile still lingering. Once, I heard her welcoming people at church, accidentally adding that they should let her know if they needed help finding anything. She blushed, then ducked into the bathroom, coming out with red-rimmed eyes.

They don't deserve this version of their lives.

Grandpa wants me to get a job because he swears by bootstrap mentality and believes that honest work will cure all ills. Grandma could be brought around to it because she thinks I'm going to make friends. I want to get a job because I don't want them to worry about me, a weight they didn't ask for, an extra person on the perimeter.

But also—this could be good. Actually good, not just I'm going to convince myself that this is good and then find out later I was wrong, like the time I went to Candace Gentry's birthday party in first grade and failed terribly at hide-and-seek because I was shushing everyone who had crowded into the closet with me . . . which was approximately zero real humans.

"The youngest Bailey kid works there, right?" Grandma turns to Grandpa.

"Jake," he says, nodding.

"Josh," I correct, not adding that Josh is a dick. "I'd really like to do this," I say, cutting off my grandparents as they have a small argument about whether Josh is George Bailey's son or his nephew. This is the kind of conversation that they excel at, and it can go on for quite a while if allowed.

"Yes?" Grandma asks, then knocks the question mark off the end, instead repeating it firmly, as if worried that her indecision might infect me. "Yes."

"Good," Grandpa adds, with a sharp, satisfied nod. "I'll talk to John tonight, see if he's got room for you."

But I know that John will, because this is East Independence and personal favors carry a lot more weight than individual merits. We finish eating in a comfortable silence, Grandma not quite able to banish a smile that hovers, perpetually, even when she's not being paid to do it.

That's one version of my afternoon, the real one, the actual one, things that happened that other people witnessed, and so an agreed-upon version of reality has occurred. There's another version, one that I indulge in once I'm at home, safely ensconced in my room, mouthing the words, mimicking the actions, as if replaying it with no audience, sotto voce, with minimal movement can make it real.

I stand at Mom's grave, located at the foot of my bed. I pull weeds alongside Grandma, my hands plucking an inch above the carpet, tossing them over my shoulder. We stand, and she tells Mom they've brought someone along today, pushes her hand against my spine. I reach back and grab it, returning the squeeze, grateful for the support.

"I really miss you, Mom," I say. It's a revision I've earned, a do-over in my mind that might make the next actual cemetery visit easier. The more I practice being normal while I am alone, the better I can get at it in public.

"I miss you and I wish you were here," I say, still speaking to Mom's grave, still feeling that afternoon's light on my face. "I don't know what you would think of me. But I bet you would be worried."

"Try again," the girl under the bed says.

I sigh and close my eyes. She might not be real, but she's not wrong. If I'm trying to get better at being normal, talking about being crazy isn't a good first step.

"I really miss you, and I wish you were here," I say, returning to my first statement.

Grandma's hand presses against mine, and I know I did it right this time. We plant the lilies together; the carpet grinding against my knees feels like cool grass.

"I talk to your mother every day," Grandpa says.

"Do you talk to Lance?" I ask.

I wanted to say it then, but had held back. Here, it comes out. I wait for a second, but there's no feedback from the girl. She must think it's a fair question, so I don't revise. I let it hang, wondering what the answer is. Even in my do-overs, there are rules. I won't put words into other people's mouths. They said what they said; it's me that has to figure out how to interact.

Lance's grave is in the corner; I push aside honeysuckle branches, my fingers pressing on wallpaper. I stand for a second, waiting for Grandpa to follow me, hand over the red carnation cross. I press it into the floor. Just like at the cemetery, it's crooked and off-balance, leaning a little to the right, resting against Lance's stone. I didn't fix it then, and I don't fix it now. Because it doesn't matter.

It's recycling.

"How long does it take?" I ask.

"This is sandstone," Grandpa says. "It's very soft, so it wears away easily. When I worked at the quarry—"

Now I stop the story, breaking through with what I need to know, what matters, what is right and real, and relevant.

"Is it because Lance looked like him?" I ask Grandpa, who has stopped talking.

"Because Lance was Dad and I am Mom, and Dad wasn't worth a good goddamn thing. I've heard you say that, you know. These walls are thin, and I have to talk softly in here by myself, but I have heard you say that more than once."

My finger is out now, and I poke Grandpa. He takes a step backward, across the cemetery grass, toward my bed. He can't answer me, because this is a revision and he is not an active part of it. This is me, redoing my day, reliving my life, doing what I wish I'd done, saying what I wish I'd said.

Sometimes, it takes hours.

Sometimes, I don't sleep at all.

"I'm Mom, and Lance was Dad. You tried, but you couldn't hide how you felt, and he couldn't help who he was. Grandma couldn't watch him eat because he held his fork like Dad. You couldn't talk to him because he sounded like Dad. He knew, and he tried to be better, tried to be less himself, until there was none of himself."

My hand is in a fist now, shaking, tapping against Grandpa's top shirt button, against my mirror, where my own face stares back, snarling.

"But I'm Mom. You tell me all the time. Look like, talk like, act like . . ." My voice rises, following Grandma's pitch and inflection, her singsong optimism twisting my lips, unfamiliar. My fist drops and Grandpa is gone; there's just me staring at me, trying hard to tell the truth. I press my forehead against my own forehead, feel the cold glass, skin on skin.

"I've got bad news, guys," I say, my breath fogging the mirror. "I'm Dad, too."

I step back, taking in myself. My index finger extends from my fist and rises, moving in a slow, small circle next to my ear.

"I'm a lot Dad," I whisper.

"Nobody likes you," the man in the closet says.

I bite my lip and choose not to answer.

FOUR

"You have a black belt in karate."

"I really don't," I mutter, and yank a pillow over my face.

The man in the closet often does this after he has told me that no one likes me, I'm not pretty, or that I probably have cancer. Guilt must be a factor even for the nonexistent, because the next day he'll convince me that I can fly a plane, won a cooking contest, or have been selected as an intern at the White House. Most of the time, I'm able to rationalize that nothing he says is true, but I had tried to board a Greyhound to DC once and was only stopped when the bus driver refused to believe that the president was comping my ticket and he'd be paid when we arrived at 1600 Pennsylvania Avenue.

That was a bad day, and I was lucky that I was only tossed to the curb and told to sober up. I'd found my way home, nobody had called the cops, and I'd made a vow not to act on anything the man in the closet said again—no matter how good it sounded. This is why I will not attempt to roundhouse anyone today. Also, it's my first day at work, so I should definitely not be kicking anyone, black belt or no black belt.

"I'm thirsty," the girl under the bed informs me, her voice seeping through the pillow, no matter how hard I pin the sides against my face.

"Fuuuuuck," I say, feeling the reverberations.

I already made a mistake by responding to the man in the closet. I will not leave out water for the girl. I am going to get up. I am going to get dressed. I am going to brush my hair, and then I'm going to go to my first day at a new job, like a normal fucking person.

Or at least I'm going to pretend really, really hard.

When I park in the employee lot, the heat is already baking up from the tarmac. There's a white Jeep there, as well as a minivan with an OSU air freshener hanging from the rearview mirror. John had told Grandpa I could start immediately when they talked last night, and that the employee entrance was to the south of the gift shop. I make my way along the brick path, swinging my keys as a tabby cat runs in front of me, then pauses, and flops onto his back, rolling over to show me his belly.

"Hey, buddy," I say, kneeling down. His sonorous purr kicks up a notch as I give him a rub, the long fur of his belly forming tight curls. "You've got a tick, dude."

He gyrates a little, and a voice comes from behind me.

"T.S., let the new girl clock in before you make her groom you."

I stumble to my feet and turn to find a tall blonde walking toward me, wearing the khaki shorts and green button-down uniform of the caverns.

"I talk to cats," I admit.

It seems like the best way to greet her, given that she just came upon me doing it. I'm also super glad that the cat is actually here, because she also bends down to give him a rub.

"All good people do," she says, then adds, "You're right. Tick."

She scoops the cat up in her arms, then eyes me over his furry head. "I'm Mila."

I actually already know she's Mila, but I don't tell her that. I've been coming to the caverns at least once a summer, and Mila is exactly the kind of girl I notice. Tall, blond, tan, muscular, and absolutely confident that everything she says is accurate.

"Neely," I say. "Yeah, I'm new."

"Cool name," she says. "How do you feel about your first duty of pinning down T.S. while I pull this tick?"

"T.S.?" I ask, following her down the path, while the cat regards me over her shoulder.

"Oh, T. S. Eliot, that's this guy's full name," she says, hoisting the cat. "His actual, legal name. It's on his birth certificate."

"Like the poet," I say, reaching for the door handle. I hold it for her, and she sweeps past, glancing at me. The air-conditioning is on full force already, the sheen of sweat that had formed on my skin dissipates, leaving behind goose bumps.

"Yeah," she agrees, pushing her sunglasses on top of her head and giving me a real look, not just the polite one from outside. "Like the poet."

Mila transfers T.S. to her other shoulder and nods toward a door that says "Staff Only." I push it open, and she follows me inside, resting the cat on a pedestal sink that has a medicine cabinet with a cracked mirror above it. Mila pulls it open and starts rummaging.

"Pick a locker," she advises. "But a tip from the initiated—not next to Brian. It's bologna twenty-four/seven in his immediate area."

"Noted," I say, scanning the strips of silver duct tape with names written in black marker before choosing an empty one.

"We'll get you a shirt and shorts in a sec," Mila says, holding up tweezers while she pins T.S.'s neck with one hand. "But first, would you like to assist or perform?"

I opt for performing, because so far, I've been doing that very well.

"All right, last interrogative and then I'll back off," Mila says as I flush the tick down a toilet in one of the stalls. "Why is a cat that lives at the caverns named T. S. Eliot? And by the way, this is a bonus round, so you don't lose points if you don't know the answer."

Maybe, maybe not. I feel like if I didn't know, I might drive back home and tell my grandparents that I can't possibly work at the caverns because there's a really hot girl there that knows a lot about modernist poetry. Luckily, for me, really depressed people do, too.

"'The Waste Land,'" I tell Mila, giving T.S. a nose scratch by way of apology. "'Come in under the shadow of this red rock,'" I recite. "'And I will show you something different from either your shadow at morning striding behind you or your shadow at evening rising to meet you.'"

"Oh damn, girl," she says. "It'll be nice to have someone else working here who isn't a total idiot."

"Who named him?" I ask, already suspecting the answer.

"I did," she says with a smile. "I'm an unapologetic English major."

I assume she goes to school at the OSU branch nearby, but I want to ask, just to keep the conversation going. I also want to know what her favorite color is, how old she is, what she likes to do in her spare time, and if she has a boyfriend—or is even into boys at all.

She's spared this onslaught of questions when Josh Bailey walks into the employee room and stops hard at the sight of me, eyes bouncing off mine awkwardly.

"Hey," he finally manages.

"Hey, shitbird," the Shitbird Man says.

So, of course, so do I. Except I don't bother mumbling it into my cupped hand. It just kind of pops out.

"Oh damn," Mila says again, clapping a hand onto my shoulder. "I definitely like you."

And I definitely like her, too.

FIVE

The owner, John, wants to talk about working at the quarry with Grandpa back in the day.

I'm extremely fortunate that the Shitbird Man does not show up during that conversation. I manage to look polite, interested, and encouraging throughout the ten-minute nostalgia tour of heavy machinery and sedentary objects. At the end of it, John asks me clothing sizes, hands over the uniform, and then tells me that he thinks everything is going to work out fine. He winks when he says this, and I'm pretty sure he's not just talking about me working here. The sympathy of strangers is something I've grown accustomed to; their well-meaning advice still grates on my nerves.

The first time I meet someone else whose brother threw themselves off a bridge after pinning a note to his shirt that said *I cannot manage*, I will listen. Until then, I'm sticking with polite blankness. Also, no one should wink. Everyone thinks they do it well, and literally no one does. I've never even tried.

"Mila's in charge," John tells me, standing up and stretching behind his desk. The fact that I can see the computer monitor reflected in his glasses and that he's playing FreeCell at eight in the morning tells me that he doesn't just mean Mila is in charge for today.

"She'll take care of training you," he goes on, leading me to the door. "Usually, I start a new person working the register in the gift shop—"

"Oh God, please don't," I say, before I can reconsider telling my new boss where he can and cannot assign me on my first day. I don't know if I can make it through eight hours of assisting small children with fake gem mining or flattening pennies in the souvenir press without losing my mind.

Well, losing more of it. And in public.

"Don't worry," John reassures me. "Ed and I had a long talk, and he says you could lead a tour right now, if I let you. Says you probably know more about this place than I do."

"It's the largest cave system in Ohio," I say eagerly, "and called America's most colorful caverns because of the crystal formations. It was discovered in 1897 by Harold Gentry, and is constantly fifty-four degrees, no matter the outside weather. There are two miles of passageways, with the lowest point being one hundred and three feet below the ground. There's the historic tour and the natural wonders tour—"

"Yeah, you're good, kid," John says, waving me off with palpable disinterest in his own business. "Get changed, then you'll do the morning walk-through with Mila. She'll take you from here."

I change into my uniform in the solitary toilet stall in the staff room, ignoring the loud applause when I pull my pants off. Sometimes their timing is really bad.

"Hey," Mila greets me right outside the door, handing off a flashlight. "John said I'm to take you on the morning sweep."

"'Kay," I say agreeably, trying to decide the appropriate amount of distance to tail her at as we walk back out into the sun. Too close and

I risk stepping on her heels; too far back and there's a good chance I get caught staring at her ass.

Mila flicks her sunglasses back down over her eyes as we follow the brick path toward the shelter house and playground, where a few early arrivals are already seeking shade. T.S. precedes us, puffy tail in the air, as if he's the one actually leading the tour.

"He stays pretty close to you," I say.

"He'd follow me underground, if it was allowed," Mila says, pushing open an iron gate. I slip in past her, and she swings it shut, leading me along the curved path that twists downward across the ridge, switchbacking toward the entrance to the cave.

"T.S. is basically the reason why we have a morning sweep now," she goes on. "Somebody has to walk the passageways and make sure there's nothing that shouldn't be there before we let the kiddos in."

"Like what?" I ask. We descend farther with every curve, trees now branching over us and shading our steps.

"Like a dead cat," Mila says as we approach the solid steel door set into a granite alcove. "This one time, somebody brought their toy poodle with them in their purse, even though we've got signs posted everywhere—no pets. Period. Dot. And mostly that's because it takes millions of years for a crystal to form in ideal conditions, so we don't need any mutts lifting their legs and ruining thousands of geologic work hours. But that toy poodle?" Mila goes on. "He got away from his mama and she was too worried about getting into trouble to say anything. So . . ."

"So . . . ?" I ask, mildly horrified as we pass beneath the jutting overhang of granite. Some wild grapevines trail downward, ten feet above our heads.

"So he wandered around down there over a weekend. Got a little lost, then a lot lost. There's miles and miles of unmapped caverns, and most of them a person can't fit into."

"But a toy poodle can," I say.

"Yep," Mila agrees, knocking her sunglasses back once again and wiping sweat from her upper lip. "And he can get into places he can't find his way back from, where no one can rescue him. Long story short, couple of years ago we're leading the first Monday tour of the morning and the little guy hears voices, starts to lose his mind. Crying and yelping, doing everything he could to get our attention. But we couldn't get to him. By the sound of it, I'd say he was at least a quarter mile under our feet."

"Jesus," I say, my skin going cold.

"Code is five-five-six-two," Mila says casually, jabbing it into the keypad next to the metal door. She yanks on the handle, and the iron door screeches open, the smell of earth and wetness, damp and decay rising to meet us.

"What did you do? About the dog?" I ask, flicking on my flashlight as she does the same with hers.

"Canceled tours for a few days until he stopped crying," she says, her eyes darkly shadowed as we pass through the door, the cold mist immediately enveloping us.

"Jesus," I say again, but it's not only for the sake of the poor departed toy poodle who is technically still with us here in the caverns. It's because I'm in the one place that my monsters don't follow. I discovered it on my very first tour, when my constant playmates weren't interested in the crystal formations, didn't screech with joy when we ducked under the small waterfalls that drip from the ceiling in spots, and there was no applause for "The Star-Spangled Banner" that is piped through speakers as you exit the tour.

"So yeah, that's part of the reason for the morning sweep," Mila continues, her tone lighter than it had been when discussing dead miniature mammals. "That and the time a third grader found a used condom near the sacrificial table. I mean, maybe we shouldn't call it that, but . . . you've been down here before, right?"

Yes. Often. I wish, always.

But I don't say that, instead I nod in understanding. "Yeah, I know about the table. It's a lot."

The sacrificial table is set off from the path, looming ten feet overhead, surrounded by a field of stalagmites, some of them as thick as my arm, reaching up from the floor. If they are the teeth of this underground world, the table is a stony tongue.

"Uh, someone had sex on that?" I ask.

"I know, right?" Mila asks, rolling her eyes. "Just thinking about it hurts my back."

I don't have a chance to think about it myself, because Mila swings the door shut, its resounding crash sealing us in together.

"Always, always, always close the door behind you," Mila says, her voice suddenly stern. "This is rule number one. Anything that gets in here other than tourists can cause massive damage. Be careful, the steps can get slick," Mila says, moving past me.

I take a deep breath as we descend the sixty-six stairs, the sound of dripping water growing louder. The steps are carved from the rock, a metal banister bolted on either side. My shoulder brushes against the wall, the beam of my flashlight bouncing off Mila's blond ponytail.

"I feel like you guys should offer a tragic animal-death tour in addition to the historic and natural wonders tours," I say as I join her at the bottom.

"You draft the speech, I'll lead. Halloween only. We'll have five hundred bucks by the end of the night," Mila says, tipping me a wink.

Okay, one person can wink well. It's her.

"Touch panel to your right," Mila says. "Give it a tap, and it'll light up the first cavern. This is the point at which I remind everyone on the tour that they are not allowed to touch anything. After that, I try to be funny. Tips, you know."

We move through each cavern, the ever-present mist floating eerily in front of the recessed lights. Mila shows me where the panels are, embedded behind rocks, and the touch of my hand plunges the cavern behind us into total darkness.

"The tour lead taps them on, the caboose taps them off," Mila explains. "John has three tourist businesses, and I'm sure that between the canoe livery, the zip-lining, and the cave tours, they make a mint. But John won't have the electricity on down here all day. You don't mind being called the caboose, right?"

I'm about to tell her I'm perfectly all right with it when she barrels on.

"My little sister, she got all upset one time and told me that a kid at school had said the c-word. She's in fourth grade and I was like '*What?!*' And then she leans in, all seriousness, and whispers in my ear." Mila leans into me, reenacting the story, her breath warm and soft in my ear.

"Caboose."

I laugh, really loud. Inappropriately loud. Loud enough that I probably just impaired the growth of the nearest crystals with my sonic blast. But I have to do something to cover the fact that an electric jolt just ran up my spine that could probably power this place for the next three months.

We cover the passageways for both tours, Mila showing me where they intersect. "That's why we never run both the historic and natural wonders tours at the same time. We bus people two miles out for the entrance to the historic tour, and they walk back to the visitors' center through the cave system; the natural wonders tour is just a circuit under the center that starts at the granite overhang and comes out—conveniently—at the gift shop. John says it's important that no one gets turned around and ends up back out there at the drop-off for the historic tour, when the bus has already come back to the visitors' center."

"But also they could just hop tours at the intersection, and get both for the price of one," I say.

"Yep," Mila says. "And then we have to drown them in one of the pools. If we don't, others will be encouraged to follow in their criminal ways."

"I see no flaw in your thinking," I say, and she smiles, the brightness of her white teeth flashing in the beam of my light.

"All right, last thing," she says as we approach the end of the passageway and another iron door set into the granite. "Everybody gets to rub the exit crystal for luck. I've usually got to yell at people during the tour to keep their hands to themselves, and sometimes Josh or Brian will have to back me up because, you know, sexism."

"Yeah, that," I say, my eyes resting on the eroded crystal that stands next to the door. It's a sad sight, a large stalagmite that the original owners had offered up as a literal touch point for guests as they left. Years of oil, salt, and acid from human skin have been absorbed, turning it a murky yellow, the top dull and rounded into a smooth dome from hundreds of thousands of palms passing over it.

"Go ahead," Mila says. "It's already ruined. You might as well get your luck."

"I'll pass," I say. I've never taken the opportunity to touch it at the end of a tour. I'd like to think it's because I have a deep respect for nature and more integrity than the average tourist. But also, it could just be that I'm easily trainable. I tear my eyes away from the stunted stalagmite to Mila, who is standing near the door, watching me.

"I'm feeling pretty lucky as it is," I say.

"Cool," she says, giving me an appreciative nod as she yanks the door open. "I kind of think it looks like a massive dildo, anyway."

SIX

"It sounds like it went just . . . just awesome!" Grandma says, a forkful of chicken breast halfway to her mouth.

This is what my life is like, living with people who try to use cool words but also subsist on low-sodium diets.

"It really did," I agree, and there's actual enthusiasm in my voice, not the fake patina I usually apply to everything I say at dinner.

"John's a good guy," Grandpa says as he lines up his green beans before scooping them with his fork. I think his own mom must have taken the machinery analogies too far when encouraging him to eat his vegetables, because he always does this.

"Yeah, John's fine," I say, "but I think Mila kinda runs the place."

"Mila . . . Mila . . . ," Grandma says, beginning the Midwestern tradition of figuring out the last name, parentage, and any possible relation of an individual who arises in conversation. For once, I don't mind. Hearing Mila's name feels good, like I brought a little bit of her home from work with me, to be discussed and examined over dinner.

"Mila Throwmire?" Grandma asks, fork still on pause.

"Honey, no," Grandpa chides. "That's Bo's daughter you're thinking of, she'd be thirty at least."

"Neely didn't say she's not thirty," Grandma shoots back.

"Thirty bucks says she's not thirty," Grandpa says. "John's hiring practices are—" He stops short, eyes cutting to me.

"Yeah, everybody at work is young and hot," I finish for him. "I mean, except for me. I'm just normal."

"Nothing wrong with normal," Grandma says, patting my hand.

I'm sure that's true. I'd also love to know what it's like.

"And besides, thirty isn't old," she protests. "I'm sure you think so right now, but jeez . . . to have thirty back." She gives Grandpa a little eyebrow wiggle across the table.

"Mila isn't thirty," I say, hoping to cut short any senior citizen flirting. They're cute and all, but I do live here and the walls are thin.

"Mila . . . ," Grandma tries again, still scanning her mental files.

"Minter?" Grandpa tosses out. "That'd be about right. Dale's girl."

"No," Grandma argues. "Dale doesn't have any girls. She'd be Kevin's kid."

I tap the name into my phone, and confirm with a social media profile. "Yeah," I say. That's her. Mila Minter."

"Dale's girl, right?" Grandpa asks, pushing his luck.

"I don't know. You don't typically include your parents' names on your bio," I inform them, my thumb scrolling through posts. A photo pops up, Candace Gentry with Tammy Jensen, their perfect tans and shining eyes don't need a filter. My stomach lurches, a bright spear of panic that starts in my intestines and jabs upward into my brain. My amygdala overreacts, and fear chemicals pour out, causing the hair on my arms to rise, my heart to take on a rapid staccato, and the blood to drain from my face in favor of my legs—so that I can run or fight, whichever I choose.

But I can't run from the past, and fighting Tammy Jensen is what got me here in the first place. Candace's birthday party in first grade was the last time I was invited anywhere, and I can't lay that blame at anyone's feet except my own. I might have a lot of undesirable qualities, but self-pity isn't one of them. I've never felt sorry for myself; I know I deserve everything that happens to me—and mild panic attacks at the sight of Tammy is a fair price to pay for what I did. Well, *almost* did to her.

Luckily, Maddie Sayers had woken up before I brought the knife down, and screamed loud enough to wake the dead. Or, in this case, a bunch of sleeping six-year-olds.

I take a deep breath, hold it, exhale slowly, searching for something to calm me, something comforting. Not surprisingly, an image of Mila pops up, her smile flashing as she rubs T.S.'s belly.

"There's a cat," I say suddenly, and Grandpa turns to look behind him. "I mean at work," I clarify. "We have a work cat."

"I'm surprised John allows that," Grandpa says, "but if it's a good mouser, I don't see why not. Cats do their work." He nods affirmatively, finding an entire species to be of value because of their contributions to society. "Wouldn't hurt us to have a cat," he decides, pointing his fork at Grandma, whose eyes go very wide, her teeth connecting audibly with her fork as she bites down.

My stomach bottoms out, the image of comfort that I had latched on to hoping to escape thoughts of Tammy Jensen morphing into a nightmare, my past sins piggybacking onto one another, filling space, stealing air.

"I'm allergic, remember?" Grandma says, eyes avoiding mine, boring into Grandpa's, willing him to understand her meaning but not her words.

It doesn't work. He shakes his head. "No, we had a cat when we first got married. And then after the kids—" He stops himself, restarts with a correction. "After Neely came to live with us we had that orange tabby. What was his name?"

"Sulla," I say, staring down at the table, where a knot in the wood looks like a mouth, teeth bared.

"Yeah, Sulla," Grandpa says, pointing the fork again, triumphant in the knowledge that he was right. It fades fast, the fork dipping. "Whatever happened to that cat, anyway?"

I open my mouth, looking for words, mimicking the knot in the wood, producing nothing.

"He ran away," Grandma says tightly, her water glass hitting the table with a resounding *crack*.

It's that noise that breaks through whatever fog is clouding Grandpa's memory, the story of Sulla's fate and the reason why we don't have a cat—or any pets, for that matter—passing over his face in a clear progression.

"Cats will do that," he says quickly, eyes dropping down to his plate. "When it's time for them to die, they run away, go find a place."

I stare back at the wordless mouth on the table, my own clicking shut, coming down hard so that I don't remind Grandpa that Sulla didn't run away.

But it definitely had been his time to die.

"You see the Bailey boy at work?" Grandma asks, quickly changing the subject and trying to look casual as she separates white meat from the bone.

"Yes," I say, making words, following Grandma's lead as we try to

35

find a way out of this mess of a conversation. "I saw Josh." I don't tell her that I called him a shitbird. "Brian Caldwell works there, too."

"Oh, that's nice," Grandma says, but there's not a lot of force behind the words. Grandpa begins to line up green beans again as we all try to filter out my mistake.

"Caldwell kids got no chance, whole pack of them," he says, shaking his head. "Everyone knows their dad drinks his paycheck each week. I see the wife trash-picking sometimes, then she shows up at craft sales trying to resell stuff somebody threw out, and she put a coat of paint on it."

"She's trying," Grandma says, now making piles of her own vegetables, uncomfortable with any conversation that isn't optimistic.

"Shouldn't have to," Grandpa says. "Any man who can let his woman go around to yard sales trying to clothe his kids should be ashamed of himself."

"He probably is," I say. Because I know the feeling. Know the fingers of 3:00 a.m. and the final count of everything you did wrong that day.

"Too drunk to feel anything, if you ask me," Grandpa says, and then seems to realize no one did.

"Sorry," he says hastily, scraping his fork across his plate, metal on porcelain.

Grandma's face is tight, her jaw clenched, but it's not because of the damage her Corelle is taking, or Grandpa's tirade about the socioeconomic misfortunes of the Caldwell family. It's the fact that I mentioned Brian—Lance's only friend.

"I didn't see him, though," I say quickly. "He was working the historic tour today, and they kept me on the natural wonders one."

"That's the shorter one, right?" Grandma asks, lunging at the opportunity to change the subject.

Applause breaks out, and I twitch.

"Yes," I say, a little too loudly. "The one right under the visitors' center."

Grandpa has exited the conversation; as usual, any dissatisfaction from Grandma makes him reconsider sharing his thoughts. The green beans continue to line up on the plate, but he's not eating anymore.

"I had a cardinal at my feeder today," Grandma offers.

Bird-feeding is her thing. I can't call it bird-*watching*, because she works too much to put in any real time observing. Also, cardinals and blue jays are the only ones she can identify. The rest she just makes up names for based on their appearance and personalities, like *small, nice brown hopping guys*, and *the ones with pointy heads and anxiety*.

All birds look anxious to me, but I do know their real names. Mom had done her best after Dad left, and a deck of flash cards with Ohio birds had made its way home with us from the thrift store. I'd spent a summer with her pointing at wrens, hawks, sparrows, and finches, tapping my finger against each card and repeating the name after her. It had worked—a little too well.

We'd been in the line to pay for our groceries when Mom had pulled a debit card out of her purse. I'd grabbed at it, proudly announcing that the bird pictured there was a cardinal. Mom had snatched it away from me, her face turning the same color as the bird. I didn't know why, I just knew that I had caused it. Later, I'd learn that it was her child-support payment card, featuring the state bird. Also, it was declined, and we had to put some things back before her personal debit card could cover our bill.

Mom had pushed the cart into the parking lot, my legs dangling from the seat, eyes focused on hers. She'd moved the few bags we'd been able to pay for into the trunk, slammed it shut, then came back to get me. I'd lifted my arms, but instead of pulling me from the cart she'd come in close, pressing her forehead against mine.

"Neely," she said quietly. "I cannot manage."

I'd put my hands in her hair, felt her shaking as she cried, warm tears falling onto my shoulders, the sun baking us. I'd cried, too, not sure why. Not sure what happened. Only that I had identified a bird and made Mom cry.

I had reassessed, her tears rolling down my shoulders, wondering if the cardinal was actually there, or if I had made a mistake in my estimation of what was real and not real. Even at that age I had known there was a certain way to behave around Mom so that her version of the world remained intact—the one where she had a happy family and all of us were sane. So I let her hold me, felt her tears on my skin, and ignored the applause that seemed to well up from the ground around us.

Lance told me, later on, that Dad had given him the longer speech, the one where he explained to his only son that constant vigilance was necessary in order to maintain the fallacy.

"I told her," Dad had said, his hands shaking as he explained to Lance. "Once we moved in together she'd know. She'd see who I really was."

And eventually she did. But not because she saw him too much.

Because he left, and none of us ever saw him again.

After dinner, I go back to my room, standing silent for a moment in the doorway, waiting for the usual greetings of the girl letting me know

38

of her eternal thirst, or whatever insult the man in the closet has been waiting all day to launch at me upon my return.

But there's nothing.

It's quiet as I change into pajamas, ears practically ringing with the silence. The Shitbird Man already got his three in for the day—he had to sneak them in between tours since my monsters don't follow me into the caverns. But he'd tacked his single, repetitive thought onto the overheard conversations of tourists waiting to be led inside, and I'd managed to repeat them into my palm, feigning a sneeze each time. Tabitha, the girl who I had been following as I learned the caboose role, finally asked if I had allergies, and I said only to boys and assholes, at which she'd glanced at Josh and told me I might want to get my prescription refilled.

"It was a good day," I tell my monsters.

No one answers. I don't pretend for one second that it's because I have become magically healed. It's more like they're just befuddled because I've never made this statement before. I do a quick tally before bed, running back through the day with T.S. and Mila, my conversation with John, and calling Josh a shitbird. That one is debatable, but amazingly, I don't have any do-overs.

For once, I go to sleep without making revisions, without replaying a scenario and trying to do better, keep up the show that began for Mom's benefit and continued for an audience of two—Grandma and Grandpa.

For once, I think I did okay.

SEVEN

"A couple of things before we start the day," Mila says, glancing at her clipboard as she balances on the boulder near the entrance to the natural wonders tour, T.S. winding between her ankles. The rest of us are gathered around her, looking up, like she's Jesus with better legs, sharing a parable. It's the beginning of my second week at this job, and I'd like to think that by the third, I'll be able to not stare.

"The first rule of the caverns is—"

"Don't talk about the caverns," Josh finishes for her.

"Incorrect," Mila shoots back. "It is, in fact, your actual job to talk about the caverns. But I'm not surprised that you don't know that, Josh."

Beside me, Tabitha groans and rubs the bridge of her nose. "Shut the door behind you," she calls out.

"Always shut the door behind you," Mila repeats, pointing her pen at Tabitha. "Last week when I led the two p.m. natural wonders tour the entry door wasn't latched all the way."

She doesn't say what day, but I feel the blood rush to my face, regardless. Tabitha and I were caboose on natural wonders all last week, and it's her second year working here. If anybody forgot to close the door, it was me. I close my right hand into a fist, fingernails digging into the soft flesh of my palm. My left hand rushes through a series of movements at my side, fingers twisting furtively, a gift from the man in my closet who had informed me this morning that I am fluent in sign language.

He's not entirely wrong. Grandma and Grandpa have been sending me to vacation Bible school every summer since I came to live with them, and if there's one thing that you learn there, it's a smattering of religious iconography ASL and not to sniff the Sharpies during art time. But knowing how to sign *Jesus*, *love*, *fish*, and *soul* doesn't exactly make me fluent. Nonetheless, my hand twitches, eager to prove itself.

"You okay?" Tabitha asks, side-eyeing me as my wrist jitters.

I tighten my jaw and nod, not looking at her.

"And this should go without saying," Mila continues, looking over her sunglasses as she surveys us. "Don't ever share the door code. Not with tourists, not with your mom, not with anybody."

"John hasn't changed that code in years, you know that, right?" Josh asks, staring at Mila with his arms crossed. "People that used to work here have it. Shit, the zips and can-doers probably have it."

I'd learned in my first week here that John's three-pronged entrepreneurial undertaking—caverns, canoe livery, and zip-lining—share a not entirely benign rivalry. The zip-liners, with their defined arm muscles, eternal tans, and permanently windswept hair are the cool kids. The canoe livery is made up of a cadre of homeschooled, deeply religious, highly positive brown-haired teens who all seem to be related.

"The zips don't have the code to the caverns," Mila insists. "And you'll have to work a lot harder to convince me that you don't sneak girls down there."

"Wasn't me," Josh says, but there's a self-satisfied smile tugging at the corners of his mouth. My fingers move furtively, spelling in the pocket of my khakis.

L-i-a-r.

"Speaking of things that definitely don't involve Josh," Mila goes on. "It seems that somebody went into the canoe livery and rotated the halves of all the kayaking paddles 180 degrees so that they were all paddling backward on one side."

"Okay, that's actually kind of funny," Destiny says. Her red hair is pulled into a high pony, her jaw muscles flickering as she chomps down on a mint.

"Until a kid floats downriver," Mila says. "Or until the can-doers decide to hit back and leave the cavern door open overnight."

"Or cut the brake lines on the History Wagon," Josh says, referring to the bus that ferries tourists to the historical tour.

"The can-doers are a God-fearing people," Mila says. "I don't think they'd cut brake lines."

"Zips might," Destiny offers from her cross-legged position in the grass, where she's busy popping the head off a dandelion. "There's a couple of stone-colds in that group."

"Stone-cold foxes," Josh says. "I'd bang Jessica, even if she tried to kill me after."

"How about I kill you and we skip the banging?" Mila offers from her perch atop the rock.

"No reason to skip the fun part," Josh says, his eyes crawling up her legs.

"I'm not," she says coldly.

"Can there be less sexual tension and violence in the workplace, please?" Tabitha groans.

"Tab's right," Mila says. "And John's a little worried about the escalation of the pranks that have been going back and forth between the groups."

"But it's a tradition," Brian says, speaking up for the first time. "And it's not like anybody's ever gotten hurt. We're not drilling holes into canoes or anything."

"Josh did put an extra twenty pounds of rocks into Hilary's backpack when she led the overnight canoe trip last year," Mila says, looking down at him. "Her boat was riding low for forty-eight hours."

"She didn't notice twenty extra, that's on her," Josh says. "Besides, she's built like a brick shithouse. But body positivity. I'd still—"

"You'd still shut your stank-ass mouth and let me finish the staff meeting," Mila says. "Back to the point—make sure you shut the door behind you." Her eyes move over the group, land on mine, then bounce away.

In my pocket, my fingers spell *s-o-r-r-y*.

"And John wants to have a get-together with the can-doers and the zips," she finishes, to a collective groan.

"C'mon, guys," she says, surveying us. "It won't be that bad."

"Oh my God, is it a potluck?" Destiny asks, popping another head off a dandelion. "It's a potluck, isn't it?"

"I'm not eating anything a zipper makes," Tabitha says, her body stiffening beside me.

"I volunteer to be roofied," Josh says, raising his hand.

"Shut up, Josh," Mila hisses as the first carload of the day begins to unpack nearby, toddlers spilling out of a minivan. She tosses her clipboard into the grass and puts her hands on her hips. "We're going to shut doors behind us, we're going to get along with our coworkers, and we're not going to talk about sex or drugs in front of children."

"You've got a lot of opinions," Josh says.

"They're called rules, dick," Mila retorts, hopping down from the rock, T.S. landing with a flop next to her. "And you can do the morning sweep. Tabitha, Destiny, you're on natural wonders today. Brian, you're caboosing with Neely while I lead historic."

"It's my rotation on historic," Josh protests.

"You've got three dick mentions before eight a.m.," Mila says. "You've relegated yourself to the gift shop."

"It turns me on when you tell me what to do," he says as Mila walks away. "And you might drive your mom's minivan, but MILFs are in, and I'm down."

"See if you're still horny after selling postcards for eight hours," she shoots back over her shoulder.

"Oh, I will be," he says, his eyes not leaving her ass as Mila heads for the staff entrance.

"Dude, maybe take the sexual harassment down from a ten to a two," Brian says.

"She rolls with it," Josh says with a shrug.

"Maybe because you're not actually any kind of threat," Tabitha says. "I bet Mila could piledrive you and rip off your bag with her teeth without breaking a sweat."

"I'm just picking up the sexual energy slack around here," Josh shoots back, stretching his arms over his head. "Brian's the world's most boring incel and makes his own shoes."

Brian doesn't hit back, which isn't a surprise. He only looks down at his sandals, which are indeed leather that he and Lance threaded themselves. When he came over to the house to hang out with Lance, he was always the follower, never the leader. If there's a louder, larger male nearby, Brian is happy to play beta.

"C'mon," Tabitha says, turning and offering a hand to Destiny, who looks up at her friend and groans.

"I don't wanna go to work," she says, eyeing the parking lot as a church bus pulls in. "And I definitely don't want to eat Jell-O salads with the zips and can-doers."

"It's Ohio. Crock-Pots and marshmallows floating in gelatin is how we bond," Tab says, pulling Destiny up by her wrist.

I watch them, Tabitha's palm sliding easily over Destiny's skin, jealous of their casual touch and smooth friendship. They've both been nice to me, but there's a wall around their camaraderie that I won't be scaling anytime soon. I'm hoping that Tammy Jensen isn't part of that. Tammy's parents had taken pity on Grandma and Grandpa, agreeing not to share details about the incident. They ticked all the virtue signaling boxes, allowing for my *recent trauma* and even going so far as to recommend a good therapist—apparently the one they would be sending Tammy to, right after switching schools so that they wouldn't have to worry about her continued exposure to her attacker.

Tammy had been in no real danger, though no one would believe me on that count. We'd disagreed over who should get the last corner piece of the cake, heavily layered in icing. Real anger had passed over Tammy's face—eyes glittering, jaw clenching, teeth coming together in a snarl. My lip had lifted in answer, baring my own teeth, my fists curling, ready for whatever would come next.

But what came next was completely unexpected—Tammy's anger passed, like a cloud that had simply floated by, leaving her in sunlight.

45

She'd given me the piece of cake and later offered an extra pillow to me as we all settled in for the night, a small apology that only drove my bafflement to deepen. And then, as I tried to fall asleep, to darken.

I wondered, lying there with other small bodies, what it must be like inside a head like that, one that could summon rage and dismiss it as easily. Unfortunately, I decided to find out, and went to the kitchen, retrieving the knife from the sink, the pale edge of blue icing still smeared across the blade.

I don't believe I would have cut her.

I have to believe I wouldn't have.

Brian and Josh walk past me, Josh's shoulder brushing against mine and pulling me back into the present. They follow Destiny and Tabitha, and I trail the two pairs toward the visitors' center, a conspicuous fifth wheel.

"Why don't we do an after-party after the potluck?" Josh says to Brian. "We'll do it the way John wants, be polite and eat hot dogs, but then later we do beer and bikinis?"

"I don't know if the can-doers are big on bikinis," Brian says.

"Bro, for real? Those girls are way more wild than you think, and you know the zips drink. Paxton, the crew leader? He told me once they zipped naked and he got windburn on his junk."

"Cool," Brian says, in a way that makes it sound very much not.

"Cool, shitbird." It's a quick, quiet one, and easy enough to hide as I drop back a few paces.

"We could take some beers to the cavern; they'd stay nice and cool down there," Josh goes on, his voice carrying back to me. "Plenty of little unlit corners, places to stock up."

"No way," Brian says, waiting for the employee door to swing shut

46

behind Destiny and Tabitha before placing his hand on it, holding it closed. "If Mila found out, she'd shit her pants, and I don't really think you want drunk people wandering around down there. Remember the dog?"

"Fuck, yeah. Good point," Josh says, apparently having some respect for animals, if not women. "What about the ledges, out on the river? Or the quarry? Nobody's done any cliff diving off those for a while. Remember? You used to jump, right?"

Brian's eyes dart to mine over Josh's shoulder, and I look away, pretending to find interest in a young mother slathering her child with sunscreen.

"I used to jump. I don't anymore," Brian says tightly. "And you've got morning sweep."

"You make it sound like an STD," Josh says, reaching past him to grab the door. "Rather have morning sweep than what you've got, which I think is called a stick up the ass. Jesus, I'm just talking to you about jump—"

Brian suddenly grabs Josh's shoulder, pushing him against the glass door. "Stop. Talking. About. Jumping."

"Fuck, dude," Josh says, twisting out of Brian's grip. "What the—"

His eyes fall on me, and it's like I've spontaneously erupted into existence, as if Josh moves through a world populated by himself and pretty girls, and now he has to suddenly recompute for this person standing before him that falls outside of those parameters. Maybe that's what it's like for someone like him. I have to constantly analyze for cracks in my sanity; he has to be on guard against anything less than perfect tens that might skew reality toward average-looking people just getting by.

"Shit. Sorry, Neely," Josh says, and something moves in the depths of his eyes, like maybe he actually means it, or that there is a synapse in there that can still fire, triggering shame.

"It's okay," I say, reaching past them both for the door. "Lance jumped from the bridge, not the cliffs at the quarry."

I jerk the door open, letting the air-conditioning hit me hard, wash over my body. Goose bumps pop immediately, and Destiny glances back as she heads into the staff room.

"Everything good?"

"Yeah," I say quickly. "Just those two, you know."

I roll my eyes and slip past her, but my hands are doing something else, telling a different story. They twist and turn, following the plummet of a body.

"You okay?" Destiny asks, her well-being check-ins apparently not over for the day.

"Yeah, I'm fine," I tell her.

Over the years, I've perfected the delivery of this line. Being *fine* cannot be perky, which comes off as trying too hard. It cannot be morose, which clearly identifies it as a lie. The trick to being fine is to hit the perfect five, which exists somewhere between anhedonia and euphoria.

"Well . . ." Destiny's voice trails off, unsure. "I mean, let me know if those guys get to you, or something else does, or anything, really. I know that things can be . . ." She pauses, a flush rising in her face as I turn to look at her, the skin of her cheeks now matching her hair.

"I know things can be not great sometimes," she finishes.

This is true. Things can be not great sometimes. Sometimes your brother throws himself off a bridge, onto trees hundreds of feet below.

In junior high, Lance had made a diorama of the Battle of Antietam, Grandma baking hills of sourdough, Lance painting plastic soldiers in shades of blue and gray, while I broke sticks into pieces and spray-painted cotton balls, making trees for them to hide behind or die under. The dining room perpetually smelled of acetone, the tips of my fingers were continuously green, Lance's a bright smear of red, once he started adding the blood. I tapped my fingers along the soft tops of the trees long after they had dried, fascinated by our miniature world, the tiny deaths, the one soldier Lance had placed alone, walking away, his back to the world, one hand to his chest, blooming blood.

Destiny is right; things can be not great sometimes.

Sometimes when I drive over the bridge I tap my fingers against the window, never reaching the soft tops of the trees. In the summer, the gorge can look like a bowl of green cotton balls, soft masses of mossy clouds, a bed to enfold you, leafy arms to catch you.

That is not what happened.

Branches went through my brother; sliding inside, taking the place of bone. He broke, and split; the trees held some of what fell out, but other parts reached the ground. The park closed down the trail, and a tree-trimming service offered their vehicles, but there was no access road. In the end, a firefighter climbed the tree and knocked my brother's body loose with a crowbar. Volunteers with trash bags and medical gloves discreetly arrived, but Lance's body had broken open and become weather, blood like rain.

Buzzards perched for weeks, finishing the job.

And Destiny says things can be not great sometimes.

F-u-c-k Y-o-u.

EIGHT

"If you're holding a ticket for historic tour number one, please gather at the bus."

Mila's voice rings out over the loudspeaker, as families, groups, and a random loner in a T-shirt that says YOUR OPINION DOESN'T MATTER make their way over to the History Wagon. Brian waits at the bus door, taking tickets as people pass by. I stand next to him, hoping that the Shitbird Man doesn't take any opportunities. He already got one in for the day and has been pretty good at sliding his specific commentary in during moments where I can do my mandatory recitation without anyone noticing.

"Second call for historic tour number one, please gather at the bus," Mila repeats. "You'll be able to find the bus easily. Because it's the only bus parked next to the visitors' center, and it has 'East Independence Caverns' on the side in really big letters."

A smattering of giggles comes from our line, and Mila runs with it from inside the visitors' center.

"Beside the bus you'll see your lovely tour guides for today, Brian and Neely. Brian will be taking your tickets, and Neely's job is to smile and nod. It's not because we're sexist here at the caverns, but because Neely is in training."

There's another wave of laughter, and my smile becomes a real one, the muscles in my cheeks lengthening and tightening past the point of social compliance, their normal resting place.

"Thank you, welcome, thank you, welcome to the historic tour," Brian says as he takes the laminated cards from the tourists as they board the bus. His voice is low and easy, with no trace of the anger that had erupted before, though I had noticed the beginnings of a blue bruise across Josh's cheekbone, and a smear of sweat and oil on the glass door where Brian had pressed him against it.

"Thanks," I say quietly, my eyes and voice directed at his sandals. "For earlier."

There's a pause as he counts the tickets, raises his hands and indicates to Mila inside how many people have boarded.

"That's twenty people on the bus," Mila announces. "And twenty tickets sold. I might be an English major, but I'm pretty sure we're ready to go."

An appreciative laugh comes from the History Wagon, and I assume that Brian is going to ignore me, pretend like nothing happened, that there is no mutual bond between us. That there is not a matching pair of sandals like his in my house, in a closet in a room with a door that is never opened.

"It's okay," Brian says. "It's fine. I mean . . ." He sighs and pushes his ball cap back. The thin white line of fish-belly-pale skin along his hairline contrasts against the summer tan that's already deepened his face.

"It's not okay, actually," Brian clarifies. "Neely, look at me."

I raise my eyes, surprised that he would ask for this. So far, we have avoided each other. So far, we have done a very good job of being coworkers who share no history.

"Seeing you is hard, okay?" he says.

"Things can be not great sometimes," I agree.

He closes his eyes, and I think it's possible I might be the dumbest person on the planet, until he nods. "That's actually a really good way to put it," he says.

Silently, I apologize for finger spelling *fuck you* to Destiny earlier. I will need to rectify it tonight, subject it to review, invent a timeline where I smile and tell her thanks, where we hug and she says she supports me and that she's sorry for everything I've been through.

But I'm not the only one who went through it.

"Do you try not to think about it?" I ask Brian.

"All right, campers, time to get this show on the road." Mila comes busting out of the visitors' center, her shorts somewhere north of the dress code, her lanyard bobbing invitingly on her chest. I try really, really hard not to look.

"Talk later?" Brian asks.

"Sure," I say, surprised that he wants the conversation to continue. Mila tosses me a smile as she waltzes past me, and I latch on to it, the flash of her teeth, the gleam of ChapStick—it's cherry; I checked her locker. I've been reading up on ticks, modernist poetry, and how long it takes small animals to die of starvation. These are the only real touch points I have to begin chatting her up, but I'm very aware of their limitations. I haven't been alone with her after our initial morning sweep, and while she's always friendly, I could never claim that she's my friend.

And I really, really want to claim that.

Brian hands over the tickets to her, and Mila pockets them, then pulls him aside. There's a quick exchange, he drops his head as she touches his shoulder, then smiles, and flicks the brim of his hat. It jerks upward, revealing the line of vulnerable pale skin once more.

"Don't worry about it." Mila finishes off their chat as she slips past me to board the bus, Brian and I following behind but waiting on the steps.

"What was that about?" I whisper to him, but he brushes me off with a shake of his head.

"Good morning, historic tour group number one!" Mila announces, spreading her arms wide. "You are called that because you are not only the first tour group of the day, but you are also number one in my heart." She clasps a hand over her chest, then spins the other in the air, prompting them with an "awwwww!"

They follow, a chorus of "awwwww" erupting from the Naugahyde seats and sunscreen-smeared faces. The guy with the shirt about opinions tries to roll his eyes but ends up smiling. Mila does this to people; even the ones that don't want to like her end up there. I'm only at the beginning of discovering what happens to people who already like Mila when they are subjected to prolonged exposure. But I'm guessing what happens is that they fall in love.

"I'll be your bus driver today," she goes on. "In addition to being an English major, I also have my CDL. Two guesses which one will actually help me make a living in the future. Also, we do allow tipping here, so remember that on your way out of the caverns, where there is a big plastic tip jar for each of your tour guides today. My name is Mila, and you like me."

She stops, pausing for effect. "You really, really like me." She nods her head up and down, and they follow in unison, hypnotized. Mila fires up the bus as Brian and I steady ourselves in the stairwell, grabbing on to the poles as we roll out onto the highway. Mila turns on the stereo system, pulling the handset from its cradle.

"We want you to feel like you got your money's worth here at the caverns, so the tour doesn't start at the cave—it starts now. If you'll look to your left, you'll see corn. On the right you'll discover corn. Up ahead is a maple tree, surrounded by corn."

The road dead-ends and Mila brakes, flipping on the blinker. There's a car coming, so she continues her spiel.

"Hey, guys," she says to the tour group. "What did the mama corn buy for the baby corn that wanted a pet?"

She's met by silence that she allows to last for only a few seconds.

"A corn dog!" she screeches into the mic, which brings on a collective groan from our passengers.

"Oh, c'mon," she chides, turning the wheel with one hand, mic held close to her mouth with the other. "You're going to traumatize me if you don't laugh. That one wasn't so bad. I told a really awful joke once about a corn tortilla and ground beef. Nobody laughed. I still can't taco 'bout it."

That one gets an appreciative chuckle, and I have to put my hand over my mouth to stifle my own. I've done this tour with Mila three times now, and I haven't heard the same corn joke yet. She told one group to come back next year when the crops have been rotated so they can hear all the bean jokes. We pull off the highway onto a gravel turnaround, where Mila kills the engine and swings the doors open. Brian and I get out, turning to count heads as our tour group unloads.

"Still twenty?" he checks with me.

"Still twenty," I agree.

"Cool, didn't lose anybody," Mila says, hopping from the last step to land next to me. "Light check?"

Brian and I both show her that we have our flashlights, and she leads the group over to a small cinder block building with an uninviting metal door, encouraging everyone to circle around her.

"And we're here," she says, holding her arms out wide "Welcome to the official starting point of the historic tour. I know it looks like a bathroom at the state park, but it's not."

There are a couple of giggles from some middle school boys, and she mockingly levels a finger at them.

"It's not a bathroom," she says again. "And if you make it one, Dad has to tip extra."

Dad only smiles, and I think he's likely to tip extra regardless of unregulated urination.

"A couple of safety tips before we go down," Mila continues. "There are sixty-six steps to the bottom, and every single one of them is wet. There are handrails bolted into the granite on both sides. If you slip, grab those. Not a person. Especially not your mom. She's tired of taking care of you. She literally came here today for a break, so let's give her one—but not her leg, 'kay?"

She surveys the crowd and gets nods from everyone before punching the code into the door, then turns back to the group.

"All right, friends," Mila says. "Last rule. No touching; as above, so below. And while the cavern is about two hundred thousand years above the age of consent, Brian, Neely, and I are her guardians, and we're here to enforce respect for geological processes. I know pretty things are pretty and you want to touch them, but I'm telling you not to. There is a sacrificial rock in there, and I will use it in the name of poetic justice if I deem it necessary.

"And lastly," Mila says, hooking her foot around the door to pull it fully open, "welcome to the underworld." Her eyes scan the group, finally landing on mine. "'Come in under the shadow of this red rock.'"

There's a furtive giggle from the trees on my right, and then I cross the threshold, closing the door behind me.

NINE

Brian taps the light pad behind us after the last person in the group has left the stairwell. He and I follow the group, Mila's voice carrying to us as she recites the script.

"Harold Gentry discovered the caverns in 1897 when he became curious about how his crop fields were draining so quickly. . . ."

"Yeah, I think about it," Brian says as we pause in the entryway to the first cavern, the tourists' gazes drawn by the carefully placed lights that throw the largest stalactites into relief, deep shadows flaring behind them like dark fingers. "About Lance."

"Me too," I say. "It sneaks up on me."

"With Josh before . . ." Brian shakes his head, eyes still trained on our group. "I've probably heard the word *jump* a thousand times since it happened, but with you being right there, it was just different. And he had no idea."

"Gentry invited locals to come take a look whenever they'd like," Mila continues. "Anyone could enter at their own risk, and he left lanterns by his barn for exploring. At the end of the day, he'd return from the fields to see if all the lanterns were back. If not, he'd have to go in after whoever was still down here."

"What do you mean?" the guy in the opinions shirt asks. "Did people get lost?"

"Sometimes," Mila says lightly. "Sometimes their lanterns ran out of oil and people were stuck in complete and total blackness until Gentry came to get them." She wiggles her flashlight. "Tips, remember?"

There's another laugh, but this one has an edge on it. Mila does this; she'll romance them aboveground to get the paying customers on her side, then pulls the rug out from under them when she's got them one hundred feet deep. She's in charge down here, and they'd better recognize it.

"I don't think Josh meant anything by it," I say to Brian, remembering the flicker I saw in Josh's eyes, the recognition of his error. "Did Mila say something to you? Is that what you were talking about before we got on the bus?"

"Eh . . ." Brian nods at Mila as she makes eye contact with him over the heads of the group, indicating that she's ready to move on. He does a quick head count, signals to her that we still have twenty, and the group progresses forward, Mila tapping on the lights in the next cavern as Brian and I switch out the ones behind us.

"Did you get in trouble?" I ask, my voice rising a notch. "Because of me?"

"First of all, no," Brian says. "I'm not in trouble, not the real kind, anyway. Destiny saw me shove Josh into the door and got all upset about it, gave Mila a 'violence doesn't solve problems' speech."

"And?" I ask, my heart rate picking up, thinking of that white line of exposed flesh near his temple, the vulnerable pulse beating there, his fist curled in Josh's shirt and how my past—and my presence—is what caused the problem.

"And Mila said that she agrees violence doesn't solve problems, but it sure can clear the air sometimes," he finishes.

I exhale, my breath joining the mist around us. "So she didn't say anything to John?"

"John's at the livery today," Brian says. "Mila agreed that if Josh is cool, there's no need to."

"Remember the rule about no touching?" Mila asks the tourists. "It hasn't always existed, which is why we're standing in what's referred to as the graffiti room."

All eyes sweep the walls, where names and dates have been etched into the stone. They sprawl across rock, proudly announcing who was here, and when.

"Because of the constant temperature and controlled climate, these etchings are virtually untouched by time and look like they could have been made yesterday," Mila goes on, sweeping her light beam along the darker edges where the canned lights don't reach.

"Josh will be cool," Brian goes on. "We'll handle it the way guys do. He'll probably give me a solid bag tag in the parking lot and we'll call it even."

I nod, feeling the relief but not really listening. Mila is at the best part, killing her flashlight so that only the dull, sporadically strung lights offer illumination.

"Remember that the caverns only became an official tourist attraction in 1925," she says. "Thousands of tons of dirt were hauled out in order to widen these rooms, and there certainly weren't poured concrete paths beneath the early explorers' feet, a light source, or any handrails. The names you see here were carved by people who slid underground, voluntarily burying themselves. They crawled with rock pressing in on both sides, as well as above and below, all while holding an oil lamp with only hours of life, and offering only a few feet of visibility."

Recognizable shudders pass through a few of the adults.

"It quickly became a competition to see who could go deeper, darker, farther," Mila continues, her voice dropping. "Who could leave their name behind, in a place no one else was willing to go?"

She taps on a hidden light panel and a spot on the far wall is illuminated. Easily fifty yards off the path, hemmed in by a field of stalactites and stalagmites, with only inches of space on either side, a name is carved deeply.

MARGARET SANDER 1898

"Huh," one of the dads says.

"Not trying to be weird," Brian goes on, his voice dropping as the group goes silent at the prospect of a woman being the best at something. "But I don't want you to get the wrong idea, you know?"

"Huh?" It's my turn to be dumb, and I look at him, confused.

"I mean, I did that to Josh because you were there. But I didn't do it *for* you, if that makes sense."

It takes a second for it to sink in, but when it does I bark a laugh that breaks the contemplative quality of the tour, my fan of spit adding to the condensation of the caves. Brian is worried that he's my knight in shining armor now, that I'm imagining a future where we're married and have twins named Lance and Lancette. That we take them to my brother's grave and talk about how we grew up together but I never really knew how I felt until I saw him assault someone that my auditory hallucinations had identified as a shitbird.

"Don't worry," I tell him. "You are very, very safe from my vagina."

Sometimes I forget that caves are excellent noise conductors.

"*So anyway, Margaret,*" Mila says loudly, casting a dubious glance toward us. I mouth *sorry* at her as Brian pulls down his cap, avoiding curious looks.

"As far as we know," she continues, "Margaret Sander, a young wife and mother, was the boldest of the bold. You can see her name throughout the cave."

At this point, the caboose is supposed to use a laser pointer and indicate each time Margaret inscribed her name, following the path of her tenacity. Brian pulls the laser from his pocket, but I snatch it from his hand.

"I've got it," I tell him. I need to recover in Mila's eyes. Need to show her that I can close doors behind me, and not talk about genitals in front of children, and be something other than the cause of staff fistfights.

"Margaret was one of the first to enter the caves," Mila goes on, nodding to me as I point the laser at an early incarnation of her name, near the entrance, which carries the date of 1897, the same year Gentry discovered the entrance.

"But as other visitors came and competition heated up, Margaret met their challenges and raised the bar."

I train the red dot along the sides of the cave, following the escalation as Margaret returned each time someone dared to go farther than her. I know the exact spots, each sharp turn and cut of her name, can imagine her teeth set, jaw hard, as she had to prove herself time and time again. The rules keep me from touching, but the crystal formations have never tempted me. It's Margaret I want to connect with, her need to claim this space and make it her own.

When I was in fifth grade I did a history project on Margaret, digging up everything I could from the county genealogy society, and the tiny public library. Grandma had helped me run the microfiche and clip out small notices in the local paper. Margaret's wedding, her children, and finally, her death. A handful of newsprint that marked this woman's journey through life, her passage from girl to wife to mother to dead the only things of note.

Down here, her name is not printed on paper but etched on stone where time doesn't pass. Margaret won't disappear like Mary has, because Margaret cut into rock herself, in a place of her choosing. A place I also choose.

A volunteer at the genealogy center had called Grandma years later, letting me know a distant relative of Margaret's had passed away, leaving family photos to the historical society. One of them was of Margaret, and she had sent Grandma a copy so that I would know what this woman looked like, this woman who had captured me as a child and held me still. Margaret's eyes were dark and deep, like the caves, and I've stared into them often, looking for a hint, a glimpse, an indication.

Wondering if her own monsters drove her deeper, darker, farther.

TEN

"Sorry, I just wanted to do a little more than tag along on caboose," I say, handing the laser pointer back to Brian once the Margaret Sander section of the historical tour is at an end.

"I get it," he says, nodding. "You probably know more about this place than I do. And by the way, me being safe from your vagina . . ." He's smarter than me, dropping his voice low on the v-word. "I kinda figured."

I stiffen, my entire body freezing as my spine begins a low vibration, rivulets of adrenaline gathering as panic forms.

"What do you mean?"

Brian pauses, too, his eyes meeting mine under his ball cap. But his have no questions, only a placid calm I envy as my fingers tremble, and something ignites in my gut, in the place where all my darkness lives. A place that must never be tapped, for fear of it spilling outward, into the light, contaminating the world.

"It's okay, it's not a big deal," Brian says.

And I'm sure it's not, to him. Because he's not gay and he doesn't live with his grandparents and his brother didn't kill himself and his family can have pets and he doesn't hear voices.

Sometimes, I wonder what it's like to be able to do just one thing the acceptable way. To have just one thing that people associate me with that is as regular as grass clippings, or country music. But when people think of me, they think of toddlers trapped in hot cars, and intestines hanging from trees. They think of dads that leave and moms that die, grandparents that never get to retire and keep smiling, not because they're finally enjoying their lives but because it's their goddamn jobs now.

"Where does that go?"

I jerk my eyes away from Brian, back to Mila, who was just about to move the tour group on to the largest room before she was stopped by a last-minute question from a dad that I'm pretty sure just wants her attention.

"To the left of Margaret's name," he goes on, pointing.

Brian lifts the laser pointer, drawing a circle around the dark mouth that opens on the back wall, about twelve inches high and two feet wide.

"Congrats, you've spotted the entry to the alien cave base," Mila says, then shakes her head. "What you see there is an entrance to the unmapped parts of the cave system. The cave system is only partially explored. East Independence Caverns is privately owned—which means that our boss is on the line if anybody gets hurt down here. So there are very strict rules about who can explore off the paths. If you're an employee who has logged over two thousand hours underground, you're allowed to do a cave crawl."

"Nice," the dad says. "Have you?"

"Jesus Christ, dude," Brian mutters under his breath, checking his phone for the time. There's no service underground, but we always carry our phones as backup lights, as well as timekeepers. Mila needs to get this group moving if we don't want to intersect with the natural wonders tour, staggered to start fifteen minutes after ours for exactly that reason.

"I have my two thousand hours," Mila says. "But you don't want to go wandering into those unexplored areas alone, and I'm the only employee who has put in the time."

"I doubt you'd have trouble finding someone to go with you," a mom says. She's young but tired, small lines of irritation and parenting have started to dig furrows around her mouth. But she shares a glance with Mila; two pretty women who know they're pretty.

"Ha, well . . ." Mila smiles. "You don't want to take just anyone into the dark with you on a cave crawl. There has to be a level of trust, and that's not lightly given. In the next room you'll see . . ."

She moves the group forward quickly, raising her eyebrows at Brian, who gives her the nod that everyone is accounted for. He taps off the general lights as we leave the graffiti room, and I take care of the spotlight that puts Margaret's name in high relief.

"Sorry," Brian says. "I didn't mean to out you a mile underground in front of a bunch of tourists."

We fall back from the group for a second, and I feel inside for the panic that had erupted at his words earlier, the vibration that had begun in my spinal cord and radiated through my body. It's not there, replaced instead by a steady hum, a constant reminder to be on guard.

"Grandma and Grandpa don't know, is the thing," I tell him, my words coming out in a rush. "And technically, you didn't out me. What I said was that you were very safe from my vagina. A girl could be straight and not attracted to you, Brian."

He laughs and pulls down on his ball cap again, shading his eyes as a blush rises. "That's where most of them seem to land."

I laugh, an honest sound that echoes off the rock around us. I could tell him that the truth is his looks likely have nothing to do with the lack of interest from girls but rather the fact that his bumper is duct-taped to his truck, and the steel in the toes of his boots is noticeable because the leather is entirely worn away. Brian is poor as dirt, and I'm not the only employee here who got hired by the pity committee.

"But your grandma and grandpa, I mean . . ." He glances ahead at the tour group, dropping his voice a little lower. "They're cool, right? I remember them being pretty chill."

"They are awesome," I concur, and don't give him anything else.

Lance and I had followed Dad's lead—acknowledging that we had a problem, each of us finding a way to deal with it, creating our own bedrock, highly aware that if we exposed our whole selves to someone else, the earth would shake, the world would move, and we would be revealed.

And in being seen, be forced to truly know ourselves.

There's a little girl under my bed, a man in my closet, and a hovering curser with me at all times. I know I'm crazy. What I don't want to know—and don't care to have anyone find out—is exactly how crazy I am.

On the other hand, I know how gay I am—completely, totally gay. Grandma and Grandpa have no clue, though, and when a local conservative group went after the library for creating a display of LBGTQ books for Pride Month, I couldn't tell if the disapproving twist of their mouths was for the library or the protestors. I don't want to add sexuality to the topics we have to avoid in our already tense household, where my brother's name feels like a swear word and cats can't be mentioned.

I can't take back what Lance did, but that second part is my own fault.

I sneak a sideways glance at Brian as we move into the largest room of the caverns, a wide space with stalactites and stalagmites like a mouthful of teeth on either side of the path. Jutting out from the far wall is a flat expanse of granite that stretches up to the path in the middle of the room, rivulets of water dripping from a thousand tiny ledges. There's so much running water in this section that Mila has to raise her voice to be heard above the million droplets.

"Watch yourself as you enter the next room," she says to the group. "You'll be passing through one of our many cave showers. Legend has it that it can wash away your sins, but if you're an atheist, the best we can promise is to get the stink off."

There's an appreciative chuckle as we move out of the hall and into the next chamber, some tourists dodging the cold water, others taking an appreciative dousing.

"Welcome to what we affectionately refer to as the sacrificial table," Mila says, the beam of her flashlight tracing the lip of rock above their heads. "There is absolutely no evidence that anyone or anything has ever died on this rock. But I'm willing to make exceptions." She crooks a finger at one of the boys she warned against peeing earlier, comically narrowing her eyes.

There's a spattering of giggles, but this one is slightly uncomfortable, and a mother pulls her toddler closer to her, away from the field of stalagmites that edge the table, pointed tips reaching for the ceiling.

"Is your number still the same?" Brian asks.

"What? No, I . . . changed it." After Lance died, I'd been flooded by the thoughts and prayers of classmates that had never given me an inch of their mental space, and I doubted spent a lot of time on their knees—at least not in devotion to God.

"Could I get your new number?" Brian asks.

"Our eagle eye from earlier spotted the crawl space next to Margaret's name, but unfortunately because of the height of the table, you can't see that there's a similar one here. The two intersect and become a wider tunnel. But that's something you'll never see, unless I give you the pics. Tips, remember?" she says, rubbing her fingers together.

"You've been up there?" a mom asks, eyes following the lips of the table, her grip on her kid visibly tightening. "How?"

"If you're a good climber, there are some toeholds on the sides. But you've got to pick your way through those first," she says, tripping her light across the stalagmites. "And . . . ," she says sternly, flashing her light across the group, "nobody gets to do that. No touching, right?"

Everyone nods, because Mila is in charge, because Mila is entrancing, because Mila makes you want to make her happy.

"So earlier I made some jokes about the electricity down here," she goes on. "But there is a section of the tour where we turn the lights off on purpose—and that's right now."

Mila shoots me a look, and it's my cue to leave the group, following a small path that branches off the trail into a recessed corner where the breaker boxes are. One of them is closed and has *natural* scrawled across the front panel. The other has *historic* and stands ajar. Mila's voice carries to me, prompting.

"I want everybody to hold hands right now," she tells the group. "I don't care if you just got into a fight with your sister or didn't bring a friend—it's time to make new ones. I'm sure that every single one of you has the heart of a lion, but when the lights go out underground, you'll be a scared kitten. So hold hands, take a deep breath, and get ready to experience true darkness in three . . . two . . . one."

I flick the breaker with my thumb.

And the world ends.

Every time, it's like this. Every time, it sucks the air from my lungs and rationality from my brain. We think we understand darkness until we are plunged into it; think we know what nothing is until everything is taken away. When the lights go out a mile below the earth, there are no options. The sun has never been here. There is no light and nothing to see, only the sound of running water and the feel of stone under your feet. Banned from touching the walls, I've heard people stomp their feet at this point in the tour, desperate for proof that their bodies still exist, even if they can't see them, that the world around them has not poofed out of existence in a breath, that they are not floating alone in an eternal nothing.

When I was a child, this part of the tour never scared me. Quiet solitude existed nowhere except here, and I was already adept at determining what was real and not real. This extended moment when others were confused about their sanity and the existence of the world around them was a nice change.

Grandma and Grandpa hated this part, would hold on to me before the lights went out, their grips tightening in the darkness. His hand on my shoulder, her fingers entwined with mine, palms and clavicles, knucklebones and phalanges soldering together in the utter blackness. In the light, we have to make eye contact. In the light, we view each other's pain. In the light, I look like their lost daughter.

In the dark, we're just bones.

"I know it's overwhelming," Mila's voice says, sliding through the utter blackness, calming and soothing. "But I want you to take a second. Let the fear settle."

It's quiet except for the drip of water, the sound of it running to a deeper, darker place.

"Now." Mila's voice floats to me as I rub my thumb over the breaker switch. I can't lift it, can't lose it. Can't risk breaking physical contact with the one thing that can bring light back to twenty people that might lose their shit if pushed one second too far.

"Hopefully you listened to me before," Mila goes on. "Hopefully you're holding someone's hand."

I think of Brian, alone at the back, holding on to no one, asking for my number.

"If you have a hand free, I want you to lift it and hold it in front of your face."

There's a small squeal, and I know that a parent just tried to let go of their child and was firmly told this was not an option.

"You can't see it," Mila says, for those who are able to participate in the experiment. "Now bring it closer to your face." She waits a second, aware of her power. "You can feel the heat coming from it, maybe even smell your own skin. But you can't see it."

Mila's quiet a moment longer, the tension rising in the cave.

"I know everyone thought they were paying sixty bucks for a history lesson and half hour of naturally occurring air-conditioning. The existential crisis is free. If it makes you feel better, you can boop yourself now," she says. "The lights are coming back on in exactly ten seconds."

Ten . . . nine . . . eight . . .

I start counting aloud, whispering to myself, the button under my thumb and my tongue moving against my teeth the only things that exist in the world. There is no little girl under my bed, no man in my closet, no trees to catch my brother, or my mother crushed between a steering wheel and a headrest, asking us to repeat our address.

Seven . . . six . . . five . . .

"Only a few seconds left," Mila goes on, her voice the only thing that creates, the world looking for the axis of her words. "If you want to commit a murder, do it now."

Four . . . three . . . two . . .

I think of her eyes meeting mine, the silent communication that it is time to move to the next room, turn out the lights, count heads, shut the door. I will do all of those things. I will do them right, and I will do them consistently, and I will make Mila aware of me. In the dark and the light.

One.

I flip the switch, and everything exists again. The red rock on either side of the panels, the stalactite dangling near my cheek, the slow drip of time as crystals form around us. A collective exhalation of relief rises up from the group as I rejoin them, nodding to Brian.

"Yes, I'll give you my number," I tell him. Maybe other things can be real. Maybe if I have one friend to talk to, I'll be less tempted to respond to the ones that aren't there.

"Going to do a quick . . . head . . . count . . . ," Mila says, tapping her finger against the air as she scans the group.

"Yep! Still twenty," she says. "Hey, guys, what do you think would be freakier? If we had one less person after the lights went out—or if we had one more?"

She uses this line every time, and it always gets a laugh. But occasionally there is one person that actually thinks about it, seriously considers the question. I watch as a shadow passes over the face of a mother, and her grip on her child tightens.

Most of us know what it's like to lose someone.

I'm the only one who understands the other half of the question.

ELEVEN

When my phone goes off at the dinner table, I grab it, flipping its face downward as quickly as possible.

"Was that a text?" Grandma asks, her eyes on the back of my phone as it vibrates.

Grandma is not asking this question because she is a technophobe, or an idiot. Her own phone goes off multiple times during the day with texts from her friends, alerts from a Facebook gardening group, and once—although she doesn't know I saw it—a very famous dick meme that she laughed at, then glanced around guiltily. So Grandma isn't asking what a text is, or why my phone would be vibrating right now. She's just genuinely confused that I'm the one being texted.

"Yeah, work stuff," I tell her.

"Work?" Grandpa asks, glancing up from the corn kernels that he is lining up like soldiers. "Don't let John steamroll you. You don't give that place a second thought if you're not clocked in. John's a good guy, but he'll let you work as hard as you want and still pay you the same."

"It's not John," I tell him.

"Oh, is it the Bailey boy, Josh?" Grandma asks. Her eyes have so much hope in them; I almost tell her the truth. Almost tell her that it's not Josh, it's Brian, and he's probably still apologizing to me for referencing my sexuality in public. But this level of truth would mean bringing the ghost of Lance into the room by mentioning his former best friend, and then following that up with the solid knockout punch that I'm gay.

So instead of allowing Grandma to revel in a heterosexual pipe dream about her great-grandchildren being Baileys, I choose a different lie, the reality that I wish were true.

"It's Mila," I tell her.

"Oh, she seems nice," Grandma says, not missing a beat. A friend for me might not be a boyfriend, but it's still something. "I remember her from the tour we took last summer."

"The Minter girl?" Grandpa asks, raising his eyebrows. "Legs?"

"Well, dear, I think her name is Mila, and that's not how you're supposed to refer to her, but yes, she has legs," Grandma says. "Do you need to answer her, Neely?"

I glance at my phone. Yes, I desperately need to answer Mila. I also need her to text me in the first place, and to have my number. None of those things have happened, but I'm basing this entire conversation on a lie, so there's no point stopping now.

"I don't know, maybe," I say, quickly wiping my mouth with a napkin and raising my eyebrows at Grandma in a question.

"Oh, go, go," she says, waving me away from the table. "We'll tidy up."

I go to my room and shut the door behind me, giving the girl and the man a moment to jump if they want; her to let me know she's still thirsty, him to either grant me a newfound ability or tell me that I am wholly, fundamentally wrong about something important.

I close my eyes, waiting.

Neither happens. I flop onto my bed and glance at the text.

> Hey. It's me

> I mean . . . Me is Brian.

> Sorry.

I sigh and save his number. He's now canonized along with Grandma, Grandpa, and a couple of classmates who have been forced to do group projects with me.

> Our conversations can't all start and end with you apologizing.

> That's going to get boring really fast.

I tell him this as if I'm currently leaving twenty other people sitting on read, like I've got someone else to talk to, or anything to do at all, really.

"This *is* boring," the girl under the bed says, and my head drops. They've been quieter since I started working, and downright silent for the past two days. The Shitbird Man had even taken a day off, and the children haven't tried to entice me to play since Monday. Even so, I don't believe in a world where I get a summer job, fall in love, and am magically cured of an intense mental illness. But also, having a little hope would be nice.

"Stop," I tell her. "I'm trying something."

"What?" the man asks, his voice soaring through the closet door. "What are you doing?"

There's real concern in his voice, and I can't say I blame him. Dad tried something once. Something that came in an orange bottle with a tamper-proof lid, something that brought hope into Mom's face and a smile to her ever-tightening lips. Because even though we all worked very hard to keep the narrative of a sane family going sentence by sentence, Mom slept with madness every night, and she was no fool.

Forty-eight hours later I was standing next to Mom in the yard while she cried, my tiny hand in hers, Lance on my other side, stone-faced, while Dad chopped down every tree in our yard, claiming that the people inside them needed to be freed, his mania so intense that protecting Mom from the truth slipped off his priorities list. It had been raining, I remember, and the only thing I could think was that if Dad freed the people in the trees, maybe they could play with the children in the grass . . . but later, when the weather was better. The orange bottle disappeared, and Dad followed suit a few weeks later.

After the Tammy Jensen incident, my grandparents wanted to talk to me about medication, but all I could think of was dead trees and Mom's tears, mud squishing between my toes and the sound of laughter from the tall grass. They did insist on therapy, but their insurance didn't cover it, and after I'd made it a few months without stabbing any other first graders, they'd decided to let that particular financial burden go to the wayside. When they found Sulla's body, there had been a long conversation, but my responses must have been sufficient—or ready cash in such short supply—that it had been chalked up to an unfortunate accident.

So the man in the closet having some reservations about my statement that I'm trying something isn't all that surprising. He's always like this when I attempt new things, unless he explicitly told me I could or I should—like the time he insisted I could fly and I jumped off the roof only to find out that gravity applies to you whether you believe it does or not.

My phone buzzes.

Well now I'm in a pickle b/c the only way I know to respond is to say I'm sorry, and you just banned me from apologizing.

"Ha," I say, glancing at Brian's text.

You didn't out me.

I appreciate it, but stop beating yourself up.

No, like I'm sorry about all the stuff. Josh being a dick. Me just kind of disappearing.

After everything.

"That's sweet," the little girl says. The man in the closet keeps his opinion to himself.

You were his friend, not mine.

Not trying to be mean but that's the truth.

You don't owe me anything.

I think about that for a second, remembering the bruise on Josh's cheekbone and the look on Destiny's face when I came into the visitors' center, the kindness at the core of her reaching out to ask the darkness inside me if I was okay, and me finger spelling *fuck you* at her. Shit. I need to put in a redo on that. This week has been pretty clean, but if I start to let the small things slip, a great big one might get by—a great big one like Tammy Jensen. My response to Destiny had felt great in the moment, but it needs correcting now, or it could escalate into me actually saying it to her face, which is eerily free of pores.

I toss my phone aside and walk to my bedroom door, watching Josh's cheek slide across it, the look of total surprise—or at least, as much of the expression as his smashed face can manage. A laugh escapes me.

"Everything good?" Destiny asks, as I do an about-face and walk into my bedroom.

"No," I tell her. "Brian and Josh got into it, and I think it's my fault."

I roll my eyes and slip past her, just like I did this morning. Except now I'm breezy and confident. I toss my hair over one shoulder instead of reenacting my brother's suicide with my palm. Destiny follows me into the corner, where Mary's grave was last week and now is the staff room at the caverns.

"You okay?" she asks.

On the bed, my phone vibrates.

"I . . ."

My mouth hangs open, and I look for the right words, the proper response, what a normal person would do. This has been my medication for years; an attempt to tune myself every night so that the next day, I can be in more perfect harmony with the rest of the world. So far, it has worked. So far, I have maintained the pact that Dad and Lance left to me alone—to appear sane, at all costs. Because if anyone ever looked inside my head, I couldn't hide anymore.

They would see.

"You okay?" Destiny asks again, and my phone vibrates with another text.

"Hold on," I say, waving her aside as I reach for it.

> No, I wasn't your friend.

> But I still let you down.

> I should've talked to you.

> I knew you were alone.

"You okay?" Destiny asks again. Her back is to me, stuck in the replay of the day, waiting for me to manufacture the right response. Except I didn't know the right response. Not then, and not now. To either one of them—her or Brian.

> I wasn't alone.

I hastily answer Brian, then move back to Destiny, standing in front of her, letting her look at me instead of avoiding her gaze.

"No, I'm not okay," I tell her.

My mouth turns down even as I say it, the corners sinking in a muscular collapse that I know too well, the prelude to tears. Pain pricks in my eyes, and I feel the swelling water, know that they're getting ready to fall.

"She really isn't," the girl under the bed confirms.

"Good days and bad." The man in the closet comes partially to my defense.

I ignore them, breathe heavily, speak the truth.

"I'm not okay," I tell Destiny. "Josh was talking about having a party with the can-doers and the zips and he was talking about going cliff diving, or jumping at the quarry."

The phone goes off again, and Destiny gives it an annoyed glance. "Sorry." I brush past her, grabbing my phone.

Yeah.

Lance told me.

"What?" I ask aloud, shock lending my voice volume, irritation that my do-over is on permanent pause adding a bite to my tone.

Lance told you what exactly?

There's an ellipsis. It goes away. Comes back. Tries again.

I said I wasn't alone. You said Lance told you.

He told you what?

Can I call you?

The answer is quick and solid, one of the only things I've ever known so clearly.

No.

No for a lot of reasons. No, because I'll start crying . . . or shit, I already am. No, because Grandma and Grandpa will hear me talking to someone, and they will think that it is Mila, or that I have friends, or that everything is fine. None of these things are true, and I am trying very hard to keep as many things as possible in the category of what is real, and what is true. No, because my heart is too full, and my voice will break.

He wasn't ever alone, either.

He told me about them.

I sit and stare, my thumbpads resting against the screen, sending a steady feed of lowercase *t*'s into the text box.

Lance told Brian. He told someone else. He talked about the thing that was between me and him, me and Dad, him and Dad, us and Dad. He talked about the thing that all of us knew but none of us talked about. He talked about it with Brian.

There's a swelling in my stomach, but it's not vomit, or panic, it's not the need to run or scream, not the ballooning urge to get away, or fight. It's the not the slick black bag that holds my darkness, ready to break. It's something else, something warm, something like comfort.

Lance had someone he talked to.

"Didn't help, though, did it?" the man asks.

He said you weren't ever alone, either.

"Oh, I'm fucking alone," I tell the phone.

"Ouch," says the girl under the bed. "My feelings."

Are you okay?

It's what Destiny asked me, and I refused to answer honestly in the daylight. It's what everyone asks me, with their eyes and their faces, the set of the mouths and the just-so position of their brows. Everyone that crosses paths with me asks, every day, in every moment, with every molecule inside of them—*Are you okay?*

"It's a stupid question," I tell Destiny, tell the girl and the man, tell Brian. But I don't type it. This isn't a redo, this is someone trying to be my friend. No one has tried that in a really long time.

I need to answer this the right away.

I accidentally send the enormous series of *t*'s.

> Shit. Sorry.

I look back at his question, deceptively simple.

> Are you okay?

I think about it, want to say the right thing, do the right thing, be the right thing—honest and truthful and open and all the things everyone else seems to be. But they are acceptable people with normal thoughts and no monsters and no shifting darkness inside them, and there's no world where I can be honest without also being a horrifically frightening human being to know.

> Sometimes I am okay.

TWELVE

I stare at my own text, the blue bubble surrounding the white letters, the concrete statement that I have just made to a person I don't actually know that well.

> Sometimes I am okay.

Mostly when I'm underground is what I should type next, but I don't get the chance. Brian's response is fast.

> Lance was okay for a while, too.

My hand shakes, the words gone bleary as tears prick my eyes. I look up, but Destiny is gone, my do-over at a dead stop. I can't make the day right with Brian interrupting me, can't think straight with my dead brother's name filling up my phone.

Lance's name is a stark white against the blue, the perfect combination of letters that drives a spear into my heart, pinning me to the ground, unable to move, or think. Every day I see *l*'s and *a*'s, along with *n*'s and *c*'s—and *e*'s are everywhere—but seeing them in that order means my brother, and my brother means that nothing else matters in the moment that he's fully present in my mind.

I want to talk about my brother.

I need to talk about my brother.

I can't look at his name.

Brian is adding something to the text when I call him, the ellipsis disappearing as he picks up, his voice bright and welcoming.

"Hey," he says.

"He told you?" I ask, skipping any greeting.

"About the . . ." Brian fades off, unsure.

"Voices," I say. "We hear voices."

I take a minute, consider what I just said, blending both my brother and me together in the present tense, a version of reality that will never exist again.

"Heard," I correct myself. "Lance heard voices." I take a deep breath, pulling in oxygen, bathing my brain in it, letting blood flow with words and truth. "I do, too."

"Yeah," Brian says, "that's what he said." His tone is low and casual, accepting my statement. It's not followed by questions, or prying. There's no gasp or awkward silence. He doesn't hang up. I picture him in the cave today, the white line of skin along the band of his hat, the fresh stubble near his ears, the blush rising in his cheeks. He's a real person, a real human who knows that I'm gay, knows that I'm crazy, and he doesn't care about either one of those things.

"He worried about you," Brian says. "He said—"

"I didn't worry about him," I blurt. "Not enough. I didn't do anything."

This time, Brian is quiet. Maybe it's because we can talk about me and my problems, the electrical misfiring in my brain that makes me hear people that aren't there, and believe things that aren't true, even if only for a little while. But we can't talk about real things in the real world, a string of events that left my brother dangling from a maple tree, the leaves turning red long before autumn.

"I didn't do anything, either," Brian eventually says, his volume fading out, like the girl under the bed when she knows I'm not bringing her a drink. Not ever. Not again, anyway.

I shake my head, as if he can see me, phone pressed against my cheek, sweating. "You talked to him," I say. "That's a lot. It's . . ." My throat threatens to close, choking off the words.

"It's everything," I manage to finish, the words coming out in a whisper.

"That's why I said something," Brian says, strength back in his voice, a staccato in his words, like he's got to say them before they evaporate. "Today in the cave. You know this job, better than me or Josh, I bet. Mila won't keep you on caboose after this week."

My heart jumps at her name, my blood warming, my eyes darting around the room, hoping no one saw, no one noticed. A blush rises, shame and guilt forcing blood into my cheeks. For the first time in my life, someone is talking to me about my brother. That's where my thoughts need to be, not on a girl with a smile that breaks me and uneven, chipped fingernails.

"I wanted to talk to you," Brian goes on. "When I heard you got hired on at the caves, I knew it was supposed to happen, like it was fate, or God, or whatever, putting you in my path. I didn't do anything, didn't do enough, for your brother. I . . ."

He's quiet again, the heat from the shame in my face answered in his, our shared failures, a long conversation with no words, only dropped eyes and slumped shoulders, the world on our backs in the form of a dead boy.

"You couldn't," I tell him. "I couldn't."

"I don't believe that," Brian says, a thread of irritation in his voice now. "Lance said . . ." There's a deep breath, a hitched sigh, the sound of tears not falling but being swallowed. "Lance was a really angry person, Neely."

I laugh. I'm not supposed to. It's not the right response, not how you react to someone who is struggling to speak, the salt water of their own tears slicking their throat. On another day I'd notch this as a do-over and fix it late at night, alone in my room. But this is do-over time, and I still owe Destiny, but I'm here instead, talking to a boy about things that are not to be spoken of.

"Lance wasn't angry," I say. "Like, ever."

Lance was a boy who put baby birds back into their nests, a boy who pulled over when he saw someone with a flat tire. Lance was a boy who took the cups of water out of my room when he realized what they were for. A boy who quietly knew, and said little, silently redirecting me to the nearest path of sanity. Or, at least, one parallel to it.

"He was sad," I tell Brian, thinking of the long stares, the endless silence from his room. The way he'd throw himself into anything, everything, all things, to fill the void. We never talked about Dad or Mom, never talked about the false worlds we moved through, or the real one not reaching us. I used my do-overs to fix things; Lance made things, hands endlessly moving as he carved bows, knapped flint, wove a hammock for Grandpa, and built a birdhouse for Grandma.

"He was the only guy I know who got excited about going to Hobby Lobby," I say aloud, and Brian laughs.

"Yeah, he took me there once, when we needed to get leather strips to sew the flaps of the sweat lodge," he says. "I mean, we could've stapled it, but your brother was like, no, it has to be legit. I think maybe there were a few reasons that Lance liked to go there. One of them was leather, but the other two were blond."

"Oh, really?" I ask, my voice surging in amazement.

"Um, yeah," Brian says. "Your brother did not have a problem attracting girls."

"Huh," I say, truly surprised. "He never said anything about anybody."

"I don't think he ever got to the part where you talk to them," Brian says. "He was worried that he'd . . . you know, slip up."

Yeah, I know.

"Maybe that's why he started to get mad," Brian says. "He saw other guys that could—"

"Lance wasn't mad," I interrupt.

For the first time, there is a silence, this one long and heavy, all the loose words and slick-throated confessions from before gone, replaced by wariness and tension, a taut line between us. Brian takes another breath, and I can hear all of it, his chest rising, lungs expanding, the exhale of carbon dioxide, adding a little poison to the world.

"Do you know what Rock Bottom is?"

"No," I say, but it is not the correct answer to Brian's question. It is simply my reaction, an iron curtain being dropped, a resistance I will not allow him to overcome.

"Okay, so Rock Bottom—"

"I know what it is," I say, the soft corners of my voice gone. I'm all bent scissor blades and crooked nails, sharp things that have been misused. "Lance wouldn't use it."

Rock Bottom is, like many things on the internet, something that was started with good intentions and very quickly went in the opposite direction. It was supposed to be a forum where someone having a bad day could start a thread about it, sharing a less-than-stellar grade on their math final, that they'd lost their job, or been diagnosed with breast cancer. The idea was that someone else who also had these experiences could share their own, then explain how they coped, got through it, overcame the obstacle, and moved on with their lives.

What it became was something quite different.

Visiting Rock Bottom now is a deep dive into the dark side, an entire user population of people who are in touch with the worst parts of themselves. Some of them feel bad about it, but most of them want to share. It's a tour of sexual fantasies where not all the participants are of age, willing, or maybe even alive by the end, a glance into a world where deep-seated hatred has a loud voice, violence is the assumed mode of operation, and if someone likes to set fire to cats, that's their choice. Rock Bottom can make you lose your faith in humanity, strip the last bit of naivete from your life, and show you things you'll never unsee.

I've never been there. Neither has Lance. I know this, like I know my full name, my social security number, and my home address. I know this, like I know that my brother held my hand, our arms stretching to reach each other from our car seats, while Mom bled out onto the steering wheel.

"Lance didn't use Rock Bottom," I say again. "He just wouldn't."

I say it in a way that makes it very clear there is a period at the end of that sentence, not a comma, and certainly not a question mark.

Brian is quiet, not because he has nothing else to say, but because I shut him down.

"Neely, it's late," he finally says. "I'm sorry if I—"

"Hey, no more apologies, remember?" I say, forcing some humor in my voice, trying to find a part of me that can mimic hallway banter from movies where the teenagers always say the right thing and have clean, shiny hair.

"Right, right," he says, following my lead, also pretending that everything is okay.

"Can we talk in the morning at work?" I ask. It's the least I can do, let him know that I want to continue the conversation.

"Yes," he says. "Definitely."

"Cool," I say. "Then I guess I'll . . . see you then?"

There's a catch in my voice, like maybe we won't see each other tomorrow because I'm not capable of getting out of bed, he quits his job, one of us jumps off a bridge, abandons their family overnight, or dies in a car crash.

"Yes," Brian says again, his voice steady, calm, something to hold on to. "I'll see you at work."

It's more than I usually have. Much more, actually. There is a guarantee that the next day, I will talk to another human being. It feels good, the warmth of expectation spreading through me even as we say our good nights, nudging aside the darkness, making it a little smaller. I hang up and stare at the ceiling for two full minutes.

"Lance didn't use Rock Bottom," I announce to the room.

"Are you sure?" It's from under the bed, high and quiet, the little girl opening the door to doubt.

I squeeze the pillow tightly, increasing pressure on my ears, narrowing my vision so that I can't see my room, and the slightly open door of the closet, where I know the man waits to add his thoughts on the matter. Somehow, I believe that covering my ears will mute the voices inside my head, a nonsensical solution to an irrational problem.

"I know my brother," I say, sitting up suddenly.

The pillow falls away as I point accusingly at the closet, preemptively striking out against the man, planting my flag on this hill, my allegiance to a dead boy. Silence follows, a long stretch of moments when an embarrassed tension hangs across the room, bouncing off me and the two others who aren't really here, swelling the air.

"You can never truly know someone else," the man says, his words borrowed from my brother's mouth, the last thing he'd said to me.

We'd been passing each other in the hallway, wordless in our usual way, when Lance bumped against me, and I'd dropped my phone. It had landed face up, the video of a popular influencer and her golden retriever still playing.

"Really?" Lance had asked, bending down to pick it up for me. "This is what you do all day?"

I'd looked at him, the sunburn blooming across his nose, a small cut where a wood chip had sliced his cheek when he was working on something new, the next thing, a project, a goal, things to keep his hands busy and his mind calm, interests he shared with Brian. I, on the other hand, sat in my room and watched videos of happy people, wondering how they managed.

"It's fun," I told him, drawing my shoulders up in defense of the use of my time, witnessing the lives of other, more successful people, taking notes. I didn't have a friend, didn't have someone I did things with. My interactions with other humans were one-sided, lasted an average of ninety seconds, and pixelated when our internet was slow. I'd swallowed, watching the girl and her dog, their beautiful life playing out in my brother's palm. I held out my hand, asking for my life back.

"I feel like I know her," I'd said.

Lance's face had changed then, a spark lighting in his eyes, the sunburned skin of his cheeks tightening as his top lip raised. "You can never truly know someone else, Neely," he'd said. His voice was loose gravel on the road, broken glass scattered across pavement, dangling electric lines. "Not in real life, and sure as fuck not like this."

He'd shoved the phone into my hand, slamming his door, as the video looped, the dog fetched, the girl laughed, and from inside his room, I'd heard a deep, hitching breath, the prelude to a sob.

I turned away. I left him alone. I did what I thought was right.

Two days later, he also did what he thought was right, his final statement ringing in my ears as my brother performed his last act, drawing the project of his life to an end, fulfilling his own prophecy, leaving me to wonder how this person that I thought I knew could have carried the will to die inside of them, and the determination to see it through.

THIRTEEN

"That is not what fucking happened."

It's the first thing I hear when I pull into work the next morning, sliding into the spot next to Mila's minivan. Her voice cuts through the air, already heavy with humidity, and I freeze, aware that I am trespassing, but unable to stop it.

"No, Patrick—no! You listen to *me*, you son of a bitch!"

I glance over when she punches her dashboard.

"I want that video taken down. And I mean *now*. I don't care if it costs the rest of my tuition, I will hire a lawyer who will shake six figures' worth of quarters out of your ass!"

It sounds good, and her voice remains on attack, but she's wiping tears off her cheeks, and I look away. I don't know what to do; Mila was so wrapped up in her conversation that she didn't see me park next to her, but she'll certainly notice my car when she gets out. And then I'll have to pretend that I didn't hear anything, or try to console her. Either way, me just sitting in the car and hovering is weird. Even I know that.

"I'll hire a lawyer who will shake six figures' worth of quarters out of your ass, shitbird." Not for the first time, the Shitbird Man hits a home run and gets one in before I'm surrounded by tourists. I issue him a silent thank-you, and then get out, shutting my door and slipping around the front of my car, glancing at Mila and offering her a feeble wave.

In another world, maybe she is a little surprised but plays everything off, and later we exchange knowing glances in the staff room, an unspoken acknowledgment that she was there, I was there, and we're not going to talk about it. In another world, maybe I take the initiative and simply walk over and ask her what's wrong, and she tells me, and that's when the patina of coworkers falls away and we become real friends, girls who trust each other and talk about things.

But we're in this world, the one where trees drip blood and fathers disappear, and in this world, at this moment, Mila throws her phone as hard as she can, and it bounces off the windshield and hits her in the face. She jerks and yells, her elbow connected with the car horn, which makes me jump and scream, and she sees me for the first time, one hand covering her nose, our eyes connecting as we both shout, "Fuck!"

There's no way around it now; we've seen each other. Both of my hands are clenched in my hair, and Mila and I just stare at each other for a second, her holding her face, me holding my skull. I move first, winding around to the driver's side just as she opens the door, straightening her green Caverns polo and brushing away the last, betraying tear as she gets out.

"It's okay," she says hurriedly, not meeting my gaze. "I'm fine."

She leans into the car, finds her phone, gets her hair up into a messy bun, rolls her shoulders back, takes a deep breath. "I'm fine," she says again, eyes finally locking with mine.

"You're not," I say quietly. Then, because it feels slightly accusatory, I add, "I'm not, either."

The sheen of pretense fades from her irises as she stares at me, barriers gone as tears rise again, the dent in the bridge of her nose a deep, irritated red. The corners of Mila's mouth turn down in an involuntary gesture, grief possessing the muscles, the heart overcoming the mind as a sob escapes, emotions with no words, just Mila, coming apart, breaking down.

Falling into me.

I'm stunned, but my own heart has taken over as well, leaving the mind and all questions behind as I wrap my arms around her, feel her strength ebbing, my body taking up the slack. Another cry escapes her, and she turns her head away from my neck, searching for air, her hair against my face, the smell of strawberry shampoo and salty tears filling my nose.

I could die right here, I could melt into a puddle with her, the sun turning us to liquid, blending with the bubbling tar of the parking lot, drowning the tossed cigarette butt at my feet as we became the purest substance on earth, two girls as one. Mila pulls away from me, the ridge of my polo imprinted on her face. Something of mine has left a mark on her skin, and I feel full.

"Shit. I'm sorry, Neely," she says, wiping her nose.

"It's okay," I say.

"It's not," she argues, shaking her head. "I don't act like this."

"I believe you," I tell her, and it's true.

I look at her, tall and strong, her chin up again, a little trickle of blood starting to escape one nostril. She is not a girl who loses her shit in minivans and throws smartphones. She is not a girl who cries on a coworker's shoulder and has to wipe her face clean before clocking in. Mila is a girl who gets things done and does them right the first time.

Mila is a girl who tells bad jokes and everyone laughs anyway, because everyone loves her. Everyone, it seems, except for someone I don't know but have decided I hate. And his name, apparently, is Patrick.

"Tell me," I say as another car pulls into the lot, John, who plucks the cigarette from his mouth when he spots us, then parks as far away as he can. Mila's eyes follow him as he gives us a small wave, then heads into the visitors' center, unlocking the front doors. T.S. rises from his overnight spot on one of the porch benches and takes a long stretch, his back arching, tail fluffing, teeth exposed in a jaw-cracking yawn. He spots Mila and hops down, trotting across the parking lot in search of his next cuddle.

"Oh, buddy, no," Mila says, and breaks into a jog, holding both hands out to stop him from crossing the lot. I follow along behind her and watch as she scoops him into her arms, then buries her face in his ruff, the cat taking my place as her comfort. She eyes me over his fur, her eyes still red-rimmed and unnaturally bright.

"Want to do the morning sweep with me?" Mila asks.

"Yes," I say.

Yes, yes, and yes.

The close, humid air of the caverns closes in around us as we move our lights, occasionally stopping to pick up a loose candy wrapper, a dropped pen, or anything else that a tourist decided they didn't want to carry anymore and *donated* to the caverns, as Mila likes to say.

"Patrick is the kind of guy that you make mistakes for," Mila says. "All through high school I was a good girl, did the right thing, worked hard. You know the story."

I do. But this one is about Mila, which means I want to hear more.

"I mean, don't get me wrong—I had fun," she goes on, not apparently needing any response in order to keep talking. A shock to the system can do that, trigger nervous chatter, some of it horribly intimate oversharing.

I remember talking to the officer in the morgue after I identified Lance's body, telling her that he had a lot of freckles, and I did, too, even around my vulva. It hadn't seemed all that ridiculous at the time, given that I'd just looked at what was left of a dead body and tried to determine if it was my brother or not, which hadn't been all that easy to do. It was the freckles that really clinched it for me, or rather, a particular constellation on his forearm. Looking at Lance had been like seeing fabric that had been unspooled and torn, then thrown together into a pile.

"I drank most weekends once I was an upperclassman, and I've smoked some pot," Mila goes on. "But my grades were always good, so I figured no harm, right?"

"Sure," I say. I don't have much to add, since I've never had a drink and don't get invited to parties. "I mean, I don't have any judgment for it."

"Didn't think you would," Mila says. "You seem cool."

Literally no one, ever, has said that.

"And boys . . ." Mila sighs, a sound that fills the graffiti room, her deep exhalation filling the silence, her breath bouncing off names and dates, brushing against Margaret's name in all its iterations.

"What can I say?" Mila shrugs, spinning her light around the room, checking the path in front of us. "They are kind of my weakness."

"Oh," I say, because this is definitely the part where I can't relate. Like, at all.

"But I got through high school without having my heart broken or getting pregnant or sleeping with anybody who wasn't my boyfriend, which I thought was a pretty good track record. And then I met Patrick."

"At college?" I ask.

"Yeah," she says. "I wanted to go to Purdue, but you know . . ." She lifts her flashlight to illuminate her other hand and rubs her thumb and forefinger together.

I imagine a world where she goes to Indiana to college, where we don't meet. Where we're not underground together, in the dark, sharing secrets. Mila might have regrets, but I don't. I consider how selfish this is, but then I lift my shoulder to my cheek, feel her tears still drying on my polo. I'm never washing this shirt.

"He's not special. I mean, there is literally not one thing about Patrick that would make you go—*that's it*. That's why I'm so into this guy." She stabs a finger in the air, pointing at nothing.

"He's not particularly attractive, or rich, or funny. He's not that smart or interesting. He's not a great conversationalist, and he's just got the standard six inches below the waist," Mila goes on. "But . . . shit . . ."

She sighs again, and this time there's a definite sexual tone to it. I tense, aware that she's thinking of a man, of his body, of her own body, of theirs coming together. A surge of heat rises within me at the idea of her skin, mixed with an unpleasant feeling I can only call rage, as ink seeps out of the dark place inside of me, leaving small blots on my soul.

"What happened?" I ask. "What did he do?"

"Fuck." She shakes her head, banishing any good memories. "I don't know. Anything. Everything. Made me think I was dumb, or not quite good enough. Always had little tiny adjustments that he wanted, small things, within reach. Things that would sound reasonable, then I'd do them, thinking I was just being a considerate girlfriend. Then the next one would come."

"Adjustments?" I ask. Darkness swirls, touring my gut, pushing out toward my elbows. If it reaches my hands, I may hit something.

"Yeah, you know. In the beginning, he'd say things like, 'You look so great today. Yellow is your color.'" She smiles a little, her lips quivering. "And I'd be like—nice! A guy who hands out compliments. And the next time we went out I'd wear green or red, and he'd say, 'Nah, definitely yellow.' Like it was a joke, or something, right? And the compliments stopped, so pretty soon I'm just shopping for yellow clothes and only wearing yellow, and I even bought this bra and panty set for our three-month anniversary—"

She cuts herself off, shaking her head. "God, I sound like a fucking idiot."

"No," I tell her. "You sound like someone who's been emotionally manipulated."

Mila swings her light over to me. "How'd you get so smart?"

"YouTube," I tell her. "I watch a lot of armchair psychologists, as well as some real ones. You should see my ads."

Mila laughs, the sound bouncing off rock as we make our way into the room with the granite slab we call the sacrificial table, our beams tracing the stalagmites that surround it. Mila sighs, spotting a chipped one, its tip broken off and resting at the base.

"So much for the no-touching rule," she says.

"Is that what Patrick did?" I ask. "Break the no-touching rule?"

"Yeah, I don't really have that rule," Mila says breezily. "Not since like, junior year. But he wanted other things, stuff that I definitely *do* have rules about."

"Video?" I ask, thinking back to what I overheard.

"Pics and videos, yeah," she says, her jawline hardening. "I know it's super normal for a lot of people, but I never did that. If someone has that, they've got power over you, and I knew I'd already given enough control over to Patrick. I mean, he never *told* me what to wear—"

"But he implied his preferences," I interrupt her.

"And I complied."

"But not pictures?" I ask, as we move away from the table, into the last cavern, where stalactites and -mites surround us, the earth a teeth-lined mouth.

"No," Mila says. "Right up until last weekend. I was at his place, got really drunk and passed out. He . . ." Her voice stutters, the words eaten by the wet air around us, the humidity of the grave.

"He did what he wanted and filmed it all. It was uploaded before I even got back to my apartment." Mila's voice is almost lost now, low vowels evaporating, hard consonants bouncing off the metal door of the exit. "Some amateur porn site, I guess. A friend of mine called me, mortified that he had to come clean about how he found it in the first place, but he let me know it existed."

"Sounds like a good guy," I say.

"I guess some of them can be," she says. "Too bad I'm not attracted to any of them. So . . . yeah." Mila throws both her hands in the air, frustration incarnate. "Now apparently anyone who wants to see every inch of me, getting railed, in any position, absolutely can."

"Also, he raped you," I tell her. "Don't pretend for a second that's not what happened."

"I know," she says, arms falling back to her sides, lips curling downward again. "That's the next step, if he doesn't take it down."

"You'll press charges?"

"I'll *threaten* to press charges," she clarifies. "C'mon, Neely. I was his girlfriend; I was at his place voluntarily; I drank alcohol I brought with me." She ticks everything off her fingers, each a strike against her in the court of public opinion, and probably even in the actual justice system.

"You and I both know how that ends," she says, finally reaching for the door. She pauses for a second, hand resting on the metal. A deeply unfunny sound comes from inside her, a self-deprecating laugh that turns into a choke and finds the air as a sob. "I'm even wearing that damn yellow bra and panty set in the video. Well . . . I start out wearing it, anyway."

I reach out, my hand on her shoulder. "You didn't do anything wrong."

"That's debatable," Mila says, opening the door with a shriek of metal. "I trusted someone."

FOURTEEN

The morning meeting goes like any other, Mila stands on the rock, telling everyone what to do, her sunglasses resting exactly where they need to in order to hide the bump on the bridge of her nose from throwing her phone. Josh has a small bruise under his eye. Brian stands closer to me than to him. Destiny and Tabitha keep their distance from all of us, braiding each other's hair and picking at the grass.

"Reminder," Mila finishes up, glancing down at her clipboard. "The mixer with our fellow employees from the canoe livery and zip-lining is tonight."

"Oh my God, seriously?" Tabitha says, falling backward into the grass and throwing one arm over her eyes. "That's a real thing that's actually happening?"

"It is," Mila says. "And I suggest you come. We're not exactly unionized here, and John doesn't have to pay us fifteen an hour. That's a choice he makes, and this is not a hard job." Mila pushes her glasses down her nose and eyes us all over them sternly. "We get away with a lot, you guys. And I mean a lot."

"I didn't flip the kayakers paddles around," Destiny protests. "If John wants everybody to get along, he needs to just say so, not make us eat hot dogs and Jell-O salads together."

"That's proper Midwestern fare, and you'll clean your plates," Mila says, pointing her pen at Destiny, while a smile pulls at her lips.

"Whatever," Destiny says, but she's smiling back as she pops the head off a dandelion in Mila's direction.

"Real party will happen afterward," Josh announces. "I talked to Jessica and Hilary. The can-doers and the zips are in."

Beside me, Brian tenses, his arm going taut. I watch as a parade of goose bumps marches across his skin, rolling under the notch of his elbow.

"Where?" he asks.

"*Not* the quarry," Josh turns to us, the hint of an apology in his eyes. "Just up the hill, in the woods. Hilary said there's a good site there for a fire." He juts his chin at the shelter house, where rolling, wooded hills rise behind.

Brian turns to me, and I glance up, our first interaction since talking last night. His eyes are a light blue, with a black ring circling the iris.

I give a small nod, and he says, "Cool. We're in."

He says *we're* like he and I are friends. The warm feeling from the night before rises again, a flickering flame that spreads some light, sending my shadows back to the dark corners inside, the smaller ones where I now harbor what Mila confided to me.

"Cool, BYOB," Josh says, and Brian's eyes darken. I think of the fact that he only ever has bologna for lunch. Last week I saw him scraping mold off the corner of the bread.

"I got you," I tell him. It's a dumb thing to say, because I don't got him—or any beer. I suppose I could show up with a bottle of Grandma's cooking sherry and tell everyone drinks are on me.

"Thanks," Brian says, and nudges his shoulder against mine.

"Sure," I say, and add *figure out how to get beer* under my list of things to do along with *become mentally well and somehow get a damaged straight girl to fall in love with me.*

"Josh, you and I are historical, Neely, you're with us," Mila says, hopping down from the rock. "Tab and Destiny, you get natural wonders."

"You're both natural wonders," Josh says, wiggling his eyebrows at the duo.

"Save it for the zippers," Tabitha says as she helps Destiny to her feet. "Your shit hasn't gotten old with them yet."

"Also, you're a total whore," Destiny adds.

"And you're in public," Mila says, giving the other girl a light swat on the head with her clipboard as she passes her, nodding to the guests that have started to accumulate in the parking lot. Dads slide out from behind steering wheels for a stretch, while moms dash after toddlers, wiping morning car snacks off their upper lips.

"Whoa, boy," Brian says, taking his hat off and wiping sweat from his brow, his eyes sweeping the lot as another van pulls in, this one from a church camp. "I am not ready for this day."

"Did I keep you up too late last night?" I ask, but he shakes his head as we walk, shoulder to shoulder, to the staff room.

"No," he says. "Just, you know . . . didn't sleep great after we talked. I felt like I upset you, and that wasn't what I wanted to do. I mean, the whole idea of reaching out in the first place is so you feel like you've got somebody."

"It's cool," I say, but my eyes are focused far ahead of us as I watch Mila slip into the air-conditioning of the visitors' center. She kept her shit together during the staff meeting, but I saw her hand go to her pocket more than once and could hear the vibrating of her phone.

"It's nice to have somebody," I say.

"Yeah, too bad we're not on the same tour today," Brian answers, apparently under the impression that I was talking about him. But I smile and let him believe it, because maybe I get to have more than one friend in this version of the real world.

"Too bad," I agree, and head for the bench near the staff entrance, where T.S. is rolling around on his back. I settle next to him on the bench, curling my fingers into the fur on his tummy. He writhes under my hand, the low hum of his purr filling the air, his body vibrating under my palm. Mila's voice comes over the loudspeaker, inviting everyone holding tickets for the historic tour to meet at the bus. Families and groups of people start to board, and I get to my feet as Mila breezes past me.

"Rock 'n' roll," she says as I join her, her mouth set in a firm line as she ignores her phone going off, once again. We walk in step to the History Wagon, where Josh is taking tickets.

"Good morning, everyone!" Mila says, her voice filling the air.

"Jesus," Josh flinches at her volume, and one of the women from the church bus gives him a nasty look.

"Nope, sorry, the historical tour doesn't cover that time period," Mila says, turning to us as the last toddler pulls herself up the bus steps. "I'll take point. Josh, you and Neely are caboose."

"I'm cool with it," he says. "As long as I get to drive." He digs in his pocket and holds up the keys to the bus, dangling them in front of Mila's face.

"Give those back!" Mila snaps. "You can't drive. You don't have your CDL."

She snatches at them, but Josh pulls away easily, holding them just out of her reach. The back of his hand bounces off my forehead, the key ring snagging some loose hairs. They tear free as he jerks the keys away from Mila again, but he doesn't notice me.

"Josh!" Mila seethes as a pale face appears in the bus window, a paying customer curious about the delay. "It's a safety issue," Mila says, crossing her arms, refusing to be baited by the dangling keys again.

"You're not actually my boss," he shoots back, and Mila grabs his elbow, dragging him around to the front of the bus, where the looky-loos can't see. I follow, watching as she backs him against the grill, her finger inches from his nose, and the self-satisfied smile that rests below it.

"Listen, you absolute dickweed," Mila says, dropping her voice low. "I've got seniority, I've got a CDL, and I've got about two seconds of patience left. Now give me those goddamn keys, or you'll have a bruise to match the one Brian gave you. But it won't be on your face."

Josh's eyes trail away from Mila's, following the curve of her collarbone, where her shirt is pulled to the side, the shiny blue strap of her bra showing.

"Damn," he says, pushing her polo farther off her shoulder, index finger tapping on the stripe of blue. "I thought it would be yellow."

He didn't know I was there when he accidentally hit me in the face, didn't know that he tore out strands of my hair and that they're still dangling from his outstretched hand, along with the keys. But he knows when I hit him with everything I've got, all his breath leaving as my forearm connects with his throat, shoving him against the front of the bus and pressing upward, his cheeks going gray as I cut off his oxygen.

Lance and Brian didn't have signs on their treehouse that said "No Girls Allowed," and they never complained when I wanted to tag along—but that also meant that I was expected to do what they did, which meant starting fires, digging up worms for fishing, and sometimes just plain old hand-to-hand combat. They'd storm my snow fort or raid my worm can, always knowing that I would attack . . . and always aware that they would win. But I learned a lot along the way, and one of them was how to choke a motherfucker out.

"Give Mila the keys," I say slowly, and Josh drops them without hesitation. Mila scoops them from the hot asphalt, and I back away from Josh, releasing him. He takes a deep breath, massaging his throat as Mila wordlessly climbs onto the bus, the engine roaring to life as her voice comes over the intercom.

"Sorry for the delay, folks," she says cheerily.

Josh eyes me warily, sidestepping past me, one hand still protectively covering his Adam's apple. "You're fucking crazy."

"Maybe," I agree. "But that won't get the shit out of your pants."

FIFTEEN

Every tour is full, so Josh, Mila, and I spend all of our time explaining the color composition of crystals, telling people not to touch them, and avoiding eye contact with each other. Mila hits her marks, makes her jokes, and her tip jar fills up, even as her smile remains strained, and Josh and I refuse to speak to each other, the bottoms of our own jars still visible through handfuls of loose change.

It's not until I'm home that I realize I still haven't figured out the beer situation. Grandma gives me a big smile when I tell her I won't be back for dinner and explain about the coworker mixer. I don't add that afterward I'll be going into the deep woods with them and probably getting drunk for the first time in my life, but I do tell her I don't know when I'll be home. Grandma and Grandpa have never had to enforce a curfew because I've never gone anywhere, so she's left wondering if now is the time to make up rules, when my phone goes off.

"Who's that?" she asks, as she wipes down the kitchen counter. "The Bailey boy?"

I can't ignore the lilt of hope in her voice, so I decide to be honest.

"It's Brian," I say, which instantly ushers Lance's ghost into the room.

Grandma goes a little pale, and the circular motion of the dishcloth stops for a moment.

"He's been really nice to me," I add, and the dishcloth moves again, this time counterclockwise.

"He seems nice," Grandma agrees, and even though her words are positive, her tone remains staunchly neutral, discouraging conversational topics that could lead to my brother.

But maybe it doesn't have to be that way. Maybe there's a world where I say *Brian*, and Grandma thinks of him as *my* friend, not Lance's. Maybe if I keep saying his name, always with a smile on my face, they'll start to associate him with this newer version of me, the one who gets out of bed, showers regularly, and goes to work every day.

I glance down at the text from Brian, which just says, **Hey, can I call you? NSFW.**

I don't know what could possibly be not safe for work, since we work somewhere you can choke out people and talk about your vagina in front of family groups without any repercussions, so I duck into my bedroom and dial Brian's number.

"Hey." He picks up immediately. "About tonight—"

"Yeah, I don't know if I can come through with the beer promise," I admit.

"That's okay, I've got a better idea," Brian says. "Did your grandparents ever clean out Lance's room?"

They hadn't, a conspicuous absence on the to-do list. Traditional grief had been taken from us, the pall of suicide stitched people's mouths shut, and what was left of Lance couldn't have been formed into anything like a human body. There was no montage of highlight sports clips at the funeral, no mosaic of pictures with friends, no final clothes to choose to bury him in. Lance went away in an urn, only a handful of people came to the graveside service, and the door to his room has been shut ever since, 132 square feet of the house that we all simply pretend does not exist.

"No, they didn't clean it out," I tell Brian. "I don't think anyone has even been in there since . . . well, *since*."

"Not even you?" Brian asks, as if Lance and I had nightly heart-to-hearts where we talked about our days and shared our hopes and dreams. Instead, our closeness was about knowing without speaking, nodding at each other's pain, and then pushing through it alone.

"No," I say. "I haven't been in there."

"Would you be willing to do it if it meant having something to bring to the party?"

"If Lance had a beer stash, it is skunky as shit by now," I say.

"Not beer. But skunks do come into it, if you get me."

"Whatever," I say, flopping onto my bed. "Lance didn't smoke pot."

There's a long silence from the other end, one that extends to the room around me, which must mean that the girl under the bed and the man in the closet agree with me.

"Look, Neely," Brian finally says. "I don't know what ideas you have about Lance and who he was. All I can tell you is that there is pot in your brother's room, and if we bring it to the party tonight, we won't be the poor kids that are just tagging along with the better-looking people who have brighter futures."

That hits home. Mila might be borrowing her mom's minivan and can't afford to go to Purdue, but her natural beauty puts her on par with Destiny, Tabitha, and Josh, who are all operating on different levels in terms of income, social status, and genetic blessings. The truth is that John could probably do a pretty brisk business in employee calendars, with red-haired Destiny picking apples in cutoffs for an autumn month; dark-haired Tabitha slinking among the shadows for October; Josh with no shirt, soaking up the sun in summer meadow grass; and long-legged, tan Mila getting the prime spot of July, probably in an American flag bikini.

My mind rests there a little too long, and I mentally flip forward to the winter months, where Brian's ice-blue eyes could maybe get a nod. I fit wherever stringy hair, big pores, and a little extra around the middle goes. Or whenever Mental Health Awareness month is.

"Neely?"

Brian draws me back into the conversation, and away from thoughts of Mila in a bikini.

"Yeah, I know," I tell him. "We're the scholarship kids."

"Among the cavers, for sure," Brian says. "And I've got no shot with the zips, but the can-doers—"

"So this is about girls?" I ask, my eyebrows going up.

"Isn't everything about girls?" he shoots back, and I consider that for a second.

"Mostly, yes," I agree, still trying to get July out of my mind.

"If I show up in holey clothes and a beater truck, bumming beer off everybody else—"

"No, I get it," I say, rolling over onto my belly and examining some of my split ends in the light from the window. "Do you know where Lance kept it?"

"Yes," Brian says, relief evident in his voice.

"Tell me."

Lance's room doesn't exist. It's a hole in the universe, a rip in space-time, a place that I have banned from my visual plane since the door was irrevocably shut. Even Grandma, in all of her cleanliness, does not break the seal. The runner tracks from her vacuuming run right up the doorway but go no farther. I'm staring at them now, years of treating Lance's room as a memorial holding me in place.

I have successfully navigated a summer job, my personal hygiene is on an upswing, and I appear to have a friend; I can open a damn door. The sudden movement sends dust bunnies flying into the air as I push into Lance's room. The bunnies settle, one of them resting on my upturned hand like a snowflake, a dirtier version of something that was supposed to be pure. I look at it, resting there, a collection of dead skin cells that might be the most of my brother I have left. I close my fingers, compressing it as I glance around the room.

His bed is made, the navy-blue comforter tucked neatly over the pillows. The closet is shut, a stack of Louis L'Amour paperbacks rest on a shelf, along with a bird's nest, a buck knife, and a chunk of flint. Two smaller drawers line the side of his desk, and—if Brian is right— one of them has a tin of poker chips in it, and inside that, there will be a few actual chips and a lot of pot.

"He grew it," Brian had said. "Just enough for him and me, a few plants off the riverbank."

I'd listened, disbelieving. I'd never smelled it on Lance, never seen him as anything other than stone-cold sober. A lot of things can be said about both of us, but what mattered most to Lance and me was that we never gave our grandparents a reason to worry. We couldn't make other people like us, and we couldn't force anybody to date us, but we could get good grades, keep our noses clean, always show up for dinner, and never let anyone know that we heard voices.

Or were gay, in my case, and—apparently—smoked pot, in Lance's.

"Well, shit," I say as I dangle a baggie from the tips of my fingers. The low musk of skunk and heavy vegetation fills my nose as I uncurl my other hand, looking at the dust clump there.

Lance never introduced me to his monsters. I don't know who they were or what they said. I don't know what sounds followed him everywhere he went, or if he ever got the smell of Mom's blood and Dad's sadness out his nose. I don't know what he was thinking when he jumped, or if his monsters went with him, bodies falling in tandem, their voices in his ears.

I cannot manage is what his note had said.

My hand crushes the dust bunny, Lance's dead cells mixing with my nervous sweat. I blow a puff of breath over the surface of his desk, watching a swirl of what is left of my brother float in the dying light of evening. I snag a few dust bunnies from the air, rolling them into a ball with the first one, forcing them into a shape that can never be my brother but will serve as the closest approximation I can get.

I lift the dust bunny to my face, dissecting it, spotting a loose hair among the dirt.

"You could not manage," I say to it.

But the truth is that I don't know why.

And if I'm going to make it, maybe I need to know why he couldn't.

SIXTEEN

The tables in the visitors' center are usually littered with pamphlets about rocks, cards promoting local businesses, the sign-in book, and the occasional thank-you note from a visitor. Tonight, the tables have been pushed into the center of the room and filled with Crock-Pots, plastic silverware, napkins, a punch bowl, and—Destiny wasn't wrong—two different colors of Jell-O salad.

"Why do we suspend vegetables in gelatin?" a voice at my elbow asks, and I turn to find Tabitha standing there.

"Hey," I say, surprised she's chosen me as her go-to for conversation. True, John and his wife, Carol, are busily making conversation with someone's parents, and there's a group of tanned athletic teens standing in the other corner—the zips, I assume. But Tab could just pull out her phone and avoid interaction altogether. Instead, she chose to talk to me, the only other caver who is here. She exhales noisily, blowing her jet-black bangs skyward.

"This is the actual dumbest thing ever," she mutters.

"Were we supposed to invite our families?" I ask, nodding to the adults.

"Hell if I know, and wouldn't have asked my parents anyway," she says, her eyes flicking over to me. "Did you invite yours? Oh, wait . . ."

She turns red, the blood filling her cheeks and rising to her hair, like the thermometer fundraising goal board that the United Way puts in the park every summer during their annual drive.

"It's okay," I say quickly. "It's fine."

"It's not fine. Jesus," Tabitha says, hitting herself on the forehead. "I'm a fucking idiot. I'm sorry. It's not like I don't know."

Not like she doesn't know. Not like everyone doesn't know. They just forget, sometimes, because most of them have families, and they aren't used to talking around the conversational hole of someone who doesn't. These are people with labradoodles in the yard, crown molding in the living room, and cars with clean cupholders. When they ask each other how their day is going, they answer *good* or *fine*, and they are actually telling the truth.

"Don't worry about it," I say, waving off yet another apology from Tab, whose blush is just starting to recede. "Let's start over."

"Cool. You coming after?"

"Yeah, I brought pot," I blurt to Tabitha, whose eyes get big.

"Nice," she says, nodding. "Didn't know you smoked."

"I don't," I tell her. "I mean, I didn't. I'm starting now."

"Turning over a new leaf, so to speak?" she asks, cocking an eyebrow.

It gets a laugh out of me. I'm about to ask her something, anything, whether her hair is naturally that black or if she dyes it, if she likes modernist poetry or thinks Josh is a twat, when Destiny pushes through the front doors.

"Hot dogs are not real food," she announces as she joins us, giving me a once-over.

"It's not pork, it ain't beef, and I doubt it's turkey," Tabitha agrees. "But why would you call any meat a dog? That's not okay."

A sun-darkened brunette with sharp cheekbones separates herself from the zips and walks over to us. "Hey, Destiny," she says.

"Jessica, this is Tabitha and Neely," my coworker says.

"Hi," Jessica says, her eyes meeting mine. "So, we're not doing trust falls and shit, right?"

"Not unless there's something extra in that punch bowl," Destiny says, to which Jessica sneaks a glance over her shoulder at the adults.

"I got you," she says, smoothly pulling a small flask from her hip pocket, and dosing Destiny's drink.

"Ladies?" Jessica asks, but I don't have a cup.

Tabitha takes her up on the boost as Brian wanders in, followed by Mila and a group of girls I don't recognize but must be the can-doers. Josh shows up, eschewing us for the company of the zips, which I can't entirely blame him for. They could fill up the twelve-month employee calendar all on their own, and probably roll right into next year, too.

Mila finds her way to my side. "Hey, my mom needs the van tonight. Any chance you can drive me to my apartment after?"

"Yes," I say, jumping at the chance to spend more time with her.

"Cool, I'll let Mom know I got a ride," Mila says, pulling out her phone. "Thanks," she adds, giving my wrist a quick squeeze, leaving molten lava in the wake of her touch.

Mila makes her way through the different groups, pulling one person from each, making introductions, and generally forcing everyone to break away from their own camps by her sheer willpower.

"Neely," she says, coming at me with a smile. "Have you met Brigit?"

I haven't, and I have little interest in anyone in the room other than Mila, but I find myself standing by a display of antique lanterns while Brigit tells me that ponytail elastics are the most common trash floating in the river, after plastic water bottles.

"I keep a stick in the canoe, and I fish them out whenever I can snag them," she explains. "The hair ties, not the water bottles."

I don't really have anything to say to that, so I just nod and drink my punch, balancing a plate of sloppy joe in the other hand.

"The other thing is all the used needles," Brigit adds, taking another drink. "Real uptick in that lately."

"Really?" I ask, something she says finally catching my attention.

"Oh yeah," she says. "Things have gotten really bad around here, if you haven't noticed."

I haven't noticed.

Tabitha overhears us, and joins the conversation. "Last week Josh found some needles at the entrance to the historical tour. I cleared them out before the bus got there."

"Super carefully, I hope?" Brigit asks.

Tabitha only nods, and the conversation lags, all three of us looking down into our cups.

"Hey, would it be cool if I brought a plus-one to the party?" Brigit asks. "I was going to ditch plans with a friend tonight because of this, but if I could bring her along . . ." She trails off, looking at us hopefully, like Tabitha and I are the Supreme Court of Who Comes to Parties.

"Sure, whatever," Tabitha says, draining her cup. "Tell her don't come empty-handed."

A loud laugh breaks across the room; Destiny is hanging on to one of the male zippers, twisting a lock of red hair around her index finger.

"Oh my God, just don't get pregnant," Tabitha mutters under her breath.

"That's Paxton, and she's probably already in her second trimester just from being in close proximity," Brigit says.

"Great," Tabitha says. "Do I need to go save her?"

"Nah." Brigit shrugs. "He's safe; he's just slutty."

"They'll get along fine, then," Tab says, eyeing the couple over her drink, then blanches and clarifies. "Sorry, I'm not a shamer. Destiny can do whatever she wants. I'm just hitting one hundred tonight, socially." She glances at me, then looks down at her drink. "I don't know what Jessica put in this, but apparently it makes you say asshole things in public."

"Everybody! Everybody!" Mila climbs onto the table and clanks a plastic fork against her SOLO cup. "John has asked me to make a little speech. I promise to keep it short and sweet, just like Tabitha."

There's a general laugh, and Mila rolls into an impromptu speech, John nodding behind her as she talks about how lucky we are to love our jobs and to work in a fun, family-friendly environment. She says a few more things about sticking together, treating each other—and each respective camp—with respect, after which Mila effectively ends the party by announcing that we all need to pitch in and help John and Carol clean up.

Mildly bored teens are suddenly motivated, and all the Crock-Pots, cutlery, and plastic tablecloths are safely stored in Carol's hatchback within ten minutes as a few people slip away, pretending to leave, while really just pulling their cars out of the lot and down the hill, then killing the lights. Mila, Brian, and I hang back, saying goodbye to John and Carol, waving to them as they pull away. Their taillights disappear over the ridge, and a string of headlights flare to life on the road below, as everybody makes their way back up to the lot.

There's a weight on my shoulder, and I turn to see Mila resting her head there. She shifts her gaze to me, eyes wide.

"Neely, I need to get really, really drunk, and I need you to not hit anybody, okay?"

"Okay," I say.

"You either," Mila says, pointing at Brian. "Nobody is hitting Josh. In fact, if I can just make a blanket statement and say that there will be absolutely no violence tonight, that would go a long way toward me feeling like I *can* get really, really drunk, okay?"

"Understood," Brian says.

"Absolutely," I tell her.

But we're really, really wrong.

SEVENTEEN

Brian didn't need to worry about looking like a beer bum. There's more than enough for everyone, and shiny aluminum cans are being passed out freely when he and I make it up to the ridge. I'd handed off the poker tin to him at my car, happy to let him be the bearer of the group gift. There's a decent fire going inside the stone ring; Josh and all the zips have high spots of red on their cheekbones, Destiny and Tabitha are quickly catching up, while Brigit pulls a roll of trash bags out of her backpack and starts gathering empties.

Mila spots us and comes over, holding out a drink to me. I crack it open and take an exploratory sip.

"Plenty more over there," she says, nodding toward a collective pile of beer and seltzer. "But remember you're my ride, so cut yourself off when you need to."

I nod like I have any idea of how to gauge such a thing.

"Here's our contribution," Brian says, opening the lid to show Mila what's inside the tin.

"Thank Christ," she says. "Could you do me a solid and roll me one right now?"

Brian nods and heads for the light of the fire. We follow, taking a seat on one of the logs pulled around it in a semicircle. Mila lifts her can of beer to her temple, pressing it there.

"Doing okay?" I ask.

It's a stupid question, not something you ask a rape victim who just had video of the crime shared all over the internet.

"Nope," she says with authority, the single syllable popping her lips apart. Her breath is thick with alcohol, and I realized she must have taken a couple straight to the dome before Brian and I caught up with the group. "But I will be, eventually."

I nod, as if I could possibly understand, and take a deep drink. While it might not burn going down, there is a warmth spreading in my stomach, one that feels something like the comfort that had settled when Brian and I reconnected, the spreading glow of a dull coal.

"Yes, you will be," I agree. "You're in the part right now where nothing is real. You're in the part where normal things seem incredibly fake, and the only thing that has ever happened was that. There'll be a line now, a before and an after, and everything in your life will be measured according to which side it falls on."

Mila is silent, and I turn away from the flames, afraid of a blank look, or even worse—anger. The arrangement of facial features that will tell me I've never been raped, can't possibly know, and have no comfort to give. Instead, she's staring back at me, the high, protective walls of bad jokes completely fallen. There's just the pain of someone who trusted and tried, and is moving through the world doing her best.

But the world has teeth, and we are all soft meat.

"*Yeah*," she finally blurts. "I mean . . . fuck, Neely. I guess if anybody would know, it's you."

I finish off the can and pass it to Brigit, who is patrolling the party with her Glad bag of trash in one hand, a drink in the other.

"I *don't* know," I correct Mila. "Your pain is yours."

We're quiet for a minute, watching Brian across the fire, who has a piece of flat black shale in his lap and is rolling out joints. Josh had snagged the first one and carried it off to share with Jessica, Paxton, and some of the other zips. Destiny gathers up the next one and gives Brian's head an affectionate rub, which makes a blush rise that's evident even in the firelight.

"Dibs on next," Mila announces, and Brian hands the third one off to her, which she lights with a stick from the fire. She takes a deep drag, and I try not to watch her lips too much, try not to be fascinated by the interplay of paper and teeth, skin and mouth. Mila exhales, and I decide she shouldn't be July; she's August and campfires and smoke and something a lot more dangerous than flags and parades. Another puff and she hands it off to me, our fingers pressing together. I stare at it for a second, the glowing cherry, the wet tip where her lips just were.

"Ever smoke before?" Mila asks, exhaling as she speaks.

"No," I say, because I have decided that I can hurt Josh and have unkind thoughts about Destiny, but I will never be anything other than perfect and good and true for Mila.

"It's not that hard, but if it's your first time, you'll probably want to—"

I move quickly, the sudden desire to have my mouth where hers just was overwhelming any worries. I pull smoke deep into my lungs, hoping there's parts of her still there, some of Mila inside me, pot and her saliva mixing together to fill me completely, keep me together from the inside, hot glue that will make the center hold. I keep it, not letting go until I have to, finally releasing the smoke, a mixture of her, me, and something that Lance grew on the riverbed.

"Nice," she says, nodding at me. "Pretty smooth."

Behind me, in the woods, laughter erupts. It's high and light, my old friends from childhood sneaking up on me. I go in for another drag, the cherry creeping closer to my fingers, fire traveling toward my face. This time I hold it longer than before, feeling Mila, feeling Lance, identifying threads of each of them, and remembering the tangle of dust and hair, tucked securely in my pocket. I exhale, letting all of us go, me, Mila, and Lance hovering above the flames. I'm fascinated, and dive in for a third pull when there's a hard shove on my shoulder.

"Puff, puff, pass, bitch," Tabitha says, collapsing onto the log next to me and plucking the pot from my fingers. She says *bitch* the way she says it to Destiny, with the careless ease of deep connection, the alcohol concentration in her blood boosting her affection for me. The laughter behind me grows and swells, filling the clearing. I look at the groups of people, none of them reacting to it, no one noticing the exuberant joy of a disembodied child. The fire pops, small embers flying out in a starburst pattern that take forever to fade, leaving trails across my vision.

"I'm going to press charges," Mila says out of nowhere.

I turn away from Tabitha, back to Mila, whose hair is down now, a shimmering wave of light. It falls across her shoulder, the tan knob of her clavicle parting the blond sea.

"Good," I say, following her gaze to where Josh is talking to Jessica, who has one hip cocked, her head tilted to the side.

"He saw me," Mila says, the words growing out of her like a corn-stalk, slowly. "He saw that. *Josh* watched that and probably . . ." She stops talking, her lips slamming shut on the rest of the sentence. I think of Josh in his room, alone, in the dark, face lit by the dim glow of his phone, hand moving frantically.

"You know he's in my DMs?" Mila asks angrily, her eyebrows coming together. "That little fucking creep. He's been dropping me lines ever since he got hired last year, keeps saying I'll come around, just like all the other girls. Little shit."

She spits out the last word, her eyes narrowing. Mine do as well, as I remember the feeling of Josh's larynx collapsing under my forearm, the squirming of his body against mine as I made my will known. He'd been like T.S. under my hand, a living sack of skin that the right amount of pressure could end, emptying something once full.

"I mean, look at this," she says, still agitated. She thumbs through her phone, pulling up a private chat on social media. It's her and Josh, but I don't get to read much because she only flashes the phone in my face briefly, her hand shaking.

The last message from him says simply: You will be mine.

"You can't control other people," Mila goes on. "That's what my mom always said. Whenever I was upset about something that some-body said or did, she'd sit me down and she'd say, '*Mila*—'"

She puts a finger out, chastising her child self. "'Mila, what do you control?'"

Mila looks back at me, gaze unsteady. "And the right answer is *myself*. That's it and that's all. I can't make Patrick take the video down, and I can't erase it from Josh's mind, but I can control how I react. And this bitch is going to react by calling the cops."

"Did you tell him that?" I ask.

"Yeah," she nods. "He is *not* happy. Check out the texts."

She hands over her phone, but we're clumsy in the exchange, and by the time I've got it, the screen is displaying her photos, which mostly seem to be of an Australian shepherd. I stare at the dog for a second, wanting to know its name, how old it is, when she got it, and if she has any other pets. I want to read all her texts, know every person in her life and each interaction she has ever had with them. I want to eat her phone, digest everything in it, and upload the information to the encyclopedia of Mila that I'm compiling inside my brain.

Okay, fuck. I'm super high.

I don't do any of these things, partly because eating someone's phone at a party will not get me invited to more. But I'd also like to think it's because this girl has had her privacy violated in the most violent of ways, and broadcast to the general public. So I don't creep on her texts, and I am about to hand the phone back so that the temptation is removed, when something else in her camera roll catches my eye.

"Where's this?" I ask, leaning into Mila and pointing to the thumbnail.

I know the caverns, know them inside and out, each wall and wave of rock, each etching in the stone and chipped tooth of a broken crystal. Mila is somewhere else, somewhere I've never been, with black swirls of manganese and stretching columns I've never seen.

"Girl," she says, taking back the phone. "Want me to show you?"

Yes, I do. I want to her to show me. It must be written all over my face, because Mila just laughs and says, "Okay, but first I've got to pee, and I will *not* make it down to the parking lot. So give me a minute."

Then she's gone, and my head is a heavy fruit on the end of a weak stalk, it bobs and weaves, moving with the flames.

Brigit suddenly shouts out, "Hey, girl! You made it!" and crosses the clearing with her trash bag dragging behind, empty glass and aluminum making hollow music.

And Tammy Jensen walks into the firelight.

EIGHTEEN

"Oh, holy fuck," I say to absolutely no one at all.

Except there's a hand on my knee, and it squeezes. I look down and determine this new hand is not mine. I turn my gaze away from Tammy and find another girl sitting by my side. She's got brown hair, pulled back into a low ponytail, flat lips and very large, dark brown eyes.

"Hi," she says.

"What the hell?"

Tammy has spotted me, her hand clamped down on Brigit's wrist, their mutual smiles obliterated as one looks at me with horror, the other in confusion. Tammy pulls Brigit into the shadow of the trees, mouth moving rapidly, the trash bag of recycling left forgotten in the trail of this new development.

"Did you do something bad?" the girl next to me asks, her hand tightening on my leg.

"No," I immediately say, my tone easily identified as the defense of a child who has been caught doing something very bad, indeed. Tammy is undoubtedly filling Brigit in, and I'm sure the story will spread around the group faster than the weed did—and Mila will be back soon.

She can't know. She can't ever know.

I stand, swaying. "I need to . . ."

"You need to what?" the girl asks, looking up at me, her eyes wide, dark as the trash bag glistening in the firelight.

I need to disappear. I need time to stop.

But none of those things are going to happen, and I'm left with the fact that what I need to do is get my shit together and have some sort of proper response to what Tammy is sharing with everyone.

"My side of the story," I say aloud, but there are no sides to a story where one first grader stands over another with a knife, gauging where to cut first in order to see the thoughts inside.

"Tabitha?" Brigit's voice sails out from the trees, high-pitched and worried. "Can you come here?"

"What story?" the girl next to me asks as I watch Tabitha cross the clearing, join Brigit and Tammy. Their heads go together, black and blond and brown, a trio of nice girls who are about to exile the one who doesn't belong.

The one who is dangerous.

"It's not a good story," I tell the brunette. I'm sitting again, I don't know if she tugged me down or I lost my balance. Either way, it's probably the better choice. I imagine approaching the trees, seeking out the other girls, them scattering like frightened birds before the pounce of the predator.

Instead, they find courage and safety in numbers, approaching me slowly.

"Hey, so, Neely," Tabitha says, the casual *hey, bitch* left behind. "Tammy told us some things and . . . I guess she'd like to talk to you? If that's okay?"

"Yeah," I say, looking up. I've only seen Tammy in two dimensions

127

since that night; seeing her in real life is very different from the flat screen of my phone. Her eyes aren't frozen in time, and the photo op smile is gone. Something else is happening instead, her gaze roving over my face, curiously mining.

"Hey," she says, her voice small and quiet.

"Hey," I say back.

"I think we'll just leave you two alone," Tabitha says. Brigit looks like she's about to protest, but Tabitha steers her away.

"Can I sit?" Tammy asks.

"Yes," I say, and she settles, knees turned toward me, the beginning of a small smile tugging at the corner of her mouth. A girl who smiles at a girl who can't. That's who Tammy Jensen is, still a mystery, how much kindness and caring can live inside of one person, while another was skipped entirely when those traits were being handed out.

"I know this is super awkward," she says, a nervous laugh trickling out after her words.

"Yeah, kind of," I agree, and the girl next to me drains her beer, slamming it onto the bench, spraying my arm with what was left inside.

"I just wanted to talk," Tammy goes on. "I think about it still. That night. I've had a lot of therapy."

I haven't. A dark bubble grows inside of me, lifting toward my throat.

"I think about that night, too," I say, allowing my eyes to lock on to hers. "I didn't want to hurt you."

"I really do think we should talk," Tammy says, nodding. "My therapist has been telling me for years that I just needed to write you a letter, but I was like—who even does that?"

"I would have answered," I tell her, and she nods again, like maybe I'm saying the right things, like maybe there are correct answers to questions like why a child would stand over another sleeping child, intently curious. The bubble lifts higher, lodging between my collarbones.

"So let's talk now," Tammy says. "You said you didn't want to hurt me. That's a good start. Sorry—" She rolls her eyes at herself. "That's what my therapist always says."

The therapist she's brought up three times now, the one I can't afford, part of the reason why she is sitting across from me, bright and healthy, while I have been shrinking for years, hiding out, lying low.

"An animal that slinks in the night," I say, and Tammy pulls back, the first hint of alarm flashing across her face.

"Look, I know you've been drinking," she says, her tone aiming for conciliatory. "So maybe not the best time to do this. Could I get your number? Maybe we could talk?"

Each of her words leaves her mouth as a sparkling streamer, the glow of her goodness flashing from behind her teeth, emanating from inside of her. At her core is a nuclear reactor of kindness, the source that I tried to locate all those years ago, wanting to pry it free of her with the blade of a knife, claim it for myself.

"Neely?" Tammy is still talking, but I'm turning away from her, aware of the dark bubble rising higher in my chest, making its way toward freedom, wanting to collide with Tammy's light in midair. I don't know if it's something I'll say, or something I'll do, but I know I cannot look at Tammy Jensen anymore. I turn to the girl next to me, the one who is eerily familiar.

"I didn't see you before," I tell her.

"I just got here," she says.

I'm staring, trying to place her, forcing my sluggish brain to do the work, find the time and place that we have met before, the moment when we crossed paths and noticed one another. Because I know this girl, have seen those dark eyes staring back at me from somewhere. I take a deep breath, filtering my memories, wondering if we glanced at each other over the seat of a school bus, the edge of a library book, or over a child's birthday cake. My mind stops, latches down, confirming how I know this face, those eyes.

They've looked back at me from a sepia-toned photograph.

"I'm Margaret," she says, holding her hand out. I stare at it, the outstretched fingers, the palm neatly lined. Like she's real. Like she's here.

"Neely?" Tammy's voice is back, louder, touching me, her hand on my shoulder. It's heavy and solid, harder than Margaret's. "I'm trying to get some closure here. Are you even listening to me?"

"Some things never close. And some things never end," I say, turning back to Tammy as the bubble reaches my lips and teeth, the words escaping. They rise and float above the fire, the opposite of Lance's body, falling every day, in my mind's eye.

I hold Tammy's gaze, trying hard to maintain it, even when a third eye opens on her forehead, pinning me with an accusing gaze. Laughter breaks out again, closer this time, the children in the long grass coming up to the house, tapping on my window, asking me to come out and play as I hid under the covers, trying my best to do what Lance said, to ignore them, to be good and to be right, and to never, ever answer them.

"Margaret?" I say, turning back to her, letting her name lilt upward into a question.

"Margaret Sander." She nods, confirming—and that's when I know I'm truly, totally fucked.

There's laughter directly in my ears, a smattering of applause drifts from the trees, the warmth of the fire on my face combating with the deep chill that has taken hold at the base of my spine, climbing up my vertebrae, each advance a greater foothold as it heads for my brain.

My eyes find patterns in the flames, fractals and designs, then names and dates. Letters lick the air, Margaret's name in fire. I let out a breath, alcohol tinged, the space in front of my eyes thick with shimmering heat.

"Neely Hawtrey," I say, identifying myself, one thing that I know is actually here, staring hard at the fire, willing it to melt the ice in my spine, and the not-real person sitting next to me. I need Margaret to go away and Mila to come back. I need real things, true things, actual things. I need things that matter and are solid, reliable facts. I put my hand in my pocket, fingers closing around my brother's dust.

"2865 County Road 66," I say. "East Independence, Ohio—"

I don't get to the zip code; Tammy cuts me off.

"Um . . . did you just tell me your address?"

"It's an old one," I tell her, like that's less weird. Then I start rattling off my social security number, and Tammy skitters away from me, off the log, backing into the darkness.

"Uh, Brigit? Tabitha?" she calls.

"Margaret," a voice says behind me, asserting herself. Across the clearing, brush begins to move, and a child creeps forward on all fours, another appearing behind it, their laughter a bright cloud. I close my eyes against them, against Margaret, against the sound of Tammy's voice, asking Tabitha, "Are you sure she's okay? I mean, like, safe to be around? Because—"

A hand clamps on to my shoulder, strong and solid.

"Pissin' accomplished," Mila says. "Wanna get out of here?"

Everything is silenced, my world narrowed as I open my eyes and see her, see everything, the light on her hair, the outline of her body, the smile on her face, the length of her legs, the sheen of her skin.

"Yes," I say.

Yes, yes, and yes.

We're leaving the fire, walking away from the heat and the woods, the heavy weight of other people and their voices. I am content. I could walk in silence and darkness with Mila.

Forever.

NINETEEN

T.S. rises to greet us when we emerge into the parking lot, shadow reaching for us as the motion light outside the visitors' center flicks on.

"Hey, buddy," Mila says, scooping him up.

She holds T.S. above her head, bringing his face down to hers repeatedly, booping their noses. "I love you, I love you, I love you," she says.

Her hair hangs down her back, long and bright, T.S.'s velvety paws brushing her cheeks as she brings him up, then back down again. It's adorable and heartbreaking and perfect, but I'm distracted, looking behind us, wondering if the children will come crawling out of the woods, or—even worse—Margaret will emerge from the path, the darkness of her eyes bearing down on me.

But they don't, and she doesn't, and maybe I'm not totally lost, just really high. Maybe everyone who smokes suddenly sees their childhood friends, or historical idols. Maybe everyone who smokes has third eyes suddenly erupt from the foreheads of the person they're talking to.

Mila drops T.S., says something about headlamps, and moves toward the visitor's center. I fall to my knees, the retained heat of the sun released through the asphalt, baking through my jeans. T.S. presses against me, the low rumble of a purr rising from his chest. He steps closer to me, his pads light on the asphalt, his nose wet when it touches mine. His purring rises in a wave that is still in my ears when I'm standing in front of the metal entrance door, Mila adjusting my headlamp.

I don't remember walking the switchback, I don't know where T.S. has gone, or why my knees are burning. I just know that Mila is here, tucking my hair behind my ears, tapping the code into the keypad—5562—and wrenches the door open, the scream of metal against rock sending crows flying from a nearby tree, voicing their anger into the night. I take a deep breath, welcoming the smell of the earth, the cool air, and the promise that no matter what was in the woods, it cannot follow me here.

There are rules.

"Hey," Mila says, putting her hands on both sides of my head, staring into my eyes. "You're okay to do this, right?"

"Yes," I say, pressing my cheek against her hand, feeling a callous in her palm.

"Lights on," she says, reaching up and pressing the button on my headlamp. She steps inside the cavern first, then hesitates, turning back.

"This is between you and me, okay?" she says.

"Yes," I say. Because we have things between us now, Mila and me. Pain and secrets and broken rules and me squeezing a boy's throat shut.

The caverns are no different at night, and time doesn't matter down here. The world above can be boiling or freezing, at war or in peace, and this place remains the same. The air is utterly still and heavy, wet to the touch, the exhalations of everyone who passed through trapped forever. Even the sounds remain stagnant, as if the same water is falling from the same rocks, stuck in a loop.

"Nothing changes," I say as we arrive at the junction of the natural wonders and the historical paths.

Mila goes to the right, headed for the graffiti room. I told Tammy that some things never close, and some things never end. Those words were tinted with sorrow; Lance's body still falling, Mom's car still careening off the road. But down here, where nothing changes, I feel peace.

"Nothing changes," I say again, closing my eyes, appreciating the safety, fingers curling around the wad of dust in my pocket, dead skin cells and strands of hair. Up there changed him. Up there turned him into this. Up there destroyed him.

"Not down here," Mila agrees. We move into the graffiti room, and the names seem to be etched more deeply in this light, as if blades from long ago are still working, ensuring the immortalization of the wielder. Margaret surrounds us, her tenacity scarring rock, forever marking herself as part of the caves. As the one who would go deeper, darker, farther, crawling toward nothing to make something her own.

"All right." Mila trains her headlamp onto the farthest spot Margaret had reached, off the trail and surrounded by stone teeth, her name defiantly carved forever. Mila's light moves to the crawl space to the left, barely twelve inches high, a dark mouth leading nowhere.

"Sure you're up for this?" she asks.

"Yes," I say, my heart rate picking up, palms sweaty. The caves are my haven, my refuge, the only place my monsters cannot follow. Even now the drip of the water, the hollow echo of my voice fills my world, and I know that they could be the only things, forever. No light, no pain, no people or things. I could stay here and be at peace.

Or I could go farther.

Mila nods, stepping off the path and pulling herself onto the ridge of rock that stands at hip height. Her shirt pulls up, and she rolls onto her back, palms behind her, facing me. There's a smear of dirt across her midriff, following the light lines of her abs, trailing down to the low-cut line of her shorts.

"I've done this a lot, so it's totally safe," she says. "I wouldn't bring you down here if it wasn't."

"I know," I say, and it's true. Mila is safety and trust, compassion and laughter, sunlight and warmth, and why she wants to be down here with me in the dark and the wet, crawling through dirt and wedged in the maw of the earth, I have no idea.

"I'll lead," she says, rolling over onto all fours and pushing forward. "There are a few little side shoots, but they don't go far. You literally can't get lost, okay?"

"Okay," I say, pulling myself up onto the rock ledge to follow. My feet leave the poured-concrete path, the known spaces, the safe routes. An electrical thrill runs through my body as I creep forward, concentrating on the soles of Mila's shoes. She gets to the rim of the crawl space and looks back at me, a small smile on her face. Then she lifts herself up and over, rock scraping at her clothes above and below, her hip bones brushing against the pillars of the earth.

The darkness in front of her is illuminated, a kept secret uncovered, new paths opening to me. I look to my right where Margaret's name is etched. I've seen it so many times, reveled the moment when her courage is revealed, the catch in the throats of strangers as they appreciate this woman and what she did.

I close doors and don't touch crystals. I follow rules, ignore children that don't exist and try to fix the mistakes of the day when I am alone at night. I am that person, but I am also a person who holds knives over sleeping children, can't be trusted with pets, and cuts off people's airways. So there's some hesitation when I reach toward Margaret, finger tracing the first letter of her name, my hand moving where hers had been, my breath against the rock where she once was.

There's some hesitation.

But not much.

Because rules are made to be broken.

The rock presses down on me as I shimmy forward, following Mila, cold stone against my back, dirt that has never known seeds or sunlight pressing into my belly. New patterns of rock, fingers of red and rivulets of black move past me, as my haven grows deeper, and I crawl toward its heart. Mila moves in front me, hips shifting, a metronome I mimic, as we move. I watch the rise and fall of her as she paves the way, muscle straining, breath catching, pressure above and below, more intimate than anything Patrick and Josh will ever know. She stops, and I do as well, waiting for cues.

"There's a drop ahead," Mila explains, not able to look back at me or turn her head in this tight space. "It opens into a room. Don't freak out when I disappear, okay?"

"Okay," I say.

Mila pushes forward, and I hear dirt and small pebbles striking a stone floor as her shoulders are eaten, then her torso and hips, her feet the last thing to go as she pushes away from me. There's a light grunt as she hits the ground, her body lost from my sight as she moves through a world I'm not in yet.

"Come on through," she calls, and I go, putting my hands and elbows where hers were, finding the same holds, traces of her heat, melding my body to where hers had been, rock to flesh. I fall into the open air, tumbling forward, and Mila catches me like a child, hands in my armpits.

"You okay?" she asks, stepping back.

"Yeah," I say, all other words lost as my head moves, light following the curve of these new walls, inaccessible to almost everyone. I have no words here in this place, and I spin, taking it in, learning the new curves, a wing of solace I hadn't known existed. Mila is silent as I turn, understanding my awe as no one else can.

My light passes over Mila, and she shields her eyes, my gaze catching on another crawl space above her head, this one even smaller than the one we came through.

"Where's that go?" I ask.

"Uh-uh," Mila says, shaking her head. "We can save that for another time, when we're both fully functioning. Trust me, you'll love it. There's a column in there thick as my wrist, but there's also a drop-off. I'm not sure where the bottom is, but I can tell you that when I toss a rock, I can't hear it hit."

"Sounds like something John could make a mint off of," I say.

"Yeah, which is why I've never told him it's there," Mila says. "He'd probably dig out all of this, add a third tour. Some things are sacred, you know."

"Yes, they are," I say, my light coming to rest on her. She's perfect in this moment, with a dark smear of dirt across one cheek, a scrape on the other, and dent in the bridge of her nose from something that happened, and a boy that hurt her.

"Thank you," I tell her. "Thank you for sharing this with me."

Mila shakes her head, hair swinging.

"This is me thanking *you*," she says, and then she lifts her light to the crevice we came in through, and dark markings to the side.

MARGARET SANDER

"Fucking yes, Margaret," I say, under my breath. "Deeper, darker, farther in."

"There's more," Mila says, her light shifting slightly to illuminate another name there, pale scratches adjoining Margaret's.

ANNA

My breathing stops, my heart stalls, blood ceases to flow. I am stilled, like the air in the caves.

"I think they came here, together," Mila says, her voice quiet. "I think it was the only place they could be . . . themselves." Her light shifts again to hash marks below their conjoined names, moments recorded forever, not ceasing, never known, buried together. My hand goes to my throat as I will my body to life, ask for breath, beg my heart to beat.

"I heard what you said to Brian during the tour," Mila goes on. "It kind of cemented what I'd already thought."

"I'm gay." The words come out, never said before. My lips move, teeth against tongue, soft tissue of the mouth and breath forming a statement under the earth, where no one will hear.

"I know," Mila says. "It's okay."

"I know it's okay," I say, turning away from Margaret and Anna, the record of their love. "I don't feel bad about it. I don't think it's wrong or weird, or anything like that. I just . . ."

My hands move to my face, on either side of my mouth, as if they could reach in and fish out the words, pull them into the air. I'm helpless as I stare at Mila, her gaze and accepting silence a language no one else speaks.

"My grandma and grandpa," I explain. "With everything else that has happened . . . it's too much. I think it would break them, and nothing else in my family needs to be broken."

"I understand." Mila nods, her light moving the world, her eyes meeting mine. "I knew your brother."

"What?" My hand goes to my pocket and what's there, the piece of Lance I carry with me.

"Not much," Mila says quickly. "I'm not trying to claim that we had this deep connection or anything. But we had a class together at the branch. And he . . ."

She's quiet for a second, and we stand, waiting for her to go on. Me and Lance; Margaret and Anna.

"I think he tried really hard," she finally says. "The first time he said *hi* to me I thought he was going to bolt in the other direction."

Her mouth quirks at the memory, and I picture her and him, standing near each other, his arms at awkward angles, her leaning in, an invitation.

"When he was gone, no one said anything," Mila goes on. "Class just kept going, and the professor never mentioned it, and no one looked at the place he sat, and his name came off the roster, and that was that."

"He was just gone," I say. "Gone and forgotten." Gone like Mary, her grave not far from his, both of them forgotten, even though his name still stands sharply out from stone. The memory of Mary and who she was faded from the world; his has been rejected.

"It was wrong," Mila says. "I wanted to tell you that. And I wanted to thank you for what you did, with Josh. I was so stunned, I just . . ."

Her hand goes to her collarbone, the side his finger had traced, and she shudders at the memory. She has lost her words, thoughts going somewhere her tongue can't follow.

And while I can voice my desires here, standing near Margaret's and Anna's names, feeling the warmth of Mila's body even through the chill in the air, I cannot tell her this other thing. That Margaret sat next to me tonight, that people who don't exist clapped for me, that the children came through the grass, that there's a girl under my bed and a man in my closet, speaking with mouths that aren't there.

But Margaret disappeared when Mila touched me, her hand harder, heavier, more real than anything that has ever been against my skin. The caverns are safe, but maybe there can be new rules, too. New places to explore. Maybe Mila has been here so long and so often, breathed in the air, brushed against the stone, stood under the dripping water, that she carries them with her when she leaves. I think of the silence in her presence, and the cool comfort that rolls off her, the caverns in human form, standing in her perimeter, a safe haven.

"Neely?" Mila asks.

I wonder what happens when worlds collide.

"You okay?" she asks.

And I step toward her.

TWENTY

I had hoped the quiet would extend to my bed, but what happens is quite different.

If the little girl is thirsty, I do not know.

If the man has an opinion, I do not hear it.

My world is entirely filled with her, and I have no room for monsters.

We move together, and it is as I had thought it would be, her mouth humid as the caves, skin cool next to mine. She has not been with another girl, and though I have thought of nothing else, I haven't, either. But I know what I like, and think she might, too.

She does, and we learn together, in the dark, like Margaret and Anna. There are small sounds and light gasps, soft skin and her hair across my face, a smooth rhythm and a sudden jolt, fingernails digging into me.

I move with her and say her name, the only word that exists.

Mila.

TWENTY-ONE

When I wake up, there is a man in my bed.

I jolt upward, yanking the covers to my chin, knees pulled to my chest.

"What the fuck?" I say, but the words are loose and light, coming out as an exhale of surprise, no weight behind them. I pull air in, ready to scream for Grandpa, when the man looks at me from where he sits at my feet.

"You have your pilot's license," he says, and my heart bottoms out, dropping into stomach acid. My eyes cut to the closet door, which hangs open.

"I don't," I say, coming forward onto my knees, stabbing an index finger at him. "I can't fly planes and you aren't real."

I say it with conviction, with the absolute certainty of truth. But the bedspread is creased where he sits, real weight pulling against it. There's a white flash of skin through the hole in his jeans, and a pearl of fuzz on the shoulder of his red-and-black flannel. He scratches at his chin, and I hear fingernails against stubble, can see a mole on his cheek peeking through.

"You're not real," I say again.

"That's not nice," comes a small voice from under the bed, and I glance over the side.

The girl is on her back, halfway out from underneath the bedframe, shoulders and head visible, a cloud of light hair spilling across the floor. A ragged teddy bear is tucked against her, a tuft of cotton pushing through the seam of his nose. One eye hangs loose, dangling against the girl's nightgown, a faded cotton shift in a tiny strawberry print. Her lips are cracked, the thin skin bubbled and white. Her eyes, deeply sunken and bruised, find mine.

"I'm thirsty," she says.

"You're not real," I tell her.

Her thin eyebrows come together in confusion, the shadow of pain crossing her eyes. "But I *am* thirsty," she insists. "And you're mean."

And of course she is, she must be, for her lips to look like that. Am I mean? I think of Josh's skin going gray, Tammy asking me to heal the past and me turning away. The little girl might not be real, but that doesn't mean she's wrong. I *can* be mean, and my mind can be slipping away, and two people that don't exist might be in my room with me right now.

But it's not the most important thing.

"Where's Mila?" I ask.

"You shouldn't have done that," the man says, shaking his head.

"Weird thing for someone who just came out of the closet to say," I shoot back.

The little girl snorts, and I grab for my phone, ignoring a text from Brian and going straight for Mila's social media. I don't know what I'm expecting, maybe a series of vague posts about falling in love, finding someone new, or the thrill of taking a risk, or maybe even *Slept with a girl last night, oops!* followed by corn jokes. But there's nothing. She hasn't posted in days, and one of her last pics is of her out with friends, sitting on a guy's lap, cheeks red, head thrown back in laughter, tank top askew, the cup of a yellow bra just visible.

I shoot her a DM, thumbs hovering over the buttons. I have no idea what to say, or what comes next. I just know that she was here and the universe aligned, and there were no monsters. And now she's gone and they have mouths and eyes and teeth, and they're all pointed at me. She's offline on all her platforms, and I stab at my phone, switching over to my messages. I've never had Mila's number, didn't want to be too forward by asking. So instead, I kissed her in a cave and brought her to my bed and did something to her she liked enough to leave scratches that run from my shoulder to the middle of my chest.

"Damn, you two really got after it," the man says, leaning forward with me as the red streaks catch my eye in the dresser mirror.

"Shut it," I say, fishing my T-shirt off the floor with my toes, and yanking it over my head before sliding out from under the covers. He might not be real, but his gaze feels heavy as I search for my underwear.

"Here you go!" the girl says, cheerily emerging from the shadows under the bed, holding my basic white Hanes. Shit, was that really what I was wearing when I finally got laid? I snatch them from her and am about to remind her—and myself—that she doesn't exist when there's a knock on my door.

"Still half naked!" I shout, which is a great way to keep both of my grandparents out of my room.

"It's one in the afternoon, and it's just us girls anyway," Grandma announces, letting herself in. I glance at the man on the bed, who only shrugs.

"Have a good time last night?" Grandma asks, and it takes all my willpower not to look at the askew pillows, the half-untucked mattress cover. "You must have been out late. We didn't hear you come in."

"Yeah, it was nice," I say casually. I'm less worried about what they might have heard *after* I got home, but Grandma's face is still set on pumpkin-spice bland, so I think I'm probably okay. And the fact that she didn't mention Mila means that she must have left early this morning, before either of them were awake.

Or should I say *snuck out*? I didn't get a goodbye, a note, or even a message online. If Mila's having morning-after regrets, I want to know. And then I want to talk her right the hell out of them. My hand shakes as I pull on my jeans, nervous fingers closing around the clump of dust in my pocket, asking Lance for reassurance in a way I never dared when he was actually here.

"Soooo . . . ," Grandma says lightly, her voice floating higher than usual. I pause, fumbling with the button on my jeans, eyes meeting hers in the mirror.

"What?" I ask, squeezing the word out past my heart, which has relocated to my throat.

"Well . . ." Grandma pauses, folds her hand in her lap. Next to her, the man does the same thing. "Your grandpa and I were talking, and while we're absolutely thrilled that you're making new friends—"

"We really don't think you should fuck them," the man finishes for her.

"It looks like we'll need to make some new rules in order to make sure that everyone is safe and happy."

I exhale, *absolutely thrilled*, as Grandma would say, that she didn't call me out for having athletic sex with another girl under her roof.

"Yes, new rules," I say, looking at the man. "I think that's a very good idea."

After Grandma lays out some reasonable guidelines—home by eleven, call or text if it will be later—I take a shower, mulling over some new rules of my own, hoping to hear my phone go off while I stand under the hot water. I'd turned notifications on for all my apps, plus pushed the volume to the limit.

Just in case.

I breathe in the steam and run a washcloth across my body, taking stock. The scratches across my chest burn, but it's a pleasurable reminder of the night before. There are some scrapes on my elbows that must be from crawling through the caverns, and two red splotches on my knees where—I think—I knelt in the parking lot and burned my skin on yesterday's sunbaked pavement while petting T.S., focusing all my attention on him and hoping Margaret wouldn't emerge from the woods behind us. My hands stop moving, soap bubbles slide down my legs as I remember her dark eyes, the knowing half smile.

"Okay," I say to myself, swallowing a little water. "Okay, okay."

The water snaps off, and I breathe, the air in here hot and close, not cool and clinging like the caverns. I had a conversation with my favorite historical figure last night, the memory just now resurfacing, and while the man in the closet and the girl under the bed making themselves visible might smack of the inevitable, the sudden emergence of a new delusion can't be good.

I need to find Mila, talk through what went on last night.

I also need to find her because it seems her presence reinforces my sanity, the double-locking steel plates of our connection not leaving room for anything else. I wipe a spot clean on the mirror, stare at my reflection.

"New rules," I say to myself sternly, raising a finger in the air. "One: I will not talk to my dead heroes."

Technically, this isn't the problem. The problem is them talking to me. But the least I can do is not start the conversation.

"Two . . ." A second finger joins the first but I can't seem to pinpoint anything else I've done wrong. I stare back at myself, at the scratches on my shoulder that disappear underneath the towel.

"Maybe don't smoke pot." I give my reflection a tap, striking the point home.

My phone goes off, and I grab for it, knocking it to the floor, where it skids behind the toilet. I go after it on my hands and knees, sliding across the wet linoleum and hitting my head against the porcelain. Ignoring the jolt, I reach behind the toilet and grab my phone, along with a handful of wet dust bunnies, a collection of dead skin cells from Grandpa's ass and Grandma's ass, and my own ass.

I'm not keeping that one.

I shake it free of my hand only to see that it's not Mila, not the reason I got out of bed this morning—or, for that matter, went to bed last night. It's another text from Brian, a follow-up from the one I'd ignored earlier.

> Thanks for coming through, it was a good night!

It definitely was, but he must be an early-bird-gets-the-worm kind of person under all circumstances, because that text came in around

6:00 a.m. His follow-up from just now indicates his amusement that I haven't answered him yet.

> Maybe TOO good? How's your Saturday? lol

I shoot **I'm fine, just tired** back immediately, then realize that's probably what all people say the morning after their first party. In my case, though, it's mostly true; I don't have a hangover, however I can suddenly see people that I previously could only hear. Grandma passes by the bathroom door, humming a Kesha song that must be on this week's Walmart playlist.

I pull up a private browsing window on my phone and do a quick search for pot and auditory hallucinations. The first hit I get is from a thread on Rock Bottom, where a guy linked to an article about a man who claimed to have murdered his wife while under the influence of MDMA and makes the statement that if he thought he could get away with this for pot, he'd go get his medical card right now.

"Not helpful," I mutter, clicking off the site to skim through my other links, not finding anything more useful than the effects of marijuana, like heightening your senses, distorting time, and lowering inhibitions, all of which I can attest are quite true, but not exactly what I was looking for. I click on a different link, this one from a university study.

> It's not uncommon for some users to experience psychotic symptoms after smoking, such as hearing voices, feeling paranoid, or believing one has some type of special ability, says Dr. . . .

"Thank you," I say to my phone, tapping it against my forehead and accidentally zooming in on the next sentence.

However, such symptoms typically last only an hour or two. If a preexisting mental condition is present, cannabis could worsen psychotic symptoms, possibly even triggering a break.

I close the window, erase my history, and open the bathroom door.

"Hello," the little girl says, fingers spinning the dangling eye of her teddy bear.

TWENTY-TWO

"New rules," I inform the man and the girl.

They are sitting shoulder to shoulder on my bed, facing me, as the girl nervously pulls stuffing out of her bear's nose. Her lips are turned down at the corners, fully expecting me to inform her once again that she is not real.

"I made a mistake," I explain, softening my tone.

"Getting high?" the man says, giving me a hard look. "That was stupid. You're stupid."

"But I can fly a plane, right?" I shoot back.

"Not if you pop hot on a piss test," he says smoothly. "They'll take your pilot's license like that." He snaps his fingers, and the little girl jumps.

"New rules," I say again, trying to maintain control over a conversation with imaginary people. "You have to stay in this room."

They're more like negotiations than rules, but it's the best I could come up with as I walked the girl back down the hallway from the bathroom. If last night really did amp up my delusions, I need to know if it's going to be a lasting thing, or if it will fade in time. I've been dealing with the girl and the man for most of my life; seeing them was a shock, strengthening monsters that already existed, problems I've been handling for years. My plan is to give them new parameters that at least put them in a holding pattern, and deal with other issues first.

I'm prioritizing, ranking my monsters according to the biggest threat and working up. Giving the man and the girl a little more freedom now will allow me to wrestle with larger problems, like Margaret Sander showing up at parties and Mila Minter disappearing from my bed. Later, I'll coax them back into unreality, relegating him once more to the closet and her under the bed. I'll stop talking to them, opting for real humans instead. Real humans like Mila. Once she's back by my side, the monsters will not only be unseen but silent, my world in harmony with hers, everything as it should be.

I don't know where Mila lives, don't have her number. I can stalk her social media all day, but if she's gone underground, then—

"Gone underground," I say aloud, and grab my keys.

The parking lot is empty, my hope that Mila might have gone for a cave crawl on her own, seeking out silence and solitude while she pondered what we did last night evaporating like the heat shimmer rolling off the asphalt.

"Well, shit," I say, tapping my thumbs on the steering wheel.

"Well, shit, shitbird," the Shitbird Man agrees. My skin ripples with goose bumps despite the baking sun, and I sneak a glance at the passenger seat. But there's no one there, and I silently thank him for—as always—being the most manageable of my monsters.

"Well, shit, shitbird," I repeat, following our rules.

I'm checking the back seat—just in case—when Brian pulls in and parks next to my car. He gets out and raises a hand in greeting.

"Hey," I say getting out of my car to join him, wiping sweat from my upper lip. "What's up?"

"John asked me to double-check that the doors got locked last night,"

152

Brian says, walking toward the visitors' center. "Said his hands were full of Crock-Pots and leftover chicken noodles and he wasn't sure he locked up. What are you doing here?"

It's a great question, and I don't have an immediate answer, but a stray tuft of fur clinging to the splintery seat of T.S.'s bench supplies me with a ready lie.

"T.S. is due for his flea treatment," I say. "Thought I'd do it now. I think the schedule is pretty full on Monday. Don't want to forget. You know how fleas are. You get one and then there's two and then there's a thousand."

I follow this up with a nervous laugh, attempting the casual throat noises of a normal person. It's difficult, because my only childhood pet has resurfaced, along with a thousand fleas crawling up my arms, jumping, leaving tiny bites from minuscule mouths, burrowing deep into orange fur, going places I couldn't find them unless I dug—really dug. Sulla's lips raised, teeth bared, the dark spot of a flea running inside his mouth. Going deeper, darker, farther, escaping the greater threat.

Me.

Brian jerks on the double doors, and they shake under his hands but don't open, jerking me back into the present. "Wasted trip," he says. "Dad'll be thrilled that I stopped working on his truck for no reason."

I glance at my phone. No messages. No notifications. No Mila. It's almost six o'clock, and I can't keep telling myself that she's just sleeping it off. She's choosing not to talk to me, pretending last night didn't happen. A lump grows in my throat as my stomach slips lower.

I can go home, where a man and a girl that aren't real—but are getting closer—will try to get me to interact with them. Or I can ask Brian if he has Mila's number, prompting questions that I don't want to answer.

I look at him, at the dark ring around his light blue eyes. "Do you need to get back?" I ask. "Or could you hang out for a little bit?"

"Uh . . ." Brian adjusts his hat. "I mean, I can. I guess."

"No, never mind," I say quickly, seeing his hesitation. "I'm fine."

Those words hang between us, something Lance said often, something that became less and less true.

"I can," Brian says. "But what do you want to do? I can't . . ." His eyes drop from mine, the toe of his worn boot scraping the ground. "I can't exactly afford to go out to eat or to a movie or anything."

"Can we just . . ." My eyes sweep the grounds, the shaded spot under a huge maple. "Can we just sit over there and talk for a bit? Kill some time? T.S. might show up."

"Sure," Brian says. We fall into the grass together, and he begins to pluck clover, rolling it between his fingers like I did with the dust bunny from Lance's room. I reach into my pocket, feel it there, what's left of my brother, who said he was fine, even when he wasn't. Who told me no one can ever truly know someone else, and then proved it.

"Rock Bottom," I say. "Lance was on Rock Bottom." It's supposed to be a question, but it comes out flat.

"I shouldn't have told you," Brian says. "He wouldn't have wanted you to know."

I think of all the things I didn't know, who his monsters were and what they sounded like, what they said to him and encouraged him to do.

"He was angry." I repeat what Brian had said, what I had rejected, what I hadn't known. I think of Josh's pulse growing thinner because I want it to, his cheeks going gray because I can make them. The blackness inside me, spilling out.

"I told you sometimes I am okay. Sometimes I'm not," I admit.

Brian nods, the silence between us stretching.

"I need to know," I tell him. "So that I can . . ." I think of rushing wind, passing traffic, iron girders and a final decision made with a single movement, trees reaching out, welcoming arms. "So that someday I *don't* . . ." But there aren't words for the crash, the breaking of limbs, both human and deciduous.

"His username was 'hillwalker,'" Brian says, adjusting his cap, the bright flash of white skin visible for a second. "The posts are still up. I'm not telling you to look. I mean, I don't even know if it's a good idea. But if you want to know Lance better, it might be a way."

I think of small, bloodied fingers entwined with mine, a constellation of freckles pressed against my arm, the truck bed rattling under us on a gravel road. I didn't think I could know him better, but I don't know who else was with us then, or what they were saying to him.

I watch Brian flick a wad of clover into the air. "Is it bad?" I ask.

"Lance's posts?" Brian takes a second, lays back on the grass, hands crossed behind his head. "There's nothing sexually fucked up, or anything, if that's what you're worried about."

I let out a breath, relieved, and Brian shoots me a shy smile. "It's okay, I get it. You really don't want to know what other people are into. I stumbled onto my dad's porn stash when I was a kid, and all I can say is that tan lines and big hair will never be my thing, because they are *definitely* his."

I laugh, a small amount of tension escaping me, the sound a surprise that trips out, joins the clover and the slant of the sun as it sinks. I laugh, today, after I was ghosted by the first girl I ever slept with, and my monsters stepped into the light.

"You help," I say to Brian, knowing I don't have to elaborate.

"Good," he says. "Do you think it would be easier to look at Rock Bottom when you're not alone? I mean—"

"When I'm with someone who is actually there? Yeah." I nod, agreeing. "Probably."

I close out my messages and all the social media apps, congratulating myself on the fact that I actually can and ignoring the nagging feeling that if I kill enough time talking to Brian, maybe Mila will have surfaced. I pull up the Rock Bottom site, averting my eyes from the home page, and whatever posts might have the most views today in order to be featured.

"Here," Brian says, reaching out. "I'll do a search on his posts, that way you don't run across anything you don't want to see."

I hand my phone to him, and his thumbs tap along the screen while he talks. "I won't claim to be a saint, I'm not entirely unfamiliar with the layout. The site gets a bad rap, and there is some extreme stuff, but most of the posts are just angry people, and sad ones. A lot of them don't have anyone to talk to, so they get it out online."

He hands the phone back to me, the screen showing hillwalker's account page, which is just an empty avatar with the broad location of Ohio. Lance made 783 posts, and I can filter them according to which forum page he posted on, or simply view them all in chronological order. I choose that, eyes crawling the dates.

"The last time he posted was the day he died," I say, scrolling through.

"Maybe you should start at the beginning," Brian suggests.

"Yeah," I say, my throat swelling as I do the exact opposite, clicking on Lance's last post, a simple, one-word statement in a forum titled /violence.

Never mind.

TWENTY-THREE

rb/despair

hillwalker—First post, gonna be a downer, but I guess that's what this is for, am I right? I don't see the point, don't understand. Nothing matters and we're all running in our hamster wheels, but we think they're moving forward. Inertia is king, nothing changes. We think we are important but really we are just moving things from one place to another, calling it work and taking a shit paycheck for it, then going home tired and feeling like we did something. We do nothing. We are nothing. It's pointless.

Johnboy (MOD)—Welcome to RB! Seems like you'll fit in just fine in rb/despair, which may not exactly be comforting. But we're here. Keep talking. Sounds like things are hard right now.

prodigal_sun—Is this about a girl? Sounds like it's about a girl.

hardwoodworker—Isn't everything about girls?

I snort at the echo of the conversation I'd had with Brian earlier and am about to share it with him, but he's fallen asleep, head tilted back into the grass, mouth slightly open.

hardwoodworker—To the OP: whack off, it helps.

hillwalker to Johnboy—Sounds like things are hard right now?? I just said nothing matters and that's what you've got??!?! Great fucking mod job.

prodigal_sun—He's a mod, not your free fucking therapist.

hardwoodworker—Definitely whack off dude

hillwalker to prodigal_sun—I don't need a therapist. I need other people to suck less.

hillwalker to hardwoodworker—No, it doesn't help

hardwoodworker to hillwalker—Did you put my theory that whacking off helps through rigorous scientific experimentation? I have. Check out rb/titsandass

Johnboy—Other people aren't the problem. It sounds like you've got a lot of anger.

hillwalker—Fuck yes I do. Every day, I'm trying. Every day, I do the right thing. Every day, I fight my demons. And every day some other guy, with a better line, or bigger biceps gets the girl. And he doesn't fucking deserve her. Why try?

prodigal_sun—Like *the girl?* or just any girl?

hillwalker—All girl, any girls. Or maybe just one. But it doesn't matter. I can't talk to her/them because the wrong thing might come out.

Johnboy—What wrong thing?

hillwalker—Like the other day I was getting groceries and there's this guy, just gross, smells like BO and piss. He's standing in front of the milk like 2% or whole is a fucking hard decision and he's got the goddamn door OPEN so the cold air is rushing out and it's sending his stink out to everyone and all I need is some damn eggs and I've got to stand there and smell this person who doesn't shower and there's this girl standing there, and she's trying to be nice, and not totally cover her nose or whatever, because she's kind. And there I am, not smelling like a septic tank, and I say people like him should be shot, and she looks at me like I'm horrible and just turns around and leaves. But probably everyone else is thinking the same thing, it's just I said it.

hardwoodworker—Okay, I think I see the problem

hardwoodworker—Try this thread instead rb/gunstitsandass

prodigal_sun—Yeah maybe don't tell girls you want to shoot people

prodigal_sun—Hot take? It turns them off.

hillwalker—Fuck you all. Thought I could come here and say my piece.

Johnboy—You can. Free speech. But the girl has the right to walk away from you if she doesn't like what you say. Sounds like you need to modulate your thoughts versus what you actually say.

hillwalker—No shit. If I said it all . . .

There's nothing after the ellipsis, and the thread dies out after hardwoodworker feeds Lance a few more porn threads to try, the theme of them growing darker. I tap through to the next time Lance had posted, which is in the rb/rageshameburn group.

hillwalker—Demons raging hard today. I'll never be good enough, never matter, never rise above. Below seems more like it.

I look away from my phone, thinking of my monsters and Lance's demons, the fact that he would finally give in, rise above for an instant only, and then find his permanent below only six months after that post. I minimize Rock Bottom, not wanting to read more. Brian is still asleep, so I reach inside my pocket and find the dust ball, pulling it out, letting it breathe and feel the sun. When a breeze rustles the leaves overhead, I cup my hands protectively around it, putting my mouth to a crack between my fingers.

"You mattered," I say. "You mattered to me."

In the distance, someone applauds my statement, laughter rises, a child yells, "*Wait for me!*"

And I have no idea what is actually happening, and what isn't.

Sunday is supposed to be a day of rest. I don't think that means you're allowed to lay in bed all the daylight hours and look for signs of your lesbian lover online. But that's what I'm doing. Refreshing. Rechecking. Recycling her old posts, desperate for a new one. Desperate for an indication of what she's thinking, how she's feeling.

Desperate.

At the foot of the bed, the girl plays with my toes, calmly reciting "This Little Piggy," over and over. The man stands at the window, staring out. Vigilant against . . . something. I want him to go back to the closet, the girl to slide under the bed. In my quest to know my dead brother better, success has come by joining him in experiencing visual hallucinations—something we were not supposed to talk about.

He had promised that his first trip after getting his driver's license would be to take me out for ice cream. He'd flashed the newly minted ID in my face and told me to be at the car in five minutes or I'd miss my ride. I'd jammed bare feet into sneakers, running with them untied, the laces flapping around my ankles.

"Shotgun!" I yelled, which was unnecessary, since we were going to be the only two people in the car.

Except we weren't.

Lance turned to someone who wasn't there and ushered them into the back seat, opening the door for them. His eyes landed on mine, the bright shine of excitement gone, extinguished in the moment that I'd caught him doing something we weren't supposed to—interacting. I'd slid into the passenger seat, silently buckling my belt. When he got behind the wheel, he drummed his fingers against it, then turned to me, all pretense gone.

"Sometimes you have to" was what he said, his eyes flicking to the rearview mirror, and the person back there, his monster, one he'd never be able to get away from, no matter how fast he drove.

"You see them?" I ask.

"You don't?" he'd shot back, surprised.

"No, I—" I'd tapped my ear then, not wanting to say *No, I just hear voices*, like my brand of crazy was somehow less than his, with two of his five senses vulnerable to madness. I wanted to ask how many and what they looked like, what they said and how they acted. I wanted to know what his rules were and if the monsters broke them.

But I didn't, because we weren't supposed to, and Lance had his hand on the gearshift, backing out of the driveway and telling me that chocolate was better than vanilla—a lifelong argument of ours—and he'd prove it by eating more scoops than me. I informed him that that only showed he was a greedy and had no self-control, our sibling banter falling into the play we had been cast in, although we wrote our own dialogue, trying hard to figure out what normal people say to each other and then deliver our lines.

"Sometimes it's really hard," I say, glancing up at the girl, as she squeezes my pinky toe.

"I know," she says, her hand sliding down to the arch of my foot. "I'm sorry."

"Sometimes you have to," I remind myself, echoing Lance's words, allowing the girl to rub my foot, acknowledging that it feels nice.

That it makes me feel less alone.

My fingers drum against the back of my phone, willing myself not to refresh Mila's profiles again, not to see if she has posted, has reached out, made a comment, moved a muscle. My need to know seeps from my gut, a deep wondering of where she is and what she is doing right now, what she's thinking about, and—most important—if it's me.

This isn't what was supposed to happen.

I put my phone down, stare at the ceiling, pick it back up.

And I never, never hear from Mila.

TWENTY-FOUR

I don't have to worry about what to wear when I see my only ever one-night stand, because we work together and there's a uniform. I tell the girl she's not actually thirsty, and correct the man when he informs me that I can deadlift five hundred pounds.

I'm nervous as shit, aware that I'm about to face Mila and that I have nothing to say, no perfect words that will set her mind at ease. There's a world where she won't even speak to me, takes someone else with her on morning sweep, avoids my eyes while she runs the staff meeting. In that world, we will act like nothing happened and never have a real conversation again. She will move through her life without me, and I will remain, listening to lost children stuck in a loop, eventually bringing cups of water to my room that no one will drink, and having increasingly longer heart-to-hearts with a handful of dust.

But there's another world, one where she hip-bumps me the second we see each other, eyes the tail of a scratch—scabbing over now—that can just be spotted through the V of my polo. She'll tip me a perfect wink, and I'll tell her it's a travesty I don't have her phone number, and we'll right that wrong and never be separated again. I like that world better and am enjoying the daydream of it when I pull into the lot.

Mila's not here.

She's always first, always early. Always, always, always.

"She doesn't have the minivan," I remind myself, speaking aloud. "She got a ride from someone else." And while this could be true, it is also upsetting, because that someone else was not me.

"And then there's what that Tammy girl said."

I stop short of the staff room door, recognizing Destiny's voice.

"We don't actually know her," Tabitha says. "It might not be true."

"Uh, we don't *actually know* Neely, either, do we?" Destiny argues. "I'm telling you, that girl is not right in the head. Did I tell you about how I caught her talking to herself behind the bathrooms?"

"No," Tabitha says. "But I saw you call yourself a sexy little piece while making duck lips in the mirror last week."

"I was giving myself a pep talk," Destiny sneers. "That's not the same thing. I'm telling you—she was asking herself questions and then answering them in a different voice. I legit thought she was talking to somebody until I came around the corner and it was just her being a psycho."

I flatten myself against the wall in the hallway, heart racing. I thought I'd gotten away with that particular redo, a quick one-off that I'd tried to slip in between tours after a kid had caught me doing a mandatory shitbird repeat. He'd side-eyed me, then gone over to his mother, who had glanced over with pursed lips. But that had been a good week; I hadn't heard the children or random applause in days. In an effort to stay ahead of the game, I'd done a quick redo.

Unfortunately, it seems Destiny heard *that*—which is way worse.

"People talk to themselves all the time," Tabitha says, still defending me, even though she sounds more dubious now.

"Girl, it was not like that, okay? She was—"

"Hey, Neely!" John says, pushing past me, and effectively ending the conversation in the staff room. He pokes his head around the corner. "You gals seen Mila?"

"No, she's not here yet." Destiny recovers quickly, eyes bouncing off mine as I go to my locker, throat closed against all the thoughts, all the things I cannot say. The things that Lance wrote in Rock Bottom, venting his wrath somewhere safe, letting his darkness spill in an online world, anonymously.

"Huh, that's not like Mila at all," John says as light flashes off the window of a bus that has pulled into the lot. "We've got a summer school camp of seventh graders today, forty of them."

"I'll do the morning sweep," Brian offers, popping into the staff room.

"I'll go with you," I say, moving to follow Brian, who hands a flashlight off to me. I fall in step beside him, trying to quiet the ill feeling in my stomach.

"You okay?" Brian asks, dropping his voice low as we walk past the kids tumbling off the bus, bleary-eyed from the early-morning trip.

"Yeah," I say, voicing the opposite of how I feel, trying to say the right thing, even if I can't fully be that thing.

A kid pounds on the back door of the bus, trying to get our attention as we slip behind it, heading for the entrance to the caverns. I turn, aware of Mila's absolute dedication to customer service, the smile she would summon for tourists at all costs, even after discovering her own rape had been uploaded. I've got one hand raised in greeting, a fake smile pasted on.

What I see, staring back at me from the bus, is Margaret.

My hand freezes, the smile stuck somewhere between a gape and a grimace, all my air gone, any hopes I had that she was a phantom born of smoke swept away in the hot breeze that sweeps the lot, rolling an empty Natty Light can along with it.

"Brigit missed one. Must've blown down from the ridge," Brian says. "Mila will have a fit when she gets here if this is out in front of the kids." He dashes after the trash, stomping it flat and taking a victory loop before he dunks it into the trash, not aware that anything is wrong until he sees me, still stuck mid-wave, still staring at Margaret.

"Neely," he says, giving my shoulder a shake. "What's up?"

She's waving, long fingers moving slowly, dark eyes holding mine, the corners of her lips drawn up in a knowing smile.

I grab Brian's hand, my nails digging into his knuckles. "Do you see her?" I ask, my voice hard and painful, a clawed thing that drags itself out of my throat. "Do you see the woman standing at the back of the bus?"

He follows my gaze, then shakes his head. "No. Sorry, Neely. I don't."

"Fuck," I say, clutching my hand over my mouth as it comes out in a sob. Brian grabs my shoulders, turns me away from the bus.

"When did this start?" he asks.

"The party," I tell him. "It wasn't like this. It was just voices and sounds. I never actually saw anybody. I wasn't like Lance. I've never been—"

I almost say *that bad*, almost compare us, and find him lacking.

"Okay," Brian says. "Lance saw them for a long time, though, right? Like he figured out how to manage it?"

I nod, the movement savage and rough, my head a pendulum measuring how much longer I can do this.

"You can do this," Brian says, hands tightening. "And I don't want to be a total dick, but we've got a bus full of kids and no Mila. Josh is a piece of shit, and Destiny and Tab just want to take the natural wonders tour and put it on autopilot. I need you functioning."

"Brian!" John leans out the double doors to the visitors' center. "I need you in here, the internet just went down, and we can't run credit cards."

"Fuck, really?" Brian says under his breath, jerking his cap off and running his hand though his hair. "Why am I the only one who knows how shit works around here?"

That's not entirely true, but with Mila gone, it is half-true.

"I'll do the sweep," I tell him, and he glances at me dubiously.

"Is your shit together?"

Not right now, no, but it will be as soon as I get underground.

"Brian!" John yells again, irritation edging his voice.

"Dammit," Brian says, jamming his cap back on. "Fine, do the sweep alone, but maybe just do natural? Don't bother with taking the historic loop. We don't have time, and everything's going to hell right now."

I agree because I need to go, right now. I practically run down the switchback, a sheen of sweat covering my skin when I get to the door, glancing behind me, terrified that Margaret has followed. She's nowhere in sight, and I yank the door open, welcoming the familiar screech of protest. But there's another sound below that, a high scream that makes goose bumps rise under the sweat.

A shrieking streak of fur shoots out of the entrance, heading straight between my legs, aiming for the tangle of brush on the hillside. The cat dives in, a low growl emanating from the ridge as I pluck a tuft of fur from a thistle. It's wet in my fingers, the moist air of the caves still clinging to it. It's bright orange, a vibrant color that stands out sharply against my skin, defiantly alive.

And there's blood.

I slam the door shut, relegating the morning sweep to insignificance.

"Kitty!" I call, crawling over the stones and up the bank, toward the brush. "Kitty, kitty!"

I try to keep my tone light, try to use the voice Mila does when she talks to T.S., boops his nose, lifts him up and down while telling him she loves him, she loves him, she loves him. But it's hard, because that voice is full of joy, and mine can't quite resonate on that level right now, because this is not T.S., and I am not Mila.

We're a different pair, a darker echo of something wholesome.

A breeze pulls the fuzz from my hands but leaves the blood behind. I stare at it, questioning if it is real, if it is there, or if this is blood from my past, drawn into the present by my addled mind. I flick my fingers in the breeze, ridding myself of it, adjusting the world so that it fits my needs. Getting rid of blood and clinging drops of wet, my hands never quite coming clean, a ridge of dirt pressed under my nails after I dug the hole, dirt that was still there when Grandma made the discovery.

"Sulla?" I ask, eyeing the scratches on my arms, red tracks returning, filling the lines that had paled into silver streaks over the years, now matching the bright trail across my chest.

"I'm sorry," I say, scrambling forward, banging my knee and scratching my face against a mulberry as I crawl on all fours, peering into the thicket where Sulla hides, glowering.

I could tell him he's not real or tell myself there are a million orange tabbies in the world. But the distinctive curl of one ear where frostbite had withered the tip won't let me deny him, or the acrid smell of fear that emanates from the brush, a smell I couldn't get off my child-size hands for days. My dead childhood pet stares out at me from a tangle of brush, and as I watch, a flea crawls out of one nostril, traverses his eye, and crawls back into his body through his ear.

"I'm sorry," I say again, tongue like sandpaper in my mouth.

Sulla holds my gaze and calmly says my name.

"Neely."

I scream and stumble backward off the ridge, falling onto the path below. Sulla bounds from his hiding place, approaches me, wet tail dragging. I skitter away from him, heels and palms burning as he lowers his head, bumps it against my knee affectionately. I raise a hesitant hand and touch him, feel the very real press of his body against my skin. A purr emanates from him, and he locks eyes with me once again.

Speaks again.

"Psychotic break," he says.

Something brushes against my side, and I yelp, turning to find another cat there, a new one, white with one blue eye and one green. It sits, tail curled around its feet.

"Neely," it says.

"Psychotic break," another cat adds, head popping out of a cluster of poison ivy.

"Neely." A third surfaces, rubbing between my ankles.

"Get away." I kick at it, breathless as I crawl to my feet, pitch forward down the path, running the switchbacks, blowing through the gated entrance as furred heads pop up all around me, joining the fray that follows, dozens of cats converging with accusatory eyes, my name on their lips. They hit the glass door of the visitors' center in a wave as I duck into the employee entrance, hands over my ears.

"What the fuck?" Destiny asks as I blow into the staff room and throw myself into the stall just in time, losing breakfast into the toilet. I wipe my lips, take a deep breath, stare down into the mess.

"I'm fine," I call. But there's no answer.

"Really, I'm just fine," I say again.

But it doesn't matter.

Because nobody cares.

TWENTY-FIVE

John doesn't make corn jokes when he drives the bus. He doesn't use the intercom or say anything to the tourists at all. His mouth is in a thin, worried line, and he's checking his phone the entire time he drives, making me wonder if he really was the best choice for the job, CDL or no CDL.

We disembark at the entrance for the historical tour, and I lead everyone to the cinder block building after doing a flashlight check with Josh and Brian. Josh won't meet my eyes, but I don't let that bother me as I launch into Mila's welcome speech, hitting it word for word, moving like her, talking like her.

The kids are shuffling their feet, couldn't care less about the caves and what waits inside for them. But they will soon. They will when I talk about Margaret. There's movement in the woods, over Brian's shoulder. It's her, peering around a tree. I let her look, let her see me, almost consider giving her a nod before I go below, where she can't.

The silence envelops me, pulls me in, draws me to it. I take a deep breath, letting it fill my lungs, the wet air drowning me. There is no random applause, or laughter from lost children.

From the back of the group, Brian clears his throat.

"Harold Gentry discovered the caverns in 1897," I say. "He became curious about how his crop fields were draining so quickly and found the original entrance to the caverns."

I tell them more, about Gentry and his barn, the lanterns and the early explorers, adventurous people who crawled on hands and knees in utter darkness.

"Like, actual fire lanterns?" a kid asks. "What if they dropped one and their clothes caught on fire?"

"Then you burned," I say.

One of the teachers shoots me an odd look, and I decide that it would be smart to stick to Mila's script. I check with Brian before we move into the graffiti room. He nods, indicating we still have twenty-two.

"Remember the rule about no touching?" I ask our group. "It hasn't always existed, which is why we're standing in what's fondly referred to as the graffiti room."

I tell them about the paths we're walking on not existing until 1925, how the people who carved their names here had to fight tooth and nail for every inch they claimed. I remember cold dirt on my belly, the scrape of rock against my shoulder blades, pressure above and below as I followed Mila. Deeper. Darker. Farther.

"It quickly became a competition," I go on. "Who could leave their name behind in a place no one else was willing to go?"

I tap the light panel, and Margaret's name is illuminated.

"Cool," says one of the girls, but most of the kids aren't impressed.

We move into the next room, and I explain the sacrificial table as Josh leaves the group, heading for the breaker box. Brian flashes his hands, showing me we still have twenty-two people with us.

"Okay," I say. "I want everyone to hold hands." There's a collective groan, and one of the teachers shushes them.

"No, seriously," I say. "My coworker is going to turn the lights off in just a few seconds, and when that happens—trust me—you want to be holding on to someone else. It's a deep kind of dark down here, and you won't care if the person whose hand you're holding is your friend or your enemy. You're just going to be glad they're there."

Hands extend, some taken; others, still proud and brazen, refuse the connection. I realize suddenly that I have no one, and that Mila has done this before hundreds of times. Stood in front of people she was responsible for and took the plunge alone, voice still strong, still carrying, still in charge. I take a deep breath and will myself to be the same.

To be Mila.

"Get ready to experience true darkness in three . . . two . . . one."

Josh hits the lights.

Everything disappears. The world is gone, and I have no reference point, nothing to hold on to. I dig into my pocket for the ball of dust, but it only feels like dirt, filthy thoughts spewed onto a keyboard, a version of my brother I didn't know existed. Maybe the real one.

You can never truly know someone else.

The darkness presses in, and my hand goes instinctively to my own face, looking for reassurance that I am, in fact, still here. My fingers brush against my nose and trace downward, following the curve of my neck, finding the ridge of scab that cuts across my chest, something of Mila with me, down here, in the dark. I rub my finger over it, comfort flooding in.

I knew her. Knew her very well, even if only for one night.

There's a gasp in the dark, deep; labored breathing. The children who didn't believe me and weren't holding hands now wishing they had listened.

"I know it's overwhelming," I say, hand still caressing my wound. "Take a second. Let the fear settle."

But someone in the tour group can't quite get ahold of themselves. There's the sound of pebbles sliding as they fall sideways, a sharp gasp as their body connects with rock.

"Josh, lights!" Brian yells.

When they come on, everyone starts screaming.

Mila hangs from the sacrificial table, blood streaming from her mouth. I stare dumbly, unable to understand. Not knowing how this girl came to be there, one arm dangling over the edge, her chin painted entirely red with her own blood, dark dirt streaking her hands and arms so that the bright white flash of bone where her thumb should be stands starkly in contrast.

There's a moment where no one else understands, either. But when they do, they panic. Everyone runs for the exit, pushing past me as I fight against them, moving through the crowd, trying to get to Mila. I force my way through the last of them, elbowing a girl in Converse aside as she breaks past me, knocking askew 200,000 years of crystal growth. The crystals rain from the ceiling and the walls, crunching under shoes as the panicked crowd makes for the exit.

"Mila!" Brian rushes for the table, stalagmites tearing at his jeans. He reaches the edge, finds toeholds, pulls himself upward. I'm right behind him, crystals breaking around me as I lurch forward, scramble up the rock, and pull myself over the lip, dirt in my mouth.

Josh comes running around the corner, eyes wide. "What the fuck?"

Brian crawls across the table, heading for Mila at the opposite edge, his back scraping the ceiling. I follow, rock grinding into my kneecaps. Mila is gibbering, her mouth a bloody mess of broken teeth. Brian reaches her, rolls her onto her back.

"Mila!" he screams, his hands in her hair. She spits, and blood flies onto his face, spattering mine as well as I come up beside him. Mila's trying to speak, but only a ragged moan emerges, a deep, primal thing that has no words. Her eyes are wide and uncomprehending, her pupils black pits that reflect my own face. She bucks against the rock, swinging at both of us, teetering on the edge.

"Wait, Mila," I say, as if the problem is that she's in a terrible hurry, not that she's been mutilated. I make a grab at her shoulder, my hand sliding across her bloody skin, looking for purchase. A bright arc slices the air, light glinting from a pair of handcuffs that dangle from her wrist. I dodge them, losing my grip on her, and go down face-first into the dirt. I come up with grit in my teeth, just in time to see Mila go over the edge of the table, Brian reaching, his hand closing on nothing.

There's a pop and a crunch, followed by a wet, gurgling noise.

"Shit!" Brian yells, crawling forward. "Shit," he says again, more quietly as he peers over.

"No," I say, rushing forward on my elbows, the ceiling scraping my spine. "No, no, no."

"Neely, don't—" But Brian isn't fast enough, and I see all the things I don't want to see.

Mila, lying across a field of stalagmites. Mila, with the teeth of the earth protruding from her chest. Mila, who can't speak, because her tongue has been replaced by stone.

"What the fuck?" Josh yells again, looking up at me as if I can explain. And I can, actually, because I know what happens when tree and stone replace flesh and bone.

"Mila?" Brian asks, sliding to the edge of the table, letting himself down slowly, picking his way through stalagmites. I follow, dropping to the ground awkwardly, rolling my ankle, falling backward onto the concrete path.

"Mila?" Brian asks again, approaching the rag doll that is left of her, pinned in place. I get to my feet, scrambling behind him, Josh following.

"Mila? I'm here," I say. Like it matters, like I can do something, like her lifeblood isn't draining out from underneath her across the cave floor. I take her hand, and she opens her eyes. They slide from Josh, pass over Brian, rest on me. She tries to speak, holding my gaze, her mouth working against the stone that protrudes from it.

There's a twinge, a last electrical storm in the brain, a shudder that starts at her toes and passes upward, sending a spasm through her body as her final breath rattles out.

"Mila?" I ask again, hand tightening on hers.

But she's not here anymore. She's gone somewhere else.

Somewhere deeper, darker, farther.

TWENTY-SIX

Everything falls apart.

Destiny and Tabitha hold on to each other in the staff room, crying. Josh and Brian stand next to the window, watching as the parking lot fills with people in uniforms, vehicles with flashing lights and blaring sirens. One of the teachers has lined up the seventh graders along the pavement, counting heads. She gets through them all, then turns around to make another pass, mouth moving with the count, touching each crown of hair as she goes past them.

I sit on the bench in front of the staff lockers, holding Margaret's hand.

She had joined me at the entrance when Brian, Josh, and I were marched out by John. The screaming, fleeing tourists had brought him down to the caves, and he'd immediately sent us away. We'd done as we were told, silent, in shock, shivering, our skin wet with the mist of the caves, and—for Brian and me—Mila's blood.

"Are you sure she's actually dead?" Destiny asks, wiping her nose.

Brian and I share a look, but Josh has no qualms.

"Uh, yeah," he says. "I mean, not at first she wasn't, because she was trying to talk. But after she fell—" He slams the top of one hand into the palm of the other, mimicking her fall, like my fingers had done in this room, tracing the path of Lance's descent.

"That was it," Josh says. "That did it." His jaw is tight, everything he has inside of him holding on to the concept of not crying in public. Josh's hands are shaking, nervous movements bringing them back to his mouth and down to his side, as he paces near the window.

"But you're sure?" Destiny pushes, still hopeful. "None of you guys are exactly medics—"

"She was impaled through the mouth by a stalagmite," Brian says, his voice in a flatline. "And there was one sticking out of her chest, too."

If Josh is frantic energy, Brian is the opposite. He's still as the stone underground, his lips barely moving when he speaks. He doesn't try to stop tears from falling or bother to wipe them away as they trace his cheeks, follow the curve of his jawline, and drop onto his hands, which are still covered in blood. It's drying now, caked into the creases of his knuckles.

"You should clean up," Tabitha says gently, rubbing Destiny's back as the other girl sobs against her shoulder.

"What?" Brian looks down, seems to realize he's covered in Mila's blood for the first time.

"You too, Neely," Tabitha says. I nod that I understand but don't want to lose the feeling of Mila's drying blood from my skin. I reach up, touching it, sliding some beneath my fingernail for safekeeping.

"You should get cleaned up," Tabitha repeats, locking eyes with me and nodding as if I were a toddler that can't quite follow the line of conversation.

"Wait," Josh says. "Should they, though?"

"What do you mean?" Tabitha asks, still cradling Destiny's head.

Josh looks at Brian, then to me, but we are statues made of stone and painted in blood.

"Mila isn't just dead," Josh says, jamming his hands into his pockets. "Somebody fucked her up."

"What?" Tabitha shrieks as Destiny sits bolt upright, hands going to her mouth to stifle a scream. "How do you know that?"

"It wasn't some freak accident, you guys," Josh says, stalking back to the window. "Somebody . . ." He glances at the girls, weighing his words.

"Just say it," Tabitha says, jaw set hard. "I want to know."

Josh looks at Destiny, who also nods, her hands curling into her hair, fingers twisting tiny braids as she looks for something, anything, to be normal.

"She was handcuffed," Josh says, and a sob escapes Tabitha, and it's her turn to collapse into Destiny, their black and red hair flowing together in a vibrant, quivering wave as they cry, emotion wringing them clean.

"Her teeth were broken," Josh adds. "And someone cut off her thumb."

"Jesus," Tabitha says, looking at her own hands, apparently in awe of the fact that they can be disassembled. "What the fuck? Why would they cut off her thumb?"

"No," Brian says, stirring to life. "That's not it. That's not what happened."

"Dude, her thumb was gone, like totally off her hand," Josh argues, moving toward Brian, ready for a fight. "I don't know how that happens other than somebody—"

"She chewed it off," Brian says dully, his eyes unfocused.

"What?" Destiny's voice is quiet and empty, the stark inconceivability of the act measurable in her tones, a girl who has lived in a world with deep-pile carpets and herbal-infused hair conditioners her whole life.

"I've seen it in animals caught in traps," Brian goes on, lifting his gaze to us. His eyes are even brighter than normal, tears pulling color, reflecting light. "If they're desperate enough, they'll do anything, gnaw through their own bones to get free."

I think of Mila's hand, the white stub of bone among the torn pink muscle. It had been splintered and shattered, an act only endured in the face of a greater terror.

"Her teeth," I say, speaking the first time. It's all I can muster, but I don't need to say more. Brian and Josh saw, and they know. There was broken enamel, edges chipped away, nerves exposed, bone fragments buried in her gums, stalactites and stalagmites stabbing outward, parts of her body transferred, jutting out from where they don't belong, tongue moving, swollen and cracked, like the girl, begging for water.

"What could be so bad that she chewed part of her own body off to get away?" Josh asks, peering out the window again.

"Well." Brian pushes his cap back, inspects the blood on his hands. "She was handcuffed, so someone was holding her there. Who knows what they did to her, and what more they had in mind? If it was bad enough, I bet she'd do anything to escape it."

The room goes quiet, all of us digesting that.

"Who all has the code to the caverns' door?" Tabitha asks, still holding Destiny's head on her shoulder.

"Everyone who's ever worked here," Josh says with a shrug. "And besides, if someone took Mila down there, they could have forced her to open it. I mean, really, it's kind of smart; lots of time over the weekend to do whatever you want, where no one is going to be looking."

"What the fuck is wrong with you?" Tabitha cuts him off, as Destiny starts sobbing again.

"Who would do that?" Destiny asks, incredulity still her cape, the mantle that's keeping her safe from reality.

"That's what the cops are going to want to know," Josh says, finally standing still, leaning against the window and watching a group of uniformed officers. "And we all need to get our stories straight, right now."

TWENTY-SEVEN

"Get our stories straight?" Tabitha repeats dumbly.

"Yeah, Tabitha," Josh says, electrical energy lighting his words. "What's the first thing you think they're going to ask?"

"When was the last time we saw her," Destiny says, pushing tear-dampened hair from her face. "They're going to want to know where we were and what we were doing the last time we saw Mila."

"Exactly," Josh concurs, voice climbing higher. "And I don't know about you guys, but the last time I saw Mila, I was high as a fucking kite."

"Okay," Tabitha says, agreeing, but she's still calm, still holding on to the idea that the world is a safe place and anyone who tells the truth through it can move through it without fear of repercussion. "But are they really going to care about that? I mean, are they going to piss-test every single one of us, and the can-doers, and the zips? How much does that matter when somebody died?"

"It matters a lot," Josh says. "Because we were all drinking, and most of us smoked, and then something really fucking awful happened. The cops are going to want to know how a bunch of underage kids got alcohol and weed."

"I brought the weed," I say quickly. "That was me; I'll own it."

"Brought the weed and then lost your absolute mind on it," Destiny adds. "After what Tammy said—"

"Stop!" Tabitha says, clapping her hands together. "This isn't helping anybody."

"I'm telling the cops the truth," Destiny says, coming to her feet and snagging a paper towel from the roller beside the sink. "Mila is fucking dead, guys. Somebody killed her. That's way more important than a bunch of kids partying, and the cops will feel the same way."

"They might feel the same way about *you*," Josh sneers back. "Your dad's the goddamn mayor. I bet by the end of this you weren't even at the party."

"No," Destiny says, spinning, her hair a red fan. "I was there, and I was drunk and I was high. But I'm also alive, asshole. Mila's not. That's all that matters."

"Jesus, even Neely is like, I brought the pot, it's mine," Tabitha adds, not bothering to hide her contempt for Josh. "She'll get in a lot more trouble than any of us, if they even care."

"It was mine," I say again, eager to take one for the team, if they'll still let me be on it.

"Where did you even get it?" Destiny asks.

"I brought it," I reiterate. "But I guess technically it was Lance's."

"Wait," Destiny says, her fingers going to her lips. "Are you telling me I smoked your crazy dead brother's pot?"

"How is that what you're worried about right now?" Tabitha asks, as Josh breaks out in jagged, uncontrollable laughter. "And why are you laughing?" Her anger transfers to Josh easily, emotion jumping across the tension-filled air, traveling between us, forcing us together, pulling us apart.

"Because we're fucked," Josh says, still laughing, the tears finally coming. "All of us are fucked. I've got a fake ID, and the person who made it for me will not be pleased when they find out we got busted."

"Oh boo-hoo, is little baby Josh gonna get smacked around?" Destiny asks, lips stuck out in a pout, fists moving at the sides of her eyes as she mimes crying.

"I'll fucking smack you around—" Josh growls, moving toward her.

Destiny shrieks, and Brian jumps to his feet, putting himself between them.

"You do that, man?" he asks, chest bumping against Josh's. "You hit girls?"

"What? No!" Josh pales as he backpedals. "I didn't mean it. I was just—"

"Because if you do, that might be something the cops would be real interested in," Brian says, his face pulling closer to Josh's, his bloodied hands curled into fists.

"Okay, guys, clam down," Tabitha says, but Destiny is attached to her again, and she can't interfere.

"You're the one that hits people, dick," Josh says, pointing at the bruise below his own eye, now yellowing. "Remember? You and that crazy fucking bitch over there. She lost her shit, nearly choked me out last week."

His gaze cuts to me, and I'm pinned, a bug on display, as everyone turns to me.

"Neely?" Tabitha asks. "Is that true?"

My tongue is dry, filling my mouth. My words are gone; I have only images, Mila's hair across my face, her hands pressing against me.

"Mila was raped," I say, and the room falls silent, Brian's fists loosening.

"Before," I clarify. "A guy she was seeing, he drugged her and did stuff to her, and he put it all on the internet."

"Jeeeesus," Tabitha says, her eyes welling full of tears again.

"He watched it," I say, lifting my hand to Josh, one finger separating from the others. "He watched it, and he teased her about it, and I went after him, and I won't apologize."

"Why would you watch that?" Destiny asks, and Josh flushes a deep red. "Why would you want to—"

"Who was this guy?" Brian asks, cutting her off, rounding on me.

"His name is Patrick," I say, shaking my head. "That's all I know. She was going to press charges," I add, aware that all eyes are on me still and that I need to find words to fill the void.

"Did he know that?" Tabitha asks.

"Yeah, I think so," I say. "She said she texted him and he was not happy."

"You've got to tell the cops that," she says, her words coming fast and tacked hard onto the end of mine. "Okay, Neely? That is really important and you need to make sure they know."

"Right," I say. "I will."

"And maybe tell them you choked out Josh and tried to stab someone at a birthday party," Destiny says. "Just so they've got all the background information."

I choose not to answer her, instead grinding my teeth against what wants to come out, the blackness unspooling toward her, reaching with dark fingers.

"So that's what we're going with?" Brian asks, surveying the group. "We're going to tell the truth?"

"Yes," Destiny says, raising her chin. "And the truth is that the last time I saw Mila, she was leaving the party with her."

A finger comes out, long and slender, the perfectly manicured nail pointed at me.

"That's the last time I saw her, too," Tabitha says quietly.

"All right, look . . ." Brian glances between us all, hands held upward in surrender. "It's not our jobs to figure this out, okay? We just tell the cops what we know. All of us are going to tell the truth, and we let them take it from there."

"Shit," Josh says, back at the window. "They just brought up a stretcher. And Mila's mom is here."

A new sound fills the air, a pure kind of truth, a high, keening wail of grief that reaches inside the walls, past bricks and glass, filling my head, blasting away children and applause, the sound of my name from the mouths of cats, the realness of her pain eradicating everything, tearing away the skin of reality and cutting to the bone. I touch my forehead to Margaret's and she presses back, anchoring me, giving me strength.

Even if she's not actually there.

TWENTY-EIGHT

The truth is supposed to set you free, but in my case it might land me in actual jail.

The cops separate us, placing me on a folding chair next to the pamphlet rack that offers trifolds illustrating all the other wonderful things tourists can do in the county, which is basically visit John's other businesses. There's also a series of safety brochures about Lyme disease and what to do if you encounter a black bear. But there's nothing to tell me what I should say to the police, and right now that is a very big question. I can't say for sure exactly when the last time I saw Mila was, and trying to explain that will mean sharing the fact that we hooked up and then she snuck out at some point.

Destiny, Tabitha, and Brian are all eighteen or over, so they don't need their parents to be present in order to talk to the cops. Destiny's come anyway, her father hauling a man in an expensive suit alongside him. Brian shoots me a text from his corner of the room.

Lawyering up.

Josh's parents show up and hover near him, issuing a series of rapid-fire questions that come out like the humming of bees;

indistinguishable, but vaguely threatening. I tap out a response to Brian.

> Your parents coming?

He glances down at his phone as it buzzes, looking around before he answers.

Doubt it. I didn't call them.

> Why not?

Because I didn't do anything wrong.

Brian shrugs when I raise my eyes to meet his, the stress of the morning showing in the deep circles below his eyes, dark half-moons like the bruise he'd left on Josh's face. Tabitha comes out of John's office, where the cops are conducting their interviews, and Destiny is called to go back, the retinue of her parents and lawyer leading the way. Tabitha's eyes are red-rimmed, and she's carrying a tissue, although it's practically shredded. She spots me and walks over, crouching beside my chair.

"Neely, listen to me," she says. "You need to be honest in there, okay?"

"Okay," I say, nodding.

"No, like, really listen to me," Tabitha says, her fingers closing around my wrist. "Destiny is going to say exactly what she saw, all right? She's going to be honest, and she's going to tell the cops what happened that night."

"Right," I agree. "That's what we're all going to do."

"You too, okay?" Tabitha says. "I know that . . . things aren't always great for you, all right? I know that sometimes you say stuff that's just weird, or hard to figure out, or whatever. I don't know why you do it." She shakes her head—my actions a mystery, my motives a puzzle. "But this is the time to tell the truth, all of it."

I look down at her, try not to laugh, try not to consider her response to my whole truth, that Margaret Sander is standing right behind her, and that Sulla is in the tree outside, saying my name, linking it over and over with the phrase *psychotic break*.

"I don't think you're dangerous," Tabitha goes on. "I know you've got problems. I don't believe you'd ever hurt anyone but . . ." Her voice drops off as Josh's parents notice us.

"Should you girls be talking to each other?" his mom asks.

"But individual results may vary?" I finish for her.

"Yeah," she says. "So be honest, okay? The truth is the easiest thing to remember," Tabitha says, coming to her feet and giving a little wave to Mr. and Mrs. Bailey, skirting around them as she heads for the door.

And maybe for people like Tabitha, the truth is easy to remember, people who live in linear time and only interact with other humans that actually exist, people who don't have animals flash-mobbing them.

I hold my phone, a neutered thing in my hand. It holds no connection to Mila, no promise of an update on her movements, actions, thoughts. My thumb hovers over social media apps, debating, before finally opening Rock Bottom.

hillwalker—It would be so easy. No one pays attention. Everyone wears earbuds. They walk in safety bubbles, believing that their sheer specialness keeps them safe, a plastic shield between themselves and the world. Between themselves and me.

189

hillwalker—You can just take something if you want it. You can have her. You can kill him. Nothing actually stops us.

Baller_87—Well, I mean, the law.

hillwalker—No, that's the punishment that comes after you do it.

hillwalker—The only things that stops me, is me.

hillwalker—And I am very tired.

I see Mila, as if she were right in front of me, her index finger pointing, firelight playing across her face, as she imitates her mother. *What do you control, Mila?*

Lance, spewing his unwanted thoughts into the dark corners of the internet, setting aside the pact that we had made with Dad. Letting himself be himself. *The only thing that stops me is me.*

Except in the end, Mila didn't have control.

Except in the end, there was only one way for Lance to stop himself.

The front doors open, and Grandma and Grandpa walk in, still wearing their blue Walmart vests, bright yellow happy faces embroidered on their chests. They haven't even taken their name tags off, announcing to everyone that they are Ed and Betsy, two people that should get to be exactly that, not just Grandma and Grandpa, not having the latter parts of their lives eaten up by an unstable granddaughter. They spot me, and I come to my feet, walking into Grandma's arms as all the muscles in my face collapse, pulled inward by the black hole at my core. I sob, her gray hair filling my mouth as Grandma holds me close, rocking back and forth.

"Neely," Grandpa says sternly, once I'm sitting back down and they've pulled chairs over for themselves. "What exactly is going on?"

"Mila's dead," I say, which feels impossible, even though I've heard it, said it, and typed it when I texted Grandma earlier, telling her I needed them to come to the caverns. That I needed them right now. That I needed them, period. That I could not manage.

"Somebody killed her," I say, wiping my nose with my sleeve. Grandma digs in her purse and pulls out a paperback, two tubes of mascara, five pens, and approximately twenty hair ties before she comes up with a tissue. It's blotted with lipstick and has a lint stuck on one corner, but I take it anyway.

"And the cops want to question you?" Grandma asks.

"No," Grandpa says. "They want to ask her some questions, not question her. Those are two very different things."

Grandpa pretty much has *Law & Order* on an IV, so I choose to trust him on that one.

"They're talking to everybody, though," Grandma says, her statement half a question, eyes sweeping the room. She sees Brian and offers a small wave, which he returns. Destiny and her retinue leave John's office, none of them making eye contact with any of us.

"Was that a lawyer? Does the Prosker girl have a lawyer?" Grandpa asks.

"I'd say so," Grandma answers, peeling the blinds apart and observing the group in the parking lot. "He's got a Samsonite suitcase and drives a BMW." Her fingers fall away, the blinds snapping shut again as dust falls to the floor.

Brian goes back to talk to the cops alone, his shoulders straight but small and slim compared to the officer who escorts him.

"Do we need a lawyer?" Grandpa asks, holding his phone up.

"Are you asking me, or Siri?" Grandma says.

"I'm asking Neely."

"I don't need a lawyer," I say, numbly repeating Brian. "Because I didn't do anything wrong."

"Of course you didn't," Grandma says. "But we're going in with you."

"We have to," Grandpa says, fingers stabbing away at his phone as he googles lawyer advice. "She's a minor; they can't talk to her without her guardians present. But, Neely, you don't have to talk to them at all, if you don't want to."

"Wouldn't that look bad?" Grandma asks, fingers tightening around her purse. "All the other kids already—"

"I don't care what the other kids are doing, Betsy," Grandpa shoots back. "One of them has a lawyer, and the others aren't—"

He breaks off, and I'm left wondering what he was about to say. Aren't crazy?

"Aren't Neely," Margaret offers, speaking up for the first time and offering a pretty good summation.

The office door opens, and Brian leaves, his hat pulled down low. He ignores Josh but nods at me. The officer glances up. "Neely Hawtrey? You ready to come back?"

I am not ready, but I'm pretty sure it's a rhetorical question, so I follow my grandparents into John's office, where the massive whiteboard on the wall shows the schedule for the next month. Mila's name is at the top, her hours stretching Monday through Friday, her constant presence an assurance that everything would run smoothly. Two cops are seated behind John's desk, and the three of us slide onto folding chairs across from them. There's a dollop of hardened sloppy joe on the corner of mine, a reminder that just a few days ago we were all eating Jell-O salad and everything was fine.

"Neely, I'm Officer Vargas," the male cop says, then nods to the woman. "This is Officer McNichols. We know it's a really stressful time right now, but we need to ask you a few questions, okay?"

I look down at my lap, at my hands folded there, the dark line of Mila's blood pressed under one fingernail, jammed against the cuticle.

"Okay," I tell Vargas, working hard to raise my eyes, to seem normal, to pretend like everything is fine, even though it really, really isn't. Grandma puts a hand on my knee, and Grandpa leans forward, elbows on the desk.

"We know that your coworkers had a little get-together last Friday, is that right?" McNichols asks, smoothly taking over the conversation.

"Yes," I say. "John wanted to get the other groups together because there had been some problems in the past with pranks . . ."

Grandpa leans toward me. "All you have say is yes, Neely. You don't have to add anything."

"Anything she has to say is potentially helpful, sir," Vargas says. "We already know from some of the other kids—"

"It was a yes-or-no question," Grandpa says tightly. "She answered it. And some of those *other kids* have lawyers."

"We're aware that there was some tension between the different groups of coworkers," McNichols says, cutting off Vargas when it seems he might come back at Grandpa. "Do you have anything you want to add to that, Neely?"

I look at Grandpa before I speak, and hope that the people who write *Law & Order* actually know what they're doing, because that seems to be our legal touch point at the moment.

"Some things happened before I came to work here," I tell them. "Just dumb things, like messing with the kayak paddles. Stuff like that."

193

"No loose body parts," Margaret says. "That would be a definite escalation."

"Okay," McNichols says, making a note on her pad. "And when were you hired?"

"Just at the beginning of the summer," I tell her, relaxing a little. I can talk about work all day without missing a beat. I can talk about the caverns and being underground, the feeling of opening the heavy metal door, hearing the welcoming screech, and knowing that I'm about to be excused from the world for a little while, or, at least, the length of a tour.

"So you're new?"

"Yeah," I confirm. "But I know more about the caves than anyone. I can—"

"Yes or no, Neely," Grandpa reminds me, and I fall silent, suddenly aware that knowing the ins and outs of the cave systems where a girl was held against her will before crawling up from the depths to die is not in my favor.

"Yes," I say, nodding once. "I am new."

"We understand there was some tension between the different factions of employees." Vargas picks up the questions as McNichols continues writing. "So your boss had a gathering for everyone, and then there was an unofficial gathering after that, correct?"

My heart dips, remembering Destiny's jutted-out chin, the fan of her red hair when she staked her claim on the truth, Tabitha's pleading as she knelt next to me, recommending honesty.

"Yes," I say, following Grandpa's advice and adding nothing more.

"And were you there?"

"Yes," I say, without faltering. Destiny and Tabitha likely already said as much, and I'm sure Josh and Brian will as well. There's also all the can-doers and zips, who the cops will certainly talk to, including Brigit . . . and Tammy.

Fuck.

Tammy won't hesitate to tell them that I'm vicious and unstable, a girl who recites her personal information into campfires, a girl who turns away when an olive branch has been extended. Kind of a mean girl, maybe a dangerous one.

"Neely . . ." McNichols leans forward, leaving the pen behind, like things just got super unofficial and we're all just talking here. "We know that there was alcohol at the party, as well as marijuana."

"That's not a question," Grandpa says, sitting straighter now, as Grandma lets out a little puff, like a balloon slowly leaking wintergreen-scented air.

"It's not," Vargas agrees. "Because it's an established fact."

McNichols folds her hands, holds my eyes. "We're not interested in—"

"Do you know how much drug trafficking passes through this county?" Vargas asks.

"That one *is* a question. He's getting better at this," Margaret says.

But it's not directed at me. It's for Grandpa, who is leaning forward now, ready to argue.

"No, I don't know," he fires back. "And Neely wouldn't, either."

"Some of her coworkers disagree," Vargas says. "They claim she's the one who brought drugs to the party."

All of Grandma's air goes out in *whoosh*, the balloon pooped. She folds in on herself, shrinking in a way that's got nothing to do with osteoporosis as I consider the fact that I will forever associate the smell of wintergreen with disappointment after this.

Or for however long forever is.

"That's not true," Grandma says, but her hand isn't on my knee anymore, and she's looking at me with an expression that does not match the happy face stitched on her vest.

But it is true, and Destiny told the truth and Tabitha wants me to be honest, and if I do that, it opens doors that should be closed to rooms that don't exist, where Lance kept his secrets and buried his anger. Telling the truth means tarnishing him further, and maybe he won't even get plastic flowers next year on Memorial Day.

"I did, I brought it," I say suddenly.

"Neely!" Grandpa's palm hits the desk. "They didn't ask!"

"No, I know," I say, flustered now, tears starting to gather. "But I want to—"

"Everyone needs to calm down," McNichols says, shooting Vargas a side-eye that includes him in that statement.

"Neely," she continues, eyes back on mine, hands extended toward me, flat on the desk. "There are much more important factors in play here. We're just trying to get a feel for what happened that night."

"You're not charging her with anything?" Grandpa asks.

"Not yet," Vargas says evenly.

"Careful with that one," Margaret advises me, her eyes narrowing at him.

"So there was a party up in the woods above the caverns," McNichols says, sticking with the narrative that she already knows. "There was drinking, and some pot. Did anything else happen at the party that you can remember?"

I think of Tammy and Brigit congregating with Tabitha and Destiny, watching me. I think of Mila's hand on my shoulder and the play of fire across her collarbone.

"Also, I showed up," Margaret offers. "But maybe don't tell them that."

Don't tell them about Margaret or a little girl with a worn-out teddy bear, the lint on the man's flannel. Don't tell them about cats who know the mistakes I've made and speak my name aloud. Don't tell them about laughing children and how there's a space of time in the evening where my bedroom holds all worlds, all people and things.

But there are other truths, and not everything can be made right.

"Mila was raped," I say, and Vargas breaks his stare-down with Grandpa, transferring it to me.

"Not at the party," I add quickly. "Before. There was a guy she was dating, Patrick."

I tell them everything Mila told me, though I can't capture the way her voice shook, or the chill that filled me as she talked.

"She was going to press charges, and he knew it," I finish up.

"And was Patrick at the party?" McNichols asked, her pen flying across the paper now.

"No," I say.

"Not that we know of," Margaret adds.

"Not that we know of," I repeat, then recant, addressing the blunder. "Not that *I* know of."

"How many entrances are there to the caverns?" Vargas asks.

"Two," I say firmly, back on solid ground. "The one for the natural wonders tour is by the visitors' center, if you follow the path. The other is for the historical tour, about two miles away. That's the original entrance that Harold Gentry found, back in 1897. His fields were draining really quickly and he—"

"And who has access codes?" Vargas asks, not interested in the tour speech.

"All of us," I say. "I mean, all the employees."

"Anybody who works at the zip lines, or the canoe livery?" McNichols follows up.

"No, I don't think so," I say, irritated that they're back onto this line of questioning, inferring too much from small rivalries and harmless pranks, even after I just told them that Mila was raped.

"Mila was *raped*."

That one got away from me, slipping out into the open when I didn't mean it to.

"Well," Vargas says, leaning back in his chair. "That's what she told you."

"And we will be looking into it," McNichols says quickly, and I swear I see movement under the desk, her foot coming down hard on his. "But right now we need to make sure we have all the information—"

"He did that, okay?" I say. "He did that, and he recorded it, and he put it online—"

"Did you attack Josh Bailey?" Vargas asks, hands laced behind his head now. "He said that you were agitated over the situation."

Agitated.

"Yes, I was fucking agitated," I say, and Grandma gasps, like my language is what's going wrong here, not that Mila is dead and in pieces and her mother was screaming in the parking lot an hour ago, loud enough to drown out the cat in the tree saying my name.

"Neely, I think maybe we should . . . ," Grandpa says, thumbs tapping against his screen as he looks for free legal advice about what to do when your granddaughter smokes pot and swears at cops.

"He also said that Mila left the party with you," Vargas finishes.

Grandpa goes still; Grandma stiffens.

Margaret leans back, mimicking Vargas, hands behind her head. "You're goddamn right she did," she says, arching her back. "Tell them, Neely."

But I can't.

I can't tell them about lips and mouths and teeth in the dark, how everything was finally silent, except for just the right things, only the ones I wanted to hear. I can't tell them about her hair in my face or my hands on her body, the end of yearning and the beginning of something entirely new, fully mine. There was a girl in my bed and a need being answered, and I can't say anything about that because Grandma and Grandpa are actually Ed and Betsy, and I can't ask them for more, can't ask them to understand, can't ask them to love me anyway.

They shouldn't have to be here, shouldn't have to hear these things. I had thought Brian looked small and alone when he walked in here, but maybe alone is best in these situations, maybe the truth is easier to speak when there isn't anyone for you to let down, disappoint. If I was here by myself, maybe I could tell them—tell McNichols, anyway—and she would hear me, and she would listen. But just because I'm a minor—

"Oh, fuck," Margaret says, coming to it at the same moment I do.

I'm a minor. Mila wasn't. And what we did together might be perfectly fine with some people, but numbers are fatally honest. I'm sixteen; Mila was in college. And maybe they can't charge her with a crime after she's dead, but I don't want her mother's screams to get any louder. My hand moves to my pocket, to the dust ball there. I don't want Mila's mom to have to consider what I have, that you can never truly know someone else. Not even your own daughter, who kissed girls back and slipped away sometime in the night.

And after that, something happened.

My fingers go to the scab on my chest, the hot scratch that still burns there.

"No," I say, my hand falling away. "Mila didn't leave with me."

"Neely," McNichols says quietly. "I've got multiple—"

"Mila didn't leave with me," I say again.

"We've got plenty of people saying otherwise, Neely. You sure about that?" Vargas asks, leaning back still farther.

"You sure about that, shitbird?"

"Now? Really?" Margaret asks, rolling her eyes toward the ceiling.

But there's some satisfaction when I lean forward, holding Vargas's gaze.

"You sure about that, shitbird?"

TWENTY-NINE

Me calling Vargas a shitbird effectively ends my interview.

Grandpa is stiff-backed and silent when we head to the parking lot, where Grandma offers to ride home with me so that I'm not alone. It's late afternoon by now, and I'm almost surprised to see my car sitting in the same parking space that I pulled into this morning, expecting to see Mila, checking my reflection in the mirror before I got out. The world is the same, and time has passed like every other day, seconds and minutes and hours slipping by, except today they mark the length of time that Mila has been dead, and that is all it measures now.

"I don't want you to be alone," Grandma says, her hand on my passenger door. I can't tell her that I'm not alone, that Margaret has been with me ever since I left the caves.

"I'm okay, really," I tell Grandma. "I could actually use the space."

Her hand slides off the car, and worry clouds her eyes, but we haven't moved entirely out of the realm of trust because she gives me a small nod. "You come straight home," she says. "I want to see your car in our rearview mirror the whole way."

I start the car and crank up the AC, looking over at Grandma and Grandpa while I wait for it to kick in. Their mouths move, forming words I can't hear but can guess at. Words like *lawyer* and *afford* and maybe even *therapist*. Or maybe I'm way off and they're actually saying things like *Florida* and *just leave* and *we deserve it*.

"They totally do," Margaret agrees. "That was pretty intense in there."

"We need rules for you," I tell her. "You can't just be in my head."

"Uh, I can't *not* be in your head, honey," Margaret says, twining a lock of hair around her fingers. "It's where I came from."

"You're not real," I tell her, as I back out of the lot, heading for the gate, following my grandparents' car and staying in sight, as promised.

"No," she agrees. "I'm not real. But I am a product of your mind, so you can't really ask me to not follow your thoughts. I know everything you know. I think everything you think. I *am* you."

"Nobody else does that," I say, falling back from Grandpa's Buick so they don't see my mouth moving in their rearview mirror, carrying on an avid conversation all by myself. "Everybody else—"

"Follows the rules?" Margaret asks.

"Yeah," I say. "I mean, mostly." The fact that they have crawled out from under the bed and left the closet stands in glaring contradiction to that, but Margaret seems content to let it slide.

"Well, I came along when you were in total freefall," she says, crossing her arms and sliding down in her seat. "So maybe there aren't rules for me."

"No," I say, hitting the steering wheel. "There have to be. You can't—"

"What can't I do, Neely?" Margaret asks, her tone cold. I glance over at her, the hard set of her jaw, the dark pools of her eyes, and I'm certain that I don't get to tell this one what the rules are. If she is me,

202

and I can smoke pot and choke Josh and touch Mila, forget to close doors and lie to cops, then maybe there is nothing I can't do, either.

Maybe the only thing that stops me is me.

Dinner is pizza, which shows exactly how far things have deteriorated for Grandma. In the past, fast food and takeout were reserved for good reports on grade cards, when I passed my driver's test, or the time she slipped on ice and had a concussion. Even that was a one-night-only event; she was slicing vegetables and baking bread the next day, with stitches on her temple and a slightly confused look on her face.

"We need to talk about this, Neely," Grandpa says. He's looking down at his plate, unsure what to do with food that can't be lined up in regiments.

I look down at my own pizza, the hot grease resting in the bowl of pepperoni. Grandma glances at Grandpa, then seems to take her cue from whatever their conversation in the car had been. "We both want you to have a normal life, Neely," she says.

"I do, too," Margaret says, turning to me, her eyes wide and innocent, even though her mouth has a little curl on the edges, a laugh barely restrained.

"And we understand that might mean going to parties," she goes on. "But if you were the one who supplied the pot, that changes things."

"I talked to a lawyer," Grandpa says, tossing his napkin on the table. "They absolutely can—and they will—charge you with possession. And if they can peg you for distribution, they will. Even as a minor, that will put you in a world of hurt."

A world of hurt is how Grandpa describes the worst-case scenario, the absolute most horrific outcome. He doesn't understand I'm already there and my world has always been tinged with hurt, ever since I watched Dad's back as he walked away, the cough of an engine, glass breaking and the sun drying Mom's blood as Lance and I held hands.

"That cop today was an asshole," Grandpa says. "But that doesn't mean he's wrong. If he can charge you with something, he will. The lawyer said . . ."

But I don't hear him anymore, because there's a groundswell of noise inside my head that is real, a roaring of relief that boils. Whatever their conversation was in the car on the way home, none of it was about leaving me, cashing in on whatever they have and finally taking that cruise. Instead, they're doubling down, digging deeper, throwing everything they've got into protecting me, investing in the sole carrier of their genes, the one person left to keep this family moving forward.

"Too bad it's you," Margaret says, reaching over to jam her finger into a piece of pepperoni, tilting it so that the grease spills out, pooling across my plate in an orange smear.

My phone goes off, a message from Brian asking me to call him. Tears fill my throat, cloying, choking, salt sealing me shut.

"Neely?" Grandpa breaks off his speech about what I could and could not be charged with. "Honey, you okay?"

"Why do you put up with me?" I ask, looking up from my plate, tears welling as my mouth pulls downward. "Why does anyone even care? It's not like I deserve—"

My voice fails, and Grandma pulls me into her arms, the tails of her shirt dragging through pizza grease as she leans in.

"You don't earn love, Neely," she says, her breath on my neck, her words a low rumble against my ear. "It's just given. We gave it to you the day you were born, and it doesn't go away."

I nod, my tears mixing with hers, the two streams threading down her neck, trickling past stretch marks, reaching the curve of her scar from open-heart surgery. She pulls away from me, brushing wet hair off my face.

"Whatever is going on, honey, we're here. We're going to stick with you."

I glance over at Grandpa, who is quietly crying, still holding a fork even though nobody eats pizza with a fork. He's set in his ways, so used to Grandma putting food on the table that requires silverware that he grabbed a fork anyway. Just like they're going to love me, even if they don't have to.

"I mean, maybe," Margaret says dubiously. "You've got a couple of real bangers you haven't dropped on them yet."

My phone vibrates again, a reminder that Brian's text is waiting on me. Grandma looks down at it, sees the name there.

"Should you be talking to him?"

Margaret snorts, and I have to fight back the urge myself. On any given day, I talk to two or three people that I really shouldn't.

"The cops didn't say not to," I tell Grandma, although, admittedly, they didn't have a lot more to say to me at all, once I called Vargas a shitbird. We both look at Grandpa, who lifts one shoulder in a shrug.

"We don't exactly have this lawyer on retainer," he says. "John just gave me a name, said he's a friend and I should give him a call. I don't know how many more questions he'll answer for free."

"Well," Grandma says, folding her napkin—cloth, because not all niceties can be abandoned, even though we are eating pizza and a girl has been murdered. "Maybe just be careful what you say for now, okay?"

I nod and get up from the table, eager to escape before the laugh that's struggling its way up makes it all the way out. I've been careful about what I say for most of my life, making rules and following them. But rules are made to be broken, and what Grandma doesn't know about love is that it can go away.

Like dads and moms, brothers and girls who let me in.

Brian picks up on the first ring, his voice low and quiet. "Hey."

"Hey," I say, falling backward onto my bed. The girl scoots over, making room for me. The man is sitting in the corner, glowering. Margaret flops onto the bed next to me, her fingers running through my hair.

"How are you holding up?" Brian asks.

"I don't know," I tell him.

"Yeah," he says. "That was a lot."

A lot. It was a lot to see stone jutting from Mila's throat and hear her mother screaming; it was a lot to leave her behind, to find Margaret waiting on the other side.

"I talked to Destiny," Brian goes on. "There's going to be an autopsy tomorrow."

Destiny, whose dad is the mayor, who gets to know things, who has a lawyer and opinions about what happened. Destiny, who likes to point at me.

"What can an autopsy really do, though?" I ask, feeling Margaret's fingertips against my temple, cool and calming. "We know she was murdered, the handcuffs show that she was held against her will. We know she was likely down there from Friday night to Monday morning, and we know that what actually killed her was the stalactite. She was still alive, right up until then."

Brian is quiet for a second, and a cat jumps onto the outside windowsill.

"Kitty!" The girl jumps up, pointing.

"Neely," the cat says.

"The autopsy isn't just to find out how she died," Brian says. "It's to figure out who killed her. There's probably skin under her fingernails, and all that blood might not have just been hers. It's Mila we're talking about, you know she fought like hell. I mean, shit, the girl chewed off her own thumb."

There's awe in his voice and a bit of pride. We knew her, were friends with someone who wanted to live badly enough to do that.

"Wonder what that feels like?" Margaret asks.

"Did Destiny tell you anything else?" I ask.

"She's pretty chatty right now," Brian says, and I can hear a smile on his face. "She's asking all of us to personally affirm to her father that she didn't smoke any weed."

"Sounds like telling the truth has a pretty hard stopping point when it comes to Dad," I say, as the girl slides off the bed and walks to the window, tapping the glass as the cat rubs against it. The dangling eye of her bear hangs over one shoulder, fixing on me.

"Yeah, well, I wasn't about to call her a hypocrite," Brian says. "She's got info, and she's willing to share it. The more we know, the better. I can't afford a lawyer, and I don't need the cops getting cute."

Vargas was definitely not cute.

"Destiny might be a dumb bitch," Brian goes on, "but she's not wrong about one thing. The cops don't care about what went on at the party; they care about what happened after, about finding out who killed Mila. They'll put the screws to us about the drinking and the pot until somebody cracks, but I'm not worried about that."

"Why not?" I ask.

"Because I didn't kill her," Brian says.

"Oh," I say, then glance at Margaret, who is spinning a finger in the air, looking at me expectantly.

"I didn't, either," I tack on.

"Did you tell them about the Patrick guy, and that porn site?"

"Yep," I say, my lips popping together.

"Okay, good," Brian says. "He sounds like a real piece of shit."

"Yeah." I tap my fingers across my phone, pull up the photo of Patrick that I lifted from Mila's social media. The absolutely averageness of him next to her is stunning, her beauty outshining him in all ways, except for his smile, which radiates in the knowledge that he has something he didn't earn.

"A real piece of shit," I repeat.

"You doing okay?" Brian asks. "Is that woman still—"

"Yeah, she's here," I say quickly, glancing at Margaret, who gives the phone a wave.

"Tell him I say hi," she mouths.

"Is that . . . Did it make things worse?" Brian asks. "Did what happened to Mila make it worse?"

"No," I say. "Listen, I have to go."

I hang up before Brian can add anything, say Mila's name again, or ask me if I'm okay. Because Mila didn't make things worse; she made them better.

And now she's gone.

I can hang up on Brian, but much like my delusions, I can't get his voice out of my head. Brian was right; Lance had been very angry. He hated how much he tried and how little it mattered. He hated that he had to run every errant thought through a mental sieve before deciding if it should be spoken aloud. He hated people who didn't instinctively understand the flow of foot traffic, or do what he thought they should, behaving in the manner he believed most appropriate in any given situation.

He posted in rb/realme.

hillwalker—We're all pretending. None of us are what we seem.

My finger trails over the last sentence, as I picture Lance tapping out messages to the only people he was honest with—strangers on the internet. There was safety in it, I'm sure, and the comfort of finally being honest, sharing his real self, alone in his room, before having to slide the mask of normality on as Grandma called him to dinner.

hillwalker—If I let people know . . . if I shared my real thoughts . . . it would be very, very bad.
SadOctopus48—You're not special.

My hand closes around the dust in my pocket, what remains of my brother. Maybe I didn't know him, and maybe he didn't share his true self with me. But he was special, the same way Mila was. They were both people that light attached to, that all the oxygen in the room flowed toward. They were people that, once gone, left behind a void.

Lance posted in rb/control.

hillwalker—People don't do the right things, don't react the way they should, don't respect what I do. I follow the rules, I behave in the expected way. I say the right things and check the boxes and jump through the hoops of social acceptability (although it is very, very hard). It's real effort, true work. And still I am just standing here. Alone.

hillwalker—I follow the rules.

hillwalker—And still, people do not do what they are supposed to do.

platosdick—What are they supposed to do, dude? Worship you?

hillwalker—They need to RECOGNIZE MY EFFORT

Lance posted in rb/violence.

hillwalker—It would be much easier if we just forced them

nightmarefire—Girls? I hear you on that. Why wine 'em and dine 'em when you can tape 'em and rape 'em?

hillwalker—Yes.

"Jesus," I say aloud, and the girl glances up, her fingers tightening on her teddy bear.

"What?" she asks.

"Nothing," I say quickly, and tilt the phone away from her, a flush rising to my cheeks. I glance around the room, embarrassed to have read this, ashamed of having a brother that would say such things. My eyes land on Margaret's, and she raises an eyebrow.

"He didn't mean that," I say. "Lance would never do anything like that." But there's a pit in my stomach that has opened, a heavy rock of doubt tumbling into it. I reach into my pocket, pull out the dust bunny, set it on my nightstand, where I regard it critically.

"People say shit on the internet; it's not real," I tell Margaret, my voice raising in volume if not conviction.

"You're not real," I remind her, as if that will clear the air of her judgment.

hillwalker—But not just girls. Others too. All people should have strings attached to them, easily pullable, something that allows them to be manipulated and controlled so that they behave accordingly.
nightmarefire—According to what?
hillwalker—My will and desires.

I close out Rock Bottom, flicking this version of Lance into oblivion with the pad of my thumb. But his words hang heavily in my head, whether they are in front of me or not. I turn onto my side, away from my nightstand, pulling my knees up to my chest. I close my eyes, willing sleep to come so that I don't have to think. Don't have to think about the brother I did not know and his need to control others, make them move in the direction of his choosing. Don't have to think about how Lance wanted everyone else to say the right things, enact his will and desires, do as they were told.

Don't have to think about the fact that if Mila were still alive, I'd want exactly the same thing.

THIRTY

"Kitty!" the little girl insists, pointing at the window, where her fingers have left smudge marks on the inside, the cat a smear of spit where it's rubbing, trying to get to her, trying to get to us, trying to get in, like the children who would come to the window when I was little, wanting to play.

"We don't need a cat," the man says, coming to his feet. "Pets are expensive."

"Only if they're real," Margaret counters.

"Guys, listen," I say, standing in the middle of the room and calling my delusions to attention. "I need to focus right now. A lot of things have gone really, really wrong."

The little girl's face falls, her hands coming together in an anxious swarm, more stuffing falling from her teddy bear's nose.

"What did you do?" the man asks, crossing his arms.

I don't answer him, only pace the room, finding my way to the door, doing an about-face and walking into the staff room, shaking and stunned, blood on my hands.

"Are you sure she's actually dead?" Destiny asks, from where she sits, Tabitha cradling her in her arms. I sit on her other side, not alienating myself from the others. Not being the loner on the bench.

I'm a girl who seeks out other people. Who needs humans and wants to be near them.

"Uh, yeah," Josh says, looking out my window into the parking lot. "I mean, not at first she wasn't, because she was trying to talk. But after she fell backward—" He moves to slam his hand together like he did this morning, and the cat follows the motion, playing a game, pawing at the glass. Josh, Brian, Tabitha, and Destiny freeze, my do-over suspended.

"Stop," I hiss at the cat.

It stares back at me through the glass, but it doesn't say my name, doesn't accuse me of having a psychotic break.

"You should wash up," Tabitha says gently, but she's not rubbing Destiny's back. Her hands are on me, warming me, pushing comfort deeper into my core, trying to reach the frozen place inside.

"Yes," I say, nodding and wiping my nose. Here, I'll cry. Here, I'll show everyone how wracked I am. Here, I'll let the tears fall, illustrative of my grief. "I want to get this blood off me."

"Do you really, though?" Margaret asks.

Tabitha's arms around me go plastic and cold, like a mannequin. I look down at my hands, at the dark red moon of drying blood that I never scraped out from under my fingernail.

"I'm trying to fix this," I growl at her.

"*Fix it?*" Margaret practically howls with laughter. "Kiddo, this is not fixable."

"Don't say that," I say, coming to my feet as the staff room disappears and we're back in my bedroom, with a cat that's not real pawing at the window.

"Kitty," the little girl says, pointing firmly, her lower lip stuck out in a pout.

"You know what? Fine!" I say, throwing open the window, followed by the screen. The sliding locks fight me, years of dirt holding them in place. They finally relent, and the cat steps over the sill and hops down to the floor, twining between my legs.

I stare down at it, a gray-and-yellow tortoiseshell with a spindly skeletal tail.

"Thank you for not being orange," I tell it.

"Is that a good idea?" the man asks, clearly skeptical.

"Does it matter, at this point?" I shoot back, throwing my hands in the air. "You're both out walking around, and I brought home a plus-one. Is it a sign that I'm getting worse if I let delusions have pets?"

"I mean . . ." Margaret holds her hand sideways in the air, wobbling it back and forth.

"Shut up," I snap at her. "You're not helping."

I walk back over to the door, shake my arms out, and turn around, making another entrance into the staff room, all the time feeling Margaret's watchful eye.

"I can do this," I tell her. "I can fix this."

"You can't," Margaret says, but she's not arguing now. The half smile is gone and there's no sparkle in her eye, just a deep, unending sadness. "You can't bring her back, Neely."

I take a deep breath, let it out, wonder if any air from the caves was in the exhalation, any of Mila's last breaths now captured in my bedroom.

"No," I admit. "I can't bring her back. But maybe I can figure out what happened."

Josh, Brian, Destiny, and Tabitha sit waiting for me. Ready for me to try again.

"Maybe I can find out who hurt her."

Margaret steps forward, into my path, blocking me.

"Are you sure you want to know?"

"What the hell do you mean—"

On the bed, my phone goes off. The staff room fades away, my coworkers with it. The cat jumps onto the comforter, one paw tapping at the phone as it vibrates.

"Get," I say, giving it a shove.

It's a group text; the only other number that I recognize is Brian's.

Hey everyone, John here. I hope you are all doing okay and recovering from the terrible events of today. Mila was a beautiful person, inside and out. She will be greatly missed.

A red heart tapback from one of the numbers I don't recognize pops up immediately, followed by the other two. Brian chimes in with his own heart and I fumble at my phone, aware that I need to react as well, but it's not a function I've ever used before, and I accidentally send a question mark instead.

"Nice," Margaret says, peering over my shoulder. "Are you questioning whether Mila was all that great, or whether she'll be missed?"

"Neither," I snipe, turning away from her and shielding my phone, for all the good it will do. She is me, after all.

Carol and I are working with the police to ensure that the investigation moves forward smoothly, and that the caverns can continue to welcome visitors as well.

No hearts welcome that statement, and there is no reaction that fits my situation. No emoticon that conveys that I absolutely must get underground again, preferably as soon as possible, so that I can settle my thoughts, think without interruption, and find a little peace.

We will be closed tomorrow.

My heart sinks, all my skin contracting as I become smaller, the vacuum inside of me pulling everything together, condensing me.

We will reopen Wednesday, but only the natural wonders tour will be available. The historic tour is off-limits to everyone. That means tourists and employees.

A series of thumbs-up from my coworkers indicate understanding, but I can't participate, can't nod and agree that this is what's best. If I can't go into the caves, I can't escape the man and the girl, Margaret and the children, cats that say my name and look at me accusingly.

The code for the doors has changed.

Carol and I will be hosting a prayer circle at the Methodist church tomorrow afternoon at two. Everyone is welcome to join in this process of healing.

More hearts pop up, but I have nothing to add. My healing happens underground.

I want to thank everyone for everything you do to contribute to the caverns. It's a beautiful place and I know Mila loved it very much. Carol and I consider all of you family, and we look forward to seeing everyone back at work on Wednesday.

Family. I think of Josh and Brian tossing a football in the front yard, Destiny and Tabitha and I sharing a room with bunk beds. Except bunks only have room for two, so maybe there's a cot for me in the corner. Maybe Brian would throw the ball when Josh wasn't looking, hitting him under the eye and leaving a bruise. Maybe Destiny points at me over dinner, insinuating things with her perfectly polished French tips.

Thank you so much, John! Mila was not just a coworker but a friend and a great asset to the community, one of the unknown numbers responds. My family and I will be at the church tomorrow. Should we bring anything?

"Destiny," Margaret and I say in unison, rolling our eyes. I add the number to my contacts, which tries to autocorrect her name to *Destroy*.

Another number replies to John's series of texts with a terse okay. I add it to my contacts as Josh, which leaves the third number unidentified. It doesn't respond to John at all and hasn't reacted since the initial heart popped up on his first statement. I tap the number into my phone, add Tabitha's name to it, and shoot her a text.

Hey, it's Neely.

She reads it immediately, but no ellipsis pops up, no indication that she has any intention of responding. I look back through the group

217

text, hoping I didn't make a mistake, didn't misidentify who was saying what, and who was saying nothing.

Hey

Tabitha doesn't give me anything else, and I drum my fingers against the bedspread, wondering if I should try for more. The cat hops back onto the bed, taking it for an invitation. The little girl follows, her nightgown lifting as she hauls herself upward, exposing dirty knees.

Are you going to the church thing?

The text from Tabitha comes in unexpectedly, and I type my answer quickly, thumbs flying.

I doubt it. Unless you are?

It's vaguely pathetic, but I'm okay with that. Pride has never been really high on the list of my faults.

"It's a long list, though," Margaret says. "With some whoppers."

No way in hell, Tabitha answers. I'm not holding hands with anyone in a circle.

A series of texts comes through from her, the phone alive in my hand, vibrating with her anger.

I'm not talking about understanding that the Lord moves in mysterious ways.

I'm not looking for hope and forgiveness in my heart.

I'm fucking pissed and I want to know who did this.

Relief washes over me, something I didn't know I could find above ground anymore.

Me too, I text back. **I can't think about anything else.**

It's true. Mila had been everything yesterday, a live wire that moved through my mind, her name a flash point. All my thoughts revolved around her, any action precluded by the question of what Mila would think of it. The fact that she's dead changes nothing. She's still everything, and someone took it away from me, from a girl who already lost too much.

"Maybe even a few marbles," Margaret adds helpfully.

Me neither.

Tabitha's answer takes me by surprise, the idea that someone who smiles and looks normal and moves through reality efficiently might also stare at her ceiling and spiral, might spin hamster wheels of different worlds, mentally exploring the universe of what-ifs.

"She probably doesn't act them out, though," Margaret says.

Do you want to get together tomorrow?

I shoot the text spontaneously, expecting rejection, expecting to have my hand, barely rising above the waters, slapped away, pushed back under with all the hair ties, plastic water bottles, and used needles. Me, drowned with the rest of the litter.

Sounds better than praying.

It's not the greatest endorsement, but nobody has ever thought hanging out with me was better than anything, so I'll take it. Nobody except Mila, that is. There's a knock on my door, and I jump, the cat skittering away under the bed, leaving behind a circle of loose hairs where he'd been lying.

"Neely?" Grandma calls. "You need to get a shower, honey, okay?"

"I will," I answer, tossing my phone aside. "Promise."

There's a moment of hesitation when I can still see the shadow of her feet outside the door, a pause while Grandma wonders if a murdered coworker means I need more time alone or less. Eventually, she walks away, and I come to my feet.

"Okay," I say, pulling my hair up into a ponytail. It moves through my hands, heavy and slick, the wet air of the caves still held there, along with the outpouring of sweat from my scalp as Vargas held my gaze, all my nerves leaking the pheromones of prey.

"I'm trying again," I tell the man, the girl, and Margaret. "Do *not* distract me."

It takes until three in the morning, but I get through the whole day, react the right way, say the correct things, convince Destiny and Tabitha and Josh and McNichols and Vargas and Grandma and Grandpa that I am okay, that nothing is wrong with me, that everything is fine, that *I* am fine, and that I haven't done anything wrong.

I fall asleep exhausted and unwashed, the half-moon of Mila's dried blood curled under my chin, a fistful of dust in the other hand, the girl lying next to me, holding her teddy bear.

THIRTY-ONE

I wake up to screaming.

Margaret and the girl sit at the end of the bed holding hands, eyes wide. The man is at my door, peering out into the hallway. He jumps back as something flashes past, followed by Grandma, who is running with a broom over her head.

"Get that goddamn thing out of my house!" she screams, and I jump out of bed, scrambling into the hallway just in time to see the cat bounce off the wall, neatly circumvent Grandma, and dash back toward the living room, where it launches itself at the curtains, climbs up onto the rod, and flattens itself there, a low, permeating growl filling the room.

"What the hell?" I ask, standing next to Grandma, staring with her.

"I don't know how it got in the house," she says, wiping sweat from her brow as she leans against the broom. "I've told Denise a hundred times, she has to stop feeding the feral cats. I know it's a kindness, but she's only encouraging—"

"You can see it?" I cut her off, pointing at the curtain rod. "You can see that cat?"

"What?" Grandma's brows come together, her eyes narrowing. "Neely, of course I can. It's right there. And it's probably spreading fleas all over, not to mention—"

Grandma doesn't get to add to her list titled "Faults of Cats" because the curtain rod gives way at that moment, sending piles of pink floral and one very pissed feral cat to the floor.

"Oh, shit!" Grandma yells, which should be the most disturbing thing of the morning, but since I just found out what I thought was a delusion is actually real, Grandma's swearing doesn't even rank. I make a dive for the bundle moving under the curtains, trapping the cat in folds of fabric. Grandma slides the curtain free of the rods and holds the door for me as I toss the curtains into the backyard, cat and all. Patterned florals writhe until it finds an opening and then streaks across the yard, making for an oak. It dashes up into the branches, then turns to look at us, a threat still percolating in its throat.

"Don't you growl at me!" Grandma yells, shaking her broom. "You're the intruder here! If I catch you, those balls are coming off, you hear me?"

"Whoa, Grandma," I say, turning to her.

"What?" she asks, blowing a lock of hair from her eyes. "It's been a long morning. And apparently your grandfather can't be bothered to close the door behind him."

"Right," I say, deciding not to tell her that I'd let a very real cat in through the window last night, after a fake little girl asked me to.

"No work today?" Grandma asks, her eyes sliding over my pajamas as the cat watches us from the tree, relaxed enough to begin a bath, letting us know that we are not a concern of his. Sulla has joined him, offers a few helpful licks behind the ears, where the stray can't reach. Sulla's eyes catch mine.

"Neely," he says. "Psychotic break."

"No," I tell her quickly, tearing my gaze away. "No work today. I guess they need time to process the crime scene."

"Of course," Grandma says quickly. "Makes sense."

There's a lull, a moment where we could talk about it, a space of time for her to ask if I am okay, and for me to answer that no, I am not, that the world is falling apart and I am going with it. But instead she straightens her shirt and asks me if I want breakfast.

Because that's what we do in this family. We pretend that everything is okay and we are all right, that there aren't children in the long grass and Dad didn't hold the door open an extra moment for someone to leave the house, someone no one else could see. We shut the doors to rooms we don't want to go into and only visit the graves of the people that did the right thing, acted normal, died accidentally and not on purpose.

Margaret, the girl, and the man have congregated on the back porch, all of them staring up at the tree, the little girl shading her eyes from the sunlight. They're supposed to stay in my bedroom, follow the rules, do as they're told. But Mila is gone, and the underground is far away, the tentative threads of my frantic do-over not holding. I walk past them, back into the house, only to find them waiting for me in my room, watching as I dress, turning their heads in unison as a small, grimy fist comes up to the window.

And knocks.

Tabitha slides into the passenger side of my car, an angry line between her eyebrows.

"Fucking vultures," she says, nodding toward the coffee shop where we'd agreed to meet. News vans are gathered there, local affiliates that smelled blood and picked up the story of a girl who died underground.

"There's one down at the ice cream place, too," I tell her.

"Hitting all the hangouts," Tabitha says with a nod. "Getting the locals to talk. What do you want to do? I don't want to go in. The lady who owns this place knows I work at the caverns, and walking in there would be like falling spread-eagle in front of a bear while I'm menstruating."

"Oh, I like her," Margaret says from the back seat.

"Definitely not going in," I agree, putting my car in reverse and leaving Tabitha's car behind in the coffee shop lot.

"Let's try the McDonald's out at the exit," Tabitha says. "Grab some coffee and then maybe drive out to the overlook?"

I head out to the interstate, highly aware that there is a person in my passenger seat, and I am very bad at small talk.

Tabitha glances over at me. "How you holding up?"

"Not good," I tell her.

"Me either," she admits, looking out her window. "I just keep telling myself that this isn't real. Like this can't possibly be happening."

"It is happening," I tell her, with all the authority of someone who has spent most of their life sorting fantasy from reality.

"You're right," she says. "Denial isn't helpful. I read this article once about a woman whose son died his senior year, and she just didn't really process it. Kept telling herself that he would have been leaving for college anyway, so it wasn't that much different. Four years later, she has a total fucking breakdown because she can't plan a college graduation, and she finally realizes he's actually dead."

"Cool story," Margaret says from the back. I don't say anything, still stuck on her first statement, rattling around in my head like a loose bullet.

Denial isn't helpful.

The three words feel large in my head, taking up more space than they are supposed to, residing beside another pair of words that have loomed large in my mind lately.

PSYCHOTIC BREAK

"Sorry," Tabitha says after a moment. "Maybe that wasn't the right thing to say."

"No, it's okay," I tell her, pulling into the drive-through.

I glance over at her, but she's turned fully toward her window, looking at dark storm clouds piling on the horizon. We get drinks, and I head for the overlook, a small lot carved out of the side of the ridge.

"Shit," Tabitha says, as the bridge grows larger through the windshield. "I didn't think about that when I suggested the overlook. I'm sorry, Neely."

"It's okay," I say again. "If I never drove over it, I'd be stuck in East Independence forever."

"Not a good fate," Tabitha says.

"No," I agree, but I can't deny the lift in my chest as the girders flash past, some of the last things Lance saw before he made his decision. Just like I can't ignore the fact that Mila will be stuck here forever, although she'll be six feet underground, not one mile. I park the car, pulling right up to the edge. There are a few other cars, standing empty, day hikers out for the afternoon. Below us run the zip lines, shouts rising from people who step off the platforms, the rising wind tearing their words away. Tabitha and I lean against the hood of my car, watching.

Her phone goes off with a notification, and she glances down, then grimaces. "Dear Lord." She turns it around so I can see a selfie Destiny just posted, her and Josh leaning in together, faces somber but equally beautiful, the less attractive participants of the prayer circle relegated to the background. In the corner, I spot a news crew.

"Gross," I say.

"Yeah," she agrees. "I love Destiny, I totally do, but she said she wouldn't touch Josh again with a ten-foot pole. Too bad a photo op came along, broke her concentration."

"Again?" I ask, as a manic shriek reaches up from the gorge below us, a zip-liner who maybe wasn't quite ready to go getting a push from behind.

"Well . . ." Tabitha leans back against the car, toes digging into gravel as she makes small rock piles. "I'd never slut shame, but Josh is a whore."

I bust out laughing, spitting out a little bit of coffee.

"No, really," Tabitha says. "Everybody can do whatever they want, as far as I'm concerned. But Josh is a walking STD factory. Take it from someone who just completed their antibiotic treatment about a month ago."

"Oh," I say, piecing it together. *"Oh . . ."*

"See, that's why I don't slut shame," Tabitha says, pointing a finger at herself. "Josh is a piece of shit, but he's a charming piece of shit who can be very persuasive when he wants to be. And also, I might have been drinking. Need to stop doing that," she says, shaking her head.

"You're not a slut," I tell her.

"I appreciate that, since you don't really know me. I don't feel great about it, but I'm not the only one who slipped and fell down the Josh stairs twice," she says, lifting her phone and the pic of Destiny and Josh.

"Is everyone at work having sex but me?" I ask, and it's her turn to spit coffee.

"I mean, not you and not Brian, unless . . ." She raises an eyebrow at me, and I shake my head. "Good, well, don't spend any time with

Josh if you want to keep your record of not sleeping with coworkers clean. The boy has a flat-out checklist."

"I doubt I'm on it," I say, but then her words settle on me, heavy in the hot air. "Wait, do you mean like an actual list?"

"Not like written down or anything," Tabitha says. "But yeah, the boy had goals. He wanted what he called the trifecta."

"Trifecta," I say, touching the tip of my finger with each name. "You, Destiny . . . and Mila?"

"Yeah." Tabitha puts her coffee down on the hood of my car, her hand shaking slightly, either from caffeine or nerves. "It's kind of why I wanted to talk to you. In the staff room you said that Josh watched the, uh . . . video of Mila?"

"Then gave her shit about it," I say, remembering his finger trailing her collarbone, the shock on her face as she froze, his words rooting her to the ground.

"That's not okay," Tabitha says, shaking her head.

"He was coming on to her pretty hard," I tell Tabitha. "She showed me the messages. She kept putting him off, but he wasn't taking no for an answer. The last message he sent to her said, *You will be mine.*"

"Wait, what?" Tabitha asks. "That's next level. I mean, being flirty and talking me out of my undies is one thing. But that verges on a threat." Her brow furrows, a memory sparking. "Remember what he said in the staff room—lots of time over the weekend to do whatever you want, where no one is going to be looking."

"Yeah, I know," I say, wrapping my hand around my own coffee, a chill running up my back as the storm clouds start to move in, a finger of lightning flickering on the horizon. A call goes out from one of the platforms, the zips pulling all the customers off the lines.

"I think maybe he watched the video because it was the only way he could have her; does that make sense?" I ask.

"Makes a lot of sense." Tabitha nods. "Did you tell the cops about this? Because I don't think Josh is capable of murder, but he was on a streak of bagging girls, and he likes to win. If that video gave him a taste of something he wouldn't normally be into—ugh, fuck."

Tabitha shakes her head, her hair a dark storm at her temples as her voice breaks, and she starts to cry. "I can't, I mean . . . this isn't possible, right?"

"I don't know," I tell her, meaning it. "I think Josh has a nasty side, but whoever did that to Mila is downright cruel."

Tabitha runs her fingers under her eyes, wiping away the tears there. I don't know if I'm supposed to offer comfort, like a hug or a shoulder squeeze. So I just sit, staring down at my feet, watching my toes curl and uncurl in my sandals while I try to decide if touching Tabitha is a good idea or not. She tears the lid off her coffee, dumps the rest out over the ridge, the wind dispersing it into individual droplets, tearing apart what once was connected.

"Did you tell the cops about Josh messaging Mila?" she asks me.

"No," I say. "But I told them about Patrick, and the video. McNichols took me seriously, I think, but Vargas basically implied that Mila just had morning-after regrets."

"Fucker," Tabitha spits as the first drop of rain start to fall around us, large and heavy, slicing through the hot air.

"I should have said something about Josh," I go on, "who would know the access code."

Thunder rolls across the valley, the car shaking underneath me as the clouds break, a wall of water suddenly moving toward us. Tabitha and I dive into the car, the rain a split second behind us. It moves across the windshield in sheets, obscuring everything.

"Can I tell you something?" Tabitha asks, her voice small and quiet.

"Yeah," I say, watching in the rearview mirror as Margaret wrings out her hair.

"The pranks thing? That's the angle they're going with right now," Tabitha says. "The cops talked to Patrick, and he said everything was consensual. They're both adults, and they were in a relationship, and Mila never actually pressed charges."

I shake my head. "She texted Patrick, she *told* him she was going to."

"Which would give him a hell of a lot of motive, so he's not exactly going to share that with the cops, is he?" Tabitha asks. "They haven't found Mila's phone, and I'm sure they can pull her texts without it, but that takes time. So right now, they're focused on sitting down the can-doers and zips, and asking them about any ill will between the different staffs."

"How do you know all this?" I ask.

"Okay, so . . . that's where the you-can't-tell-anybody-about-this part comes in," Tabitha says, her breath fogging the window. She's quiet for a beat, watching me. "I need you to say you understand that right now, Neely."

"I understand," I say, and Tabitha blows her cheeks out.

"Destiny has an OnlyFans, and one of her uncles is a paying customer."

"Fuck, that's gross," I say.

"Totally," Tabitha agrees. "But Destiny is Destiny, so she just kind of held on to that little power card until she decided to play it."

"Play it how?"

229

"Destiny told her mom she's got this little bit of info that could really reignite some old shit and blow up the family . . . or Mom could repeat everything she hears from Dad, via the cops, about Mila's murder."

"Everything you just said is really fucking horrible," I say.

"Tell me about it." Tabitha shrugs. "But how shocked are you really? I've lost the capacity. Every family's got skeletons in the closet."

Except in mine, they aren't just bones. They've got muscle and sinew, teeth and nails, and they've moved out into the world. I look at Margaret, who has gone still, simply looking back at me in the rearview mirror, her eyes dark.

"Why would her mom just let that happen?" I ask. "Why wouldn't she make Destiny take her account down?"

"Well, first of all, Destiny is a full-ass adult," Tabitha says. "She's nineteen, and her mom doesn't get to tell her what to do anymore. Secondly, have you met Destiny? Because she is a very aptly named individual, and she takes shit into her own hands. And lastly, you realize you can't make people do things, right? Sure, we can ask nicely, apply some guilt if we need to, and we all have our little games to try to get what we need. But at the end of the day, you can't make anyone do something they don't want to do."

"Not without hurting them," I say, my eyes unfocused, staring out over the dash. It's quiet inside the car, the sudden downpour over, a few angry drops still falling.

"Right," Tabitha says, fingers unrolling the rim of her coffee cup, the wet lip fraying under her nails. "So, there's something else."

"I don't know if I like her anymore," Margaret says. She's chewing her lip, one side of her mouth turned down.

"What?" I ask Tabitha.

"Mila, she was all beat up. I know you saw her and I didn't, so it's not like I need to tell you that, but . . . it seems she was being held in a cavern that's off the historic tour. I guess they had to call in some thinner cops to get back there, but apparently if you go deep enough, there's two rooms past where Margaret's name is."

"Uh-huh," I say dully, trying not to think of mist and dust, Mila in front of me, Margaret behind me, the chill of the caves and the excitement vibrating my spine.

"So, I guess whoever . . . had her . . . they handcuffed her to a column in one of those rooms, and that's where she was for three days."

"Three days," I repeat. "Without a light."

"I know, right? Fucking weird little detail, but it's stuck in my head and I can't get it out." Tabitha knocks her temple against the passenger window, a dull thump. "I'll think I've processed everything, but I keep circling back to that. I mean, I can barely take it when the lights go out for the tour. And I *know* they're going to come back on. I *know* that I'm going to be okay. But Mila . . . she didn't. For three days."

Tabitha swallows, dry throat clicking. "Three days. And I can't stop thinking about it. Is that . . . is that weird?"

"No," I tell her as I start up the car. "If you're asking me, not having control over your own thoughts is not weird at all. But I might not be the best litmus test."

"Fair point," Tabitha says, but she gives me a smile as I snake through the woods, avoiding potholes now filled with water. Steam rises from the road, the storm only adding humidity to the heat.

I drop Tabitha at her car, tapping my thumbs against the steering wheel as I drive home, Margaret silent in shotgun. I pull into the garage and kill the engine but don't get out right away. Sulla is sitting on the hood of the car, tail curled around his toes, eyeing me.

"What are you thinking about?" Margaret asks.

"You don't know?" I ask, raising an eyebrow, to which she shrugs.

"I do, but sometimes it helps to talk it out."

"With imaginary people?" I shoot back.

"Is there anyone else you want to tell?"

My eyes go to Sulla, and his tail flicks impatiently.

"No," I say, dropping my gaze. "Definitely not."

I take a deep breath, the hot, close air of the car filling my lungs. "That's my cat," I say, pointing out the windshield. "*Was* my cat."

"Pretty," Margaret says. "Too bad about the ear."

"Frostbite," I explain. "He hung around the back porch all summer, not too long after I came here. I'd slip him my leftovers. He wasn't sure, at first, wouldn't come close. But I drew him in, said the right things, gained his trust."

I remember the first time he let me touch him, my hand hovering above his head while he chomped down on the bone of a pork chop, going still, eyeing me warily. I'd dropped my palm slowly, finally connecting, and he'd pushed up to meet me, deciding he liked me.

Deciding he could trust me.

I named him, played with him, rolled him onto his belly, and let him hug my wrist, kick at my arm with his back legs. He learned what the sound of the bus meant and waited for me at the kitchen window when I got home. I would sit in the grass, watch him obliterate dead leaves while I shared what the kids at school had said and done that day, both the real ones and those who were not there.

"Then it got cold," I tell Margaret. "Real cold."

The winter brought a bone-deep cold, a wet cold, the kind that seeps into your core and radiates out later, chilling you from the inside. Birds fell from the trees, their feathered bodies littering our yard. Sulla had crawled under the porch, his plaintive cry emanating from underneath, reaching us as we ate our dinner.

"Betsy," Grandpa finally said, putting his fork down.

"Fleas," she retorted instantly, not needing context.

I stared at my plate, not daring to breathe, listening to my only friend slowly die outside.

"We don't even have a litter box," Grandma said, arguing with no one. She scanned the table, took in Grandpa's half-cocked smile, Lance's open gaze. I hadn't met her eyes, looking down, the jagged line of the messy part in my hair revealing white, unguarded scalp.

"Fine," she said, actually tossing her napkin in the air. "If you can even get him out from under the porch."

"I can get him," Lance said, swiftly rising to his feet. He returned, moments later, with snow in his hair, his front covered with dirt, a cobweb hanging from his ear—and Sulla latched on to his chest, claws digging into his heavy coat.

Grandma stood behind her chair, keeping her distance. "You clean him up," she said, eyeing the orange tabby. "If there's even one flea, pretty soon there's thousands."

"Technically, that takes two fleas," Grandpa said, then yanked on his coat when Grandma shot him a look. "Guess I'll go buy a litter pan."

I held out my arms, and Lance transferred Sulla to me, his fingers nearly blue and frozen as they brushed mine.

"No fleas," he said. "Make sure, or you know he'll be tossed right back out."

"So I made sure," I tell Margaret.

I'd run the bathtub full of water, a bottle of dish soap resting on the edge. Sulla had been curious at first, nosing around the bathroom, inspecting all the corners. He didn't fight me until I grabbed him, lowered him toward the water.

"It was bad," I say.

The trusting, soft ball of fur that I had always known had burst into a writhing mass of claws and teeth, no longer kicking at me in play but tearing, climbing my skin as I thrust him under, my arms fleshy ladders that bled.

"I tried to tell him," I explain to Margaret. "He needed to let me do it, if he didn't want to die. He had to be clean."

But Sulla hadn't understood, and my blood had mixed with water as I dunked him, over and over, pulling back hair and chasing panicked fleas, crushing them between my fingernails, lining the edge of the tub with their corpses, telling Sulla all the time that if he would just be still, if he would just listen, everything would be okay and he could be inside and we could be together and everything would be okay.

And eventually, he was still.

But everything was not okay.

"I wrapped him in a towel," I tell Margaret. "Grandpa was still out, and Grandma was doing dishes, Lance was in his room and I thought that I could get him buried and no one would have to know."

But the ground was frozen and I could barely scrape an indentation to lay him in, piling frozen chunks of dirt on top of his body, my hands aching and filthy, my arms twin pillars of fire. Grandpa came back with a pan and fifty pounds of kitty litter, disappointment clouding his face when I told them Sulla had scratched me and I'd put him back outside. Lance had closed his door, not looking at me. Only Grandma had seemed satisfied with the situation, saying that he was a wild animal anyway and had no place indoors.

But Sulla wasn't the only wild animal, and she'd already let one in.

"She figured it out, though," I tell Margaret, lifting my eyes at Sulla, who stares back at me, frostbitten ear withered. "The weather broke, and the snow melted, and he was lying there, half-buried."

And I still had dirt on my hands.

"I tried to tell them," I say. "Tried to explain that I was trying to help, trying to create the best possible world, one where he was warm and safe and where he belonged."

"Because he belonged with you," Margaret finishes for me.

"Yeah," I say softly, my throat dry. When I look up again, a second cat has joined Sulla.

"Neely," they both say.

My hand rests on the steering wheel, a line of Mila's blood pressed where dirt used to be, the silver lines of tiny scars, skating up my wrist, intertwining.

"I didn't—"

I turn to Margaret, who now has a cat on her lap, stroking it patiently. Another sits on the dashboard, toes spread, tough tongue cleaning in between them.

"I didn't mean to," I whisper, my hand going to new scratches, left by a girl who is dead now.

Fresh ones that cross from my shoulder to my chest.

THIRTY-TWO

I'm making a list of things that are real and things that are not.

Unfortunately, my delusions are trying to help.

"Me," the girl says, a dirty fingernail running down the list of things that are real. So far it has Grandma, Grandpa, Brian, the caverns, one feral cat, the fact that Mila is dead, and then a series of question marks.

There are too many, and I am tired. Compulsion drives me to Mila's social media, and I swipe through old pictures of her, the comments now blown into astronomical proportions, people leaving messages and memories, sharing their grief and typing things Mila will never read. I scroll through them, sifting through her life, tracing all the family, friends, lovers, and connections.

Everyone loved Mila.

Except someone who didn't.

I switch to Rock Bottom, continue my foray into the darker corners of my brother's brain, places I didn't know existed.

A week before he died, Lance posted in rb/violence.

hillwalker—I have a need. An unholy need.
hillwalker—There is a moment, when an animal dies, the prey knows it is beaten, and it simply . . . gives up, acknowledges

the superiority of the predator, gives over complete control,
and agrees to die.

hillwalker—I want to know if a human is the same.

hillwalker—Never mind.

It's his last post, the one I had spotted when I first came to Rock Bottom. My finger passes over his last post, this thread that he had started and no one commented on. Lance, letting his darkness out into the light, not to be vindicated, not to be villainized. Only to be utterly ignored.

I think of Josh's throat under my arm, the ease of pushing him against the front of the bus, the surprise in his face and the power that had flowed from my center. When I let myself lose control are the only times I have any over the people around me.

My hand goes for my phone, hitting up Mila's socials again, as if anything will have changed. Like the days after she left me sleeping alone, I comb through posts, no longer looking for hints of her current location or thoughts and feelings, but dissecting the past—where she had been, who she was with, and what they were doing.

Patrick pops up consistently, his commonality in high-def, Mila practically glowing beside him, his hand resting on her hip, thigh, shoulder, pieces of her he had consistent access to, whereas I only had one night, hands in the dark, bodies finding each other, needs being met. Jealous rage sends a jolt of adrenaline through my body, tightening my hands as my upper lip curls, my teeth grinding together, chewing nothing but bile.

I click over to Patrick's profile, pictures of his truck, a pit bull, memes about things that don't matter. Mila comes into his life and he's with her constantly, a visual representation of the months their lives intersected flying past. Outside, inside, with others, only together, introducing their dogs to each other, eating, hiking, drinking, canoeing—a picture of Patrick in the caverns, a doofus grin and a big thumbs-up as he suggestively rubs the tip of the exit crystal.

"Dick," I mutter.

I go back to where they met, scrolling through the timeline, watching as Mila's wardrobe becomes progressively more yellow, Patrick's preferences written on her body. In their last picture together she is holding a dandelion under her nose, glancing up at him, adoration for this unremarkable human being streaming from her eyes.

"Gross," the little girl says, her nose scrunching up in disgust.

I silently agree and flip back to Mila's profile.

Under my thumb, other pictures fly past; Mila with an Australian shepherd. Mila holding a cupcake with a candle in it, cheek pressed against her mother's. Mila with another girl, coffee cups sending steam in front of their smiles, perfect teeth mirroring each other in incandescent smiles, heads inclined toward one another. Another spike of anger, this one tinged with fear—was Mila with this girl? I never saw any indication that she was interested in women until . . .

"Until you fucked her," Margaret says, leaning over my shoulder.

"Shut up," I say, flipping Mila's happiness in the presence of this other girl into obscurity with the tip of my finger. But the next one is Mila with a guy I don't recognize, and my blood pressure surges, black dots dancing across both their faces. The next one is better, just Mila in a selfie, doing exaggerated duck lips and crossing her eyes. Then Mila hiking, holding hands with a little girl. Mila behind her steering wheel, the edge of the OSU air freshener just visible in the corner. Mila leaning against a birch tree, the river flowing in the background.

Mila. Mila. Mila.

Mila in an employee group photo shot from last summer, Josh next to her, his arm around her shoulders, pulling her in close to him, her breast pressed against his arm. I zoom in, examine her face. The smile is tight, lips pulled back uncomfortably, not quite reaching her eyes, discomfort evident. Josh's smile is open, self-satisfied, confidence emanating from inside. I scroll, inspecting the skin of Mila's arm, dimpled where Josh's fingers dig into her skin, squeezing her, holding her tight, limiting her movement, overpowering her will with his own.

"What do you control, Mila?" the little girl pipes up, leaning her head against my shoulder, echoing Mila's words from the night of the party, her finger sticking out like Mila's had, admonishing her child self.

"Myself," I repeat, taking the role of Mila, regurgitating the lifelong lesson her mother had instilled in her. "That's it and that's all."

Except Mila didn't have control in the end. Someone else did.

Another shot from the caverns, Mila with Tabitha at the meeting rock, holding up tickets for the natural wonders tour, free advertising for John that invites the public to come enjoy geology and pretty girls. In the background, barely in the frame, is another person in a green polo and khakis . . . me.

My shorts are wrinkled, baggy around the legs, tight around the waist, a curl of fat hanging over. My hair is clean but hangs flatly on either side of my face, nondescript, the part that weaves over my scalp erratic and wandering. My shoulders are drawn up uncomfortably, my posture horrible, every line of my body telling the story of someone that doesn't know what to do with their own appendages. My mouth is a flatline of deep concentration, my eyes narrowed and hyperfocused, dialing down, eliminating peripheral so that I can pay attention to the only thing that matters.

I'm staring at Mila.

"Neely," Margaret says, her hand closing around my wrist. I've been drawing, one hand doodling away on the journal page where I tried to determine what was real and what was not. Those words are overlaid now with Mila's face, her mouth pulled tight in pain, eyes closed against something horrific, one hand up, warding off something.

Warding off someone.

"What do you control?" Margaret asks.

"Myself," I say, but the word is a whisper, a half-said thing, something that barely passes my lips.

Because it's very possible that I don't.

And maybe the problem isn't that there's one person out there that didn't love Mila.

Maybe someone loved her too much.

THIRTY-THREE

Grandpa's voice jolts me out of my reverie, my phone falling from my hands, bouncing onto the floor.

"Neely? You in there?"

I am, of course, and he knows that. There is nowhere else for me to be, no one that would desire my company. Still, my tongue refuses to move, my teeth click tightly together, my lips sewn shut. Grandma comes to announce dinner, to encourage personal hygiene, and occasionally, to ask if I want to play gin rummy. Grandpa coming to my door is a very different thing that has happened exactly twice—when Tammy Jensen's mom called with a recommendation for a therapist, and when they found Lance.

"Neely?" Grandpa asks again.

"Uh-oh," the little girl says.

"Uh-oh," the man agrees.

Margaret doesn't say anything; she just looks at me, dark eyes penetrating as her thoughts—my thoughts—dance across them.

Grandpa never comes for anything good.

"Neely, you need to come out here," he says again, a formality in his tone that is reserved for church potlucks and village council meetings.

"Shit," I say, sharing a glance with Margaret.

"Someone's here," she says, voicing my suspicion.

I retrieve my phone and tuck it into my hoodie pocket, after closing out the social media apps, Mila's face filling the screen across all of them. I walk into the hallway, my retinue of unreal people trailing behind me, the little girl dragging her teddy bear, its dangling eye tapping against the floor with each step.

Officer McNichols is sitting on our couch.

"Neely, I need to ask you some questions," she says very quietly, very slowly, the way you would talk to an animal that's caught in a trap.

My gaze shoots to Grandma, who is sitting on the recliner, an abandoned sudoku book in her lap. Her hands twist each other, bone and skin grinding. Her eyes meet mine, and I see my panic reflected, fear and anticipation brewing together into a poison that has her frozen, terrified.

Lance said never let them know, never let them worry. Don't stand out, don't speak up, don't let your darkness out into the light. Be good and be kind and be faithful to the idea of what they imagined grandchildren would be—not what they actually got. But Lance isn't here anymore, and truths are floating to the surface, like drowned things, matted fur and lifeless bodies left to bob in the ebb and flow of the world, waiting to be seen.

I can't be seen. Not the real, actual me.

"Officer," I say, stiffening my spine and taking a seat in the rocking chair. Grandpa leans against the entryway, arms crossed, eyes on McNichols, as if saying he will allow this but only to a certain point. On the other side of the entryway, the man mimics him.

"Neely," McNichols says again. "The autopsy has revealed some things that make it necessary for me to ask you some more questions."

"Hopefully *Did you do it?* isn't one of them," Margaret offers up.

I take a deep breath, focus on McNichols, thankful she's the one who is here and not Vargas—or maybe this was a decision she made on her own, hoping to calm me, ease my fears.

Maybe trap me.

She doesn't know I have never been calm, and fear has been with me from the cradle. I hold her gaze, curl my fingers, nails cutting into the soft skin of my palm.

"The autopsy," I repeat, thinking of Mila's skin meeting a scalpel, Mila, splayed open, her interior now on display, just as her exterior had been. Mila, devoured by the world.

"Yes," McNichols says, eyes holding mine, a shadow passing over them as I refuse to speak further. Grandpa said don't add anything, only answer the question. I trap the soft skin on the inside of my cheek between my molars, biting down hard, the coppery taste of blood slicking my tongue. I will do what Grandpa says. For once, I will be what they need me to be, do what they want me to do.

Margaret crosses the room, takes a seat next to McNichols on the couch, mimics her posture, turns to me, trying to catch my gaze.

"Mila had heroin in her system," McNichols says, and all my determination to follow Grandpa's rules evaporates in the huff of disbelief that leaves me, followed by—unfortunately—a laugh. From her seat, Grandma lets out a small gasp.

"No, she didn't," I say, choosing denial.

McNichol ignores my attempt to force my willpower onto reality, to override the science of chemistry and the contents of Mila's blood.

"Was anyone else at the party using?" McNichols asks.

"No," I say, shaking my head, firm in this one thing at least. "No one was."

"Neely," she continues, her patience a rock that my delusions can only scratch at, gaining no purchase. "Do you have reason to believe that any of your coworkers might have access to heroin?"

"Mila didn't do heroin," I say, ignoring the question.

McNichols's gaze finally leaves mine, flicks to Grandma, perhaps looking for some kind of support against my obstinance.

"Neely," Margaret says, imitating McNichols. "Were you with Mila all night?"

All night and into the morning is what I want to say, but that's not exactly true, and it's very important that I answer questions honestly right now, because I don't think any amount of do-overs could alter the finality of anything I say to McNichols, with her sharp eyes and enduring stoicism.

I look at Margaret, aware I don't have to speak aloud. Because she is me and I am her. All I have to do is think.

No-I-wasn't-with-her-the-whole-time-she-went-away-went-into-the-trees-and-left-me-alone-and-Tammy-came-with-her-bright-eyes-and-pure-thoughts-and-then-Mila-came-back-and-she-touched-my-shoulder-and-I-can-stil-lfeel-her-hand-there

"So she could have shot up," Margaret says. "Gone off into the darkness and had her own little party, no one else invited."

McNichols clears her throat, and I look back to her, willing myself not to let my focus shift to Margaret again.

"Yes, I was with Mila all night," I say, answering McNichols's question.

"Okay," she says. "Until what time?"

In her chair, Grandma is utterly still. In the entryway, Grandpa stands vigilant. This is not a yes-or-no question, and I am left wondering what the answer is.

"I can't say," I tell McNichols, my chin lifting.

"What did you do, Neely?" Margaret asks.

I-brought-her-here-and-we-were-together-finally-and-it-was-as-it-should-be-and-I-was-whole-and-she-was-everything-and-with-Mila-next-to-me-the-monsters-were-gone

"You can't say because you don't know, or you're not willing to tell me?" McNichols's voice rises in pitch slightly, the needle of her question hovering over my bubble, the world I've built for myself.

"Were all the monsters gone, though?" Margaret presses, leaning forward. "Or was there one left?"

"I can't say because I was high as shit," I say, biting off my words. "I have no idea what time it was when I—"

"When you what?" McNichols and Margaret ask in tandem.

When-I-bought-her-to-my-bed-and-had-my-will-be-done

"When I took her home," I say.

"Mila didn't go home," McNichols says. "Her apartment has a porch camera. Mila never came back from that party."

"Neely," Grandma says, my name a prayer that can't be found in one of her devotionals. "You need to tell the truth."

In the doorway, Grandpa remains still and silent, the way he is at Lance's grave, no words for the grandchildren who have failed him, no vocabulary that could express his disappointment.

"Where did she go that night?" McNichols presses. "She left the party with you. She didn't go back home. Where did she go?"

I think of the car ride, Mila in the passenger seat, smiling over at me, anticipation tingling in my veins. Driving with one hand, the other reaching for her, receiving an answer, our fingers entwined.

It's so real. I can see it.

The little girl taps my knee, holds up her arms, wanting to climb onto my lap.

But then again, sometimes I see things that aren't there.

And sometimes, it seems, I have psychotic breaks.

I've stopped breathing, don't realize it until spots appear in my vision. I pull in air, one large gasp, oxygen to the brain, searching for clarity. Which is a hard thing to attain with all your delusions staring at you.

"I don't know," I say, shaking my head. Tears have gathered, hover on my eyelashes; all it takes is gravity for me to weep.

And I *don't* know, because she left me as I slept, leaving me alone with the monsters, leaving me to fend for myself, as I have, for all this time. Pushing back, against the darkness.

"I don't know," I say again, looking away from Margaret, from McNichols, their accusatory stares and barrage of questions I can't answer.

Or don't want to know the answers to.

"Neely," Margaret's voice is cold, demanding my attention. I raise my eyes, locking with hers. "What did you do?"

I-dont-know

THIRTY-FOUR

Grandma and Grandpa have never sent me to my room before; I usually go there willingly, and they often have to pry me from it. But after McNichols left I was told that they needed to talk and that I should go to my room. Their concerned faces send a spike of anxiety through my body—stomach lifting, hands shaking, heart fluttering like a rabbit in my chest. But I can't console them right now, can't comfort them and try to be the version of Neely that will calm their fears and reassure them that everything is fine. Or, at least, that I have not done something awful.

I also need to believe this.

Tabitha answers on the first ring, a little breathless, like she ran for the phone. "Hey, what's up?"

"The cops were just here," I tell her, skipping any greeting. "Mila had heroin in her system."

"Get the fuck out," Tabitha says her shock matching mine. "Did they say anything else?"

"Was anyone at work using?" I ask, highly aware of the inner circle, and the fact that I stood outside of it.

"Oh, hell no," Tabitha says with conviction. "But it was definitely around. I mean, we'd find needles sometimes. And it's not like it would be hard to get, if she wanted some."

"Mila didn't do drugs," I shoot back.

"Uh, sorry, Neely, but if the coroner says she did, then she did. I don't think a tox screen can lie."

I ignore that, dismissing facts that don't fit my framework, my preferred sequence of events.

"What do you mean, it wouldn't be hard to get?" I ask.

"Hold on," Tabitha says, and I hear movement, a door shutting, and then the sound of running water.

"Okay, so," she continues, her voice dropped low. "This is some not-to-be-repeated-shit, you understand?"

My stomach bottoms out, the lift of anxiety from before dropping into a chasm of despair. I don't want to hear what Tabitha is going to say, don't want further proof that the people around me aren't who they seem.

But maybe you can never truly know someone else.

"Neely, I need you to say you understand," Tabitha says.

"Yes, I understand," I tell her.

"Back when I was hanging out with Josh, we would hook up at the motel out by the interstate, you know which one I mean?"

"Yeah," I tell her.

"So we did our thing and were just kind of chilling out, and he asks me if I want to party. I had some weed on me, and I was like yeah, sure, and I pulled it out, but he laughed and said he had something else in mind."

"Something else?"

"Yeah, he flat-out said he could make one phone call and we'd have it in twenty minutes."

I picture Tabitha, hair mussed, a sheet pulled up to her chin. Josh sitting up, leaning in.

"Wanting more," I accidentally say out loud.

"You got that right," Tabitha says with a snort. "That's how he rolls. Like, when we were hooking up, I did everything with him I'd ever done with any other guy. And that was always enough to get the job done, you know?"

I don't know, but I can imagine.

"But with Josh it was like regular sex was just foreplay for him. If you ask me, he probably had unsupervised internet access at way too young of an age. He needed something more, something different."

"Something dangerous?" I ask.

"Look, I'm not getting into his kinks, okay?" Tabitha says. "I don't exactly like Josh, but I'm also not going to just share his preferences with everyone like it's a joke."

"Was it handcuffs?" I ask, and Tabitha goes silent.

"Did he want to hurt you?"

There's a long pause before Tabitha says, "Neely, I'm telling you this because you asked about heroin, and yeah, I think it's possible that he was using."

"Because he had to raise the stakes in other arenas," I say.

Tabitha sighs loudly, the sound carrying over the running water. "I mean, it's actually kind of sad. He's way too young to need escalating—"

"Did you tell the cops any of this?" I ask.

"Uh, no, I didn't tell the cops that I have kinky sex with my coworker at hotels and turn down offers of heroin," she says, an edge in her voice. "I don't really see how it's relevant."

"It is if Mila was using," I say.

"It doesn't necessarily mean she got it from Josh," Tabitha counters. "We don't know this Patrick guy she was with. He could have been into anything, and from what I could see, he kind of led her around by the tit."

"That's a really horrible visual," I tell her.

"Am I wrong?" Tabitha shoots back. "If Patrick had told her to jump off a bridge . . . Fuck—" She cuts herself off. "Sorry, Neely."

"It's okay," I say. And suddenly it is okay, because Josh is a pervert and a user and Patrick is a rapist and abuser. There were bad people in Mila's life, bad guys who maybe did horrible things.

And needed more.

"What if she wasn't using?" I ask, and the sound of running water on the other end of the phone suddenly snaps off.

"There's no way my parents will believe I'm washing my hands this long," Tabitha says, followed by the squeal of shower curtain rings, then more water. Her voice drops again.

"I know it doesn't fit who she is—*was*," she corrects herself. "But if the autopsy showed she had heroin in her system, then Mila did heroin."

"But what if someone forced it on her?" I say, and Tabitha is quiet for a second.

"What do you mean?"

"What if they shot her up to keep her quiet, keep her under control? To give themselves 'lots of time over the weekend to do whatever they wanted'?" I say, repeating Josh's comment in the staff room.

There's a sudden intake of breath, and I know Tabitha recognizes the words.

"You need to tell the cops," I press. "You need to tell them about Josh using and . . . whatever it is he was into."

Maybe then McNichols will show up in his living room—or better yet, Vargas—and they can ask intrusive questions that make Josh look very bad. Except in his case there probably won't be a local historical figure who takes an active role in the interrogation.

"Nope, no way," Tabitha says resolutely. "It's got shit to do with shit, and I'm not about to start airing my own dirty laundry."

"What happened to telling the truth?" I ask, and Tabitha laughs.

"There's the truth, and then there's things that nobody needs to know, because it'll just hurt people. Don't be in a hurry to advocate a scorched-earth policy of brutal honesty, Neely, because Josh might not be the only one who looks bad. We've *all* got our things."

I look up, glancing at my things. A dehydrated little girl, a man with terrible mood swings, and a woman that died a hundred years ago.

"Yeah, I know," I say.

"What did *you* tell them?" Tabitha asks, a tremble of fear in her voice.

"Nothing they didn't already know," I reassure her.

We say goodbye, and I attempt a redo, stepping around Margaret, who sits cross-legged on the floor, picking at her nails. In it, I'm straightforward with McNichols, answering all her questions, then sharing more. Telling her about Josh and Patrick, about what boys are willing to do to girls to get what they want, throwing their scent into her path, hoping she'll follow, hoping it will be enough.

Except it might not, because I was the last person anyone saw Mila with, and she never made it home that night.

THIRTY-FIVE

"We're just running natural wonders," Brian says in the morning. He's leaning against the sink in the staff room, as our usual morning meeting spot at the boulder is currently occupied by a news van.

"Nobody talk to the press," he says, letting his gaze linger a little longer on Destiny than the rest of us. "The cops are still working here." He stops, resituates himself on the sink. "The historic tour is off-limits, so we're running double the natural wonders today."

"Sorry, but why?" Josh asks.

"Because we sold out online tickets yesterday after the news got a hold of the story, and now everybody across three counties wants in. The whole week is sold out, and with only half the tours available, we'll run natural every twenty minutes. So that's two teams. Neely, you and Josh are running one of the natural legs."

"Seriously?" we both say at the same time, neither one of us bothering to be polite about it. Tabitha shoots me a glance, then shakes her head. She might think she knows Josh, believes he isn't capable of killing Mila.

But the truth is no one ever knows anyone.

"Guys, I need you to do this, okay?" Brian says, putting his hands together, pleading with us. "Carol is going to need Tabitha in the gift shop. Josh and Neely. Me and Destiny. That's the deal, and it's probably going to be the case all week, so everybody get okay with it right now."

"Fine," I say, grabbing a flashlight and tossing one to Josh. "Let's do the sweep."

We take the staff door out the side of the visitors' center, keeping our heads down as we walk past the news crew, who John is arguing with about whether they have a right to be there. He's keeping his tone conversational, but his face isn't red only from the early-morning heat. Josh and I don't talk, shutting the gate to the switchback behind us and picking our way down in silence. When we get to the door, Josh punches in the code, then steps back when the light flashes red.

"Big Boss Brian forgot to tell us the new code," he says.

"I got it," I say, pulling out my phone and tapping a text to Brian.

"We should just skip it," Josh says, yawning and stepping underneath the rocky overhang, finding some shade. "Does the morning sweep really matter right now?"

"It matters," I say, staring down at my phone, willing Brian to text me back immediately. Right on the other side of this door is peace and quiet, a place where Margaret won't follow and the children can't come, a place where Sulla's accusing stare doesn't reach.

"Two-six-nine-one," I say tersely to Josh, punching in the new code when it comes through from Brian.

"Got it," Josh says, tapping his temple as if it's a repository for all sacred knowledge.

I pull open the door, letting the coolness wash over me. Josh slips past, then pauses and turns back, motioning for me to go first.

"What?" I ask, wrenching the door closed. "Don't tell me you suddenly have a 'ladies first' attitude."

"For the record, in my world, ladies always come first," he says. "And no, it's got jack shit to do with that. It's more I don't like the idea of having you behind me at the top of a flight of stairs."

"Guess that won't be too much of a problem, since I'm lead," I say, breezing past him.

"Yeah, that's right," he says, voice echoing around and below me, Josh filling everything, Josh with his mouth and his words and his attitude. "You know all there is to know about the caves. You've got this place memorized. You're the real winner here."

I sigh and block him out, looking for the cool air, the floating mist, the persistent sound of running water to relegate Josh to the background, where he belongs. He's mercifully quiet as we move through the rooms, leaving the lights on behind us. The mad dash for safety from the last tour had ended with people bouncing off rock walls in the dark, running for a door they didn't know how to get to. With the threat of a few lawsuits and full tours blocked out all day, John's erring on the side of caution versus conservation, allowing the lights to remain on, illuminating things that usually remain hidden, dark corners now visible.

I think of my sketch last night, Mila's face, contorted with pain, light flowing from Tammy Jensen's mouth as she spoke freely, me clamping my teeth, trying to keep my darkness inside. Lance's post on Rock Bottom—*I have a need. An unholy need.*

Do I, too? Did Lance and I share more than delusions?

We get to the connection point for the two tours, the path that leads to the historical side dark and forbidding. Josh swipes his light across it, illuminating yellow crime scene tape a few feet into the opening. Names and dates flash brightly, past residents of East Independence leaving their mark, family names that persist today—Otto Gentry, Bob McClelland, Psychotic Break.

Wait, what?

I run my own beam across the walls, pulse pounding, blood rushing, heat filling my body as panic stokes flames.

It's gone.

It was never there.

I'm fine.

The crime scene tape flutters. Below it, hundreds of broken crystals are scattered on the ground, some of them crushed into a powder, detritus of a panicked evacuation.

"Shit," Josh says under his breath, taking a few steps down the historic path, crouching in its now-toothless mouth. He runs a hand along the ground, the tiny broken stalactites and stalagmites rolling away under his fingers.

"This is bullshit," he says. "All of it."

I play my light across his face as he picks up a larger crystal, runs it over his finger like a poker chip.

"What do you mean?" I ask.

"It's insane, everything is fucking nuts," Josh says. "Mila is dead. It's just . . ." He shakes his head, his hair brushing against crime scene tape. "I can't get my head around it. I mean . . . people don't just die."

And I suppose for someone like Josh this is true. Someone with parents and siblings and two sets of grandparents and probably a dog and maybe a cat that is actually real.

"People don't just die," I repeat, my voice a monotone. "Especially not before you get to fuck them, am I right?"

"What?" Josh looks up, squints against my light. "What the hell?"

255

"Don't get cute," I tell him, coming closer. "I know you were going after Mila hard, and she wasn't interested. I saw your last message to her—*You will be mine*?"

Josh comes to his feet, wiping dirt off his hands. "You don't know shit," he says, his voice a coarse whisper, his face coming closer to mine.

"I know enough," I say. "You watched—"

"*Fuck!*" Josh suddenly yells, and throws a punch, his fist hitting solid granite. I jump back, surprised, my light following the path of his fist as he pulls back, takes another shot at the wall of the cave, knuckles bloody.

"You don't fucking know!" he howls at me, heaving breaths sending his shoulders up and down, in long, rhythmic pulls. "You have no fucking clue how—"

He breaks off, bloodied hand coming to his face to wipe at his eyes. "I showed the cops everything I ever sent to Mila, I told them I fucking dogged her, I told them that I wouldn't give up and that I was totally into her playing hard to get."

"But she wasn't playing," I tell him.

"Yeah, well . . ." Josh shakes his head. "I owe her an apology that I'll never get to make. Do you know how that feels?"

I think of Lance sitting at dinner, head down, not talking. I think of his loneliness and the fact that I would have understood, but some things aren't talked about, and so we don't encourage conversation at dinner and we don't knock on closed doors.

And sometimes people die because of it.

"Yeah, actually," I say. "I do know."

"Right," Josh says, eyes meeting mine. "Maybe you do."

We're silent for a moment watching each other, water that will never see the light again dripping around us, flowing downward, leaving the world behind.

"I can't take it back," Josh says finally. "I can't unsay things, and I can't change the fact that I watched that video, and yeah—I liked it. I know you think I'm a piece of shit, Neely, and maybe I am. But I did what I did, and now I can't unsee it, and she's fucking dead, and it's all . . ."

Josh goes quiet, eyes going to the ceiling, tears pooling, hands curled on either side of his head. "It's all tangled together in here now, and I can't unfuck myself."

I should step forward, touch his shoulder, should tell Josh he's not a horrible person and we all make mistakes. I should see another human being in pain and do something to help them, or, at least, feel something myself. But all I've got inside me is the need to look away, to ignore the better parts of Josh, the parts that are upset about broken crystals and treating Mila's body like a playing field. Because I need him to be horrible, I need him to be capable of awful things.

So that I can keeping telling myself I'm not.

"Welcome to the natural wonders tour!" I say, smiling bright, ignoring the circles of sweat already ringing the armpits of my polo. I'm standing on the rock, facing a group of thirty people who are ticket holders and ignoring the dozen or so children that speckle the lot, staring at me. They don't have tickets, their dirty fists conspicuously empty.

"I'm Neely, your tour guide. And Josh will be assisting me today." I nod toward the back where Josh stands, sunglasses hiding his red-rimmed eyes. He gives a nod and a half-hearted wave to the group. I run through the safety instructions, hop down from the rock, and lift

257

the latch to the metal gate, just as John calls over the intercom for the next tour to gather, Brian and Destiny already making their way to take my spot on the rock.

Historic might be my jam, but despite what Josh thinks, the natural wonders tour is no slouch. I caboosed for Mila on just as many of these as I did historic, and I've got all her jokes down. I open the gate and start walking the switchback, calling over my shoulder.

"Got a little walk here," I say. "There's a quicker way down, but it's a straight drop of fifty feet, so I can't say I recommend it."

I get a few giggles, Josh's face stoic and unmoving as he latches the gate behind the last tourist. I switch stances, walking backward now, explaining that the caverns were discovered in 1897, and that the new entrance with the tiered gardens is planted entirely with native plants.

"Who can tell me the official wildflower of Ohio?" I ask.

There's an awkward silence, until a lady in a sundress meekly raises her hand. "Carnation?"

"Close!" I say, smacking my hands together the way Mila would, an *aw, shucks* gesture that doesn't make anyone feel stupid and welcomes more guesses. "But that's the official flower. There's also an official *wild*flower."

"The buckeye tree?" a guy in an OSU hat takes a stab.

I resist the urge to inform him that a tree is not a flower, instead announcing "White trillium."

A lot of people look at me blankly, and I indicate the flower beds, the sun pounding on the back of my neck.

"Normally, at this point I would show you what a white trillium looks like," I say. "But unfortunately, poison ivy grows much faster and tends to choke everything else out."

"Like you choked Josh," Margaret says. "Remember that?"

I ignore her, aware that the door is only a few feet away, the caves and the darkness and a place where she can't follow. I turn to face the tourist group at the door, remind them that there is a very strict no-touching rule when it comes to the crystal formations and punch in the code, then look to Josh for the head count. On a typical Wednesday, we might have six to ten people in the morning tours. Today, we've got thirty.

"It's the new business plan," Margaret says, leaning against the stone next to the door and biting her nails. "I call it the murder model."

A handful of pebbles tumble down the ridge face, as Brian brings the second group around at the top of the switchback. His voice carries as he talks about 1897 and Harold Gentry, and everything I know that is absolutely true and right and real fills the morning air, settling my nerves and calming my mind. My gaze lands on the thicket Sulla dove into, and a tangle of loose fur that hangs there, matted and dirty.

I jerk open the door, explain that the steps are wet and handrails exist for a reason, borrowing all of Mila's words, my mouth forming the same way, tongue clicking against teeth, our shared language of the caverns. We get to the first cave shower, which is running on full blast, fueled by yesterday's storms.

"We highly encourage everyone to never, ever treat the caverns like a bathroom," I say. "However, we do offer complimentary showers. Legend has it that—"

I stop cold, watching as a child slips to the front of the group, eyes wide, listening, one dirty hand cupped near his ear, scratching. I look to the back, at Josh, who has slipped his sunglasses on top of his head. I flash both hands at him three times, palms out, fingers extended.

Thirty?

He nods, confused, eyes scanning the group, then returns the head count, confirming thirty.

Except I come up with thirty-one.

The child smiles at me, a loose tooth in the front hanging by a thin thread of bloody gum. I look away, to the cavern ceiling, at the black swirling patterns of manganese and red-stained iron oxide, the crystals casting long shadows.

"Legend has it that each drop from a cave shower will forgive your sins," I tell them, then tack on Mila's joke. "If you're an atheist, the best we can promise is to get the stink off."

There's a smattering of giggles, and I pass under the shower, moving into the next room as cold droplets trace my spine. Fingers clasp mine and I glance down to see the child. I shake him loose, turning to the group.

"If you look to the left, you can see one of the largest crystal formations in the United States, which we have named the Yellow King. As you can see, the king is a stalagmite, which is a formation that grows from the floor up, while a stalactite grows from the ceiling downward."

The child grabs at my arm again, but I slip his grip, shining my light across the field of crystals that surround the Yellow King.

"Does anyone know what we call it when a stalactite and stalagmite grow together?"

I'm greeted by a sea of blank faces, a sea that has grown from thirty to thirty-five as we moved forward.

"We call 'em a column, because that's what we call 'em," I say, or at least, it's what I try to say. I get about halfway through before the words stop, the magic of this place dying on my lips, Mila's jokes about columns no longer funny because she chewed her own thumb off to escape from one. I deliver a sob instead of the punch line and the tourists at the front of the group glance at each other, unsure what to do.

"Sorry, everyone. Sorry, look out, coming through," Josh says as he threads through the crowd, people pressing to either side of the cave wall as he separates them, finding his way to me.

"I'll take it," Josh says, bending down to speak into my ear.

"I can do this," I tell him. "It's the only thing I *can* do."

"Neely, you can't," he says. "Not right now. Take caboose. I've got this."

"You don't even know the speech," I say, words grinding out between my teeth.

"It's not why they're here," Josh says. "They don't give a fuck about iron oxide or whatever the hell it is."

A hand slips into mine, dirty fingers braiding with my knuckles. The child glances up, pulls me toward the back, urging me through the crowd until I stand behind them, surrounded by a second group that no one else can see, seven kids who circle me, somber eyes trained on my every move.

"All right," Josh says, clapping his hands together and bringing everyone's attention back to him. "So . . . rocks!"

I want to laugh but can't, because at this point, I don't know what will come out of my mouth. I can't trust my voice not to release my thoughts, give vent to dark needs and wants, vocalizing the blackest of darkness and blood spilled where no one can see.

Josh puts together a string of sentences that might be true, then glances to me, waiting for the count. I sign to him *thirty*, although that's not the case.

But I can't tell him that there are monsters here.

"*Because one of them might be you*," Margaret's voice is a whisper, not at my elbow or in my ear, not from the path behind. It flows from all around me, the black and red mineral paths, stalactites and stalagmites, speaking their truth, rejecting me.

"You can't do this," I say, falling back from the group. "You can't be here."

My voice is shaky, any authority I ever had over them utterly evaporated, my rules broken, their power growing as they move out into the world.

"I can't?" Margaret asks, she's beside me now, running her hands over the walls, reaching for the ceiling, spreading her fingers wide, knocking loose small crystals that scatter to the ground like baby teeth. "But I'm you, remember? Do you always follow the rules?"

"No," I say, hurrying to catch up to the tourists, to Josh's voice and real people and things that are actually there. I pass the conjunction of the two tours, the dangling crime scene tape fluttering with the movements of the tourists.

"Do you always do the right thing, Neely?" Margaret asks, leaning in. Hands close around my ankles, rise to my knees, small fingers dig into my spine and latch on to my wrists as the children climb me, resting on my shoulders, pressing against my skull.

I hear the door open ahead, around the curve. "America the Beautiful" starts to play, and I try to follow the path, try to make it out, but the children are hanging on my legs. I drag them, stumbling forward, nearly there. I fall under the last shower, the cold water running over me, trickling through my hair, following the curves of my neck, slipping past my collarbone and dripping over the scratch on my chest. Droplets part my lashes, fill my eyes, blur my vision. I open my mouth, drink it in, hoping it will find all the dark places inside.

And wash me clean.

THIRTY-SIX

"You okay?" Brian asks, tossing me a towel from the staff room. "Everything working out?"

Everything is not okay. I have done every possible thing to delay sections of the tour, drag my feet, catch each drop of cave water that I can. As a result, my shirt is soaked through, and my hair hangs in a straggled mess on either side of my face. Destiny shoots me a glance as she and Tabitha join us under the shade tree, while Josh rests on a bench, scrolling through his phone, bruised knuckles resting carefully on one knee.

"Why are you all wet?" Destiny asks, but I am good at pretending that people are not there.

"I switched with Josh," I tell Brian. "I couldn't lead. I had to stop at the column joke—"

"It's okay, Neely," Tabitha says, taking the towel from my unmoving hands, then squeezing out my hair. "It's been tough today."

"We've moved three hundred people through already," Brian says.

"I'd like to be happy about that, but it kind of makes me sick," Tabitha says. "We ran out of T-shirts in the gift shop. I was opening boxes that shipped five years ago when there was a screen printing sale and Carol decided to stock up."

Destiny shoots me a glance as Tabitha finishes up with my hair. "Not hungry?"

"No." I shake my head. And it's true, but what is also true is that I forgot to even bring anything for lunch, because eating is something that people do in order keep going.

"We're booked solid for the rest of the week, too," Brian adds, taking a huge bite of his sandwich.

"Uh, not good, bro," Destiny says. "I asked for two days off this week, like, way in advance."

"I saw the schedule," Brian says, but doesn't look at her.

"And am I still getting them?" she asks.

"A lot's changed—" Tabitha starts, but her friend cuts her off.

"It has," Destiny says curtly. "But my brother's wedding this weekend has not, and I've got a final fitting for my dress, and a bridesmaids' luncheon, and—"

"Some of us have to work for a living," Brian says. "Some of us aren't just doing this for thirst-trap tips."

"Excuse me, what?" Destiny asks.

"Okay, hold up," Tabitha says, putting her hands out. "We're running natural wonders the rest of the week on double, but that's it, right?"

"Yeah," Brian says. "That's the plan."

"Remember Erin and Nathan?" Tabitha asks. "They transferred over to the zips but they both worked here for a few years, and she always led natural. I bet they've still got it down. Let me see if they want to come over here for a couple of days, help us out."

Tabitha doesn't wait for Brian's permission, immediately tapping out a text.

"Maybe you should ask John?" he says. "You know, the owner?"

"John's got his hands full," Tabitha says, brushing aside his concern. "And I'm trying to help you out here. You don't want to get this bitch riled up," she says, giving Destiny a hip check.

"True, this bitch gets nasty," Destiny agrees, checking her teeth in her phone.

"I don't think—" Brian begins, but he's cut short by a notification from Tabitha's phone.

"Erin said she can cover for Destiny next couple of days. Nathan can come, too, but he'll need to find somebody to fill his shift at the zips. It's super easy, he just takes pics of people coming in off the top line."

"We don't need two—" Brian tries again, but Tabitha cuts him off, reaching over to grab my wrist.

"What do you think?" she asks. "Want to switch with him?"

"Me?" I ask, trying to catch up, pull myself back into a conversation that I didn't think had anything to do with me. "But—"

John's voice rings out over the intercom, making all of us jump as he calls the first round of afternoon tours to gather at the rock.

"Oh my God, get me off the ground," Destiny moans, falling backward and rolling around in the grass. "It's too hot to live. Oh, shit—" She covers her mouth. "Sorry, guys, that's not what I meant."

"It's okay, we're ignoring you," Tabitha says, reaching down to help me up instead.

I take her hand as she pulls me to my feet.

"Listen," she says, looping the towel around my neck and pushing hair off my face. "I think it would do you some good to not be in the caverns right now. Mila—"

"Is the most important thing," I interrupt. "This morning, Josh—"

266

Tabitha pulls down on the ends of the towel, bringing my forehead into hers, voice low. "It wasn't him," she says.

I try to pull away, but she keeps her grip, holding me close. "I got a text from Hilary, one of the can-doers?"

I nod, remembering that she is a person that exists but not what she looks like or why she would matter.

"Turns out Josh went home with her that night," Tabitha says. "Left a little something behind, too, something that rhymes with *crap*."

"I thought you weren't going to tell me his kinks?" I ask, and she stares back at me blankly.

"Not actual crap, Neely. *Rhymes with*. Like, the clap?"

My silence must be telling, because she continues.

"Gonorrhea?"

"Oh, okay," I say, finally catching up. "Why would she tell you that?"

"Because she knows that I have my weaknesses and sometimes Josh can be one of them, so maybe I should refill that antibiotic prescription."

I glance over at Josh, who is rubbing his swollen, bruised knuckles.

"He gets mad really fast," I say, breaking Tabitha's grip on the towel and backing away from her. "And he's violent. This morning, he—"

"Neely," Tabitha says slowly. "He was with Hilary all night. It's a fact."

It's a fact, and facts are reality, which I've never been good at. My mind reels, bouncing away from Josh to latch on to something else. Anything that isn't me.

"I need to find Patrick," I tell Tabitha. "I need to—"

"That's the cops' job, Neely," she says.

"They already talked to him," Destiny says, rolling onto the balls of her feet and hopping up. "He is a person of interest," she says, surrounding the words with air quotes. "But they didn't arrest him

267

or anything. Apparently, he's got an alibi. Oh, and get this—it's his girlfriend."

"Fast work," Tabitha says.

"Or he always had more than one." Destiny shrugs.

"Tabitha," I say, bringing her gaze back to mine. "I need—"

"Okay, look," she says. "Tell me you'll take a shift as photographer at the zip line instead of going into the caves, and I'll come with you to have a conversation with a guy who might be a murderer. Deal?"

"Yes," I say quickly. "Thank you. Yes. Deal."

The three of us walk toward the visitors' center together, Destiny coming in close as we approach the rock.

"And hey, Neely?"

"Yeah?" I ask, turning toward her.

"Maybe take a real shower before you get on the zip lines, okay? Someone has to go behind you, you know."

"Someone has to go behind you, you know." Destiny's voice comes from the corner of my bedroom later that night, a scruff of green grass growing over the carpet as we walk.

"Why would you say that to me?" I ask, keeping my face open, my words light. "I don't know if I deserved that."

"Debatable," Margaret says from my bed, where she sits cross-legged, the girl on her lap. "Once you get that solid base of BO, a little bit of moisture just brings everything out. So maybe the cave shower wasn't—"

"Shut up!" I spit through my teeth, jamming a palm into my eye socket. "I need to do this."

"Someone has to go behind you, you know," Destiny says again, her long legs eating up the space in my bedroom as she walks, confident, assured, absolutely aware that everyone is looking at her, and they all like what they see.

I snake my ankle around hers, and she goes down. Hard. Her head bounces off the sidewalk, and I roll her over, take in the wide-mouthed *O* of surprise, the broken fissure of skin on her forehead, the trickle of blood sliding down her perfectly freckled nose.

My first punch caves in her front teeth. The second comes in from the side and clips her temple, sending an earring flying. She spits out blood and puts her hands up, but I slap them away easily, going in for the throat as she writhes under me, trapped by my weight, enfolded in my wrath.

"Neely?"

Grandma's knock on the door freezes me—fist suspended in midair, carpet burn bright and blazing across my knuckles.

"Yeah?" I call, out of breath, chest heaving. Margaret and the girl peer over the edge of the bed at me, the child's bubbled, dry lips downturned.

"Dinner," Grandma says, her voice a high call, the beckoning song of normal life and regular rituals, a place where things might be okay if I weren't on my knees, straddling nothing and punching my floor.

"Fuck," I say, grabbing the footboard of my bed and pulling myself up.

"Neely?"

"I'll be out in a bit," I promise. "I've got to—"

"Take a shower," Margaret provides helpfully.

"Take a shower," I parrot.

"She can't argue with that," Margaret says, pinching her nose shut.

"Please, just stop," I say, falling backward onto my bed, my voice a weak, pleading thing. My hand finds my phone; I flip through my pictures, find Patrick. I cropped the picture so I wouldn't have to look at Mila, but her arm is still in the photo, draped around his shoulders, the hand that hangs over him all the more painful in its past perfection since it is now disfigured.

"Who's that?" the girl asks, cuddling against me, her teddy bear pressed into my side.

"A very bad man," I tell her, zooming in on the photo, studying his face.

"Well, we're hoping," Margaret clarifies.

"No, he is," I say, tucking my bruised hand under the covers, hiding the burns on my knuckles from myself. "He did something horrible."

I shoot Tabitha a text.

> Patrick. Tomorrow at lunch.

The ellipsis pops up, then disappears again, returns for a minute, followed by a text.

> Somewhere public, right? We gotta be smart.

> I've got it all figured out.

"And that," Margaret says, tapping the screen, "might actually be true."

THIRTY-SEVEN

"Today been okay?" Tabitha asks me, as she climbs into the passenger seat.

"Josh and I split up the tour," I tell her, as I back out of the parking lot. "I'm point for the first half, then he takes the back half. I can't do the column joke."

"Don't blame you one bit," Tabitha says. "But you won't have to after tomorrow."

Tomorrow, when I go to work at the zip lines. Tomorrow, when the underground is taken away from me.

"So what's the plan?" Tabitha asks, cranking the AC in my car to the max. "Dear Lord, working in the gift shop is making me soft," she says, pushing her face up against a vent.

"Mila met Patrick at the OSU branch," I tell her. "His profile says he's a sports psychology major, and I know he was taking summer classes. The only psych class being offered this semester lets out in about fifteen minutes, so we should be able to catch him in the parking lot."

I toss her my phone. "If you scroll through my pics, I pulled some photos, what he looks like, what he drives. He shouldn't be too hard to spot."

"Uh-huh," Tabitha says warily, eyeing me over the phone. "You're kind of freaking me out right now, Hawtrey."

I shrug, turning on my blinker when we get to the stoplight on campus.

"You said you've got it figured out," Tabitha says, putting my phone in the cupholder. "What are you going to say? I mean, screaming *You killed Mila, motherfucker!* isn't the entire plan, right?"

"I just want to see him," I tell her. "Ask him some questions."

"Like what?" Tabitha presses.

"I don't know, okay?" I say, tapping my fingernails against the steering wheel, the red, angry skin on my knuckles catching the light.

"Dude, this isn't a whole thing where you think you're going to look into his eyes and plumb the depths of his soul, is it? Because I've looked a lot of guys straight in the face, and quite a few of them are excellent liars."

I don't answer her, simply pull into the lot outside of the main building. There are only a handful of vehicles, the summer semester offerings not drawing a huge crowd.

"Oh my God, you were fucking right," Tabitha says, sitting up straighter when she spots Patrick's truck. "Shit, Neely."

I find a spot, put the car in park.

"He's in the truck," I tell her, watching as he rolls down a window, blowing out the white mist of vape.

"Wait, Neely. Shit," Tabitha says again, reaching over, grabbing my wrist. "I didn't think we were actually going to track him down, okay? I mean, I thought maybe we'd grab some coffee and get some things off our chests, but—"

"But what?" I cut her off, killing the engine. "You didn't think I'd follow through?"

"I mean . . ." Tabitha leans forward, talking fast. "Sorry, Neely. But this is legit, like, actual crazy stuff. He might have *killed* someone, okay? And if he didn't, you're straight-up harassing him."

"I'm fine with it," I say, popping open my door. "You don't have to come."

"Yeah, right," she says, unbuckling her belt. "I'll just sit here and watch you—Neely! Wait!"

I'm already out of the car, moving toward him, legs covering the space in between like Destiny's did last night when I tried another do-over. Tried to make it right. Tried to be good. My footfalls are heavy, and he hears me coming—that, or Tabitha running behind me, yelling my name. Patrick makes eye contact, offers a mildly confused but polite smile that quickly changes into alarm when I hit the driver's side door with both hands, shaking the whole truck.

"Whoa, what the fuck?" he shouts in surprise, dropping his vape pen into his lap.

"Patrick," I say, staring at him, eating him up, digging into each detail. The thin, pale line of a scar that curves around his lower lip. The remnant of an ear piercing in his cartilage that he's allowed to grow shut. One hair growing in not quite right in his eyebrow, shooting off to the left when everything else goes right.

Mila had said she didn't know why *him*, why this guy. She had said there was nothing special about him, but he got under her skin anyway. All of it.

"What did you do?" I ask.

"Um, who the hell is she?"

I pull my gaze away from his open-mouthed shock to the girl in his passenger seat, holding her phone loosely, blond hair falling around her shoulders.

"I have no goddamn clue," Patrick says, until his eyes land on my polo, and the logo stitched there.

"Aw, shit," he says, rolling his neck.

"I worked with Mila—" I say just as Tabitha comes up behind me.

"We're sorry," she says breathlessly, her hands clamping on to my shoulders, trying to pull me away. "Really, sorry to bother you."

"No!" I shout, hands curling around the doorframe, into the open window. "I want to hear him say it!"

But it's more than that, I need him to say it. Better yet, I need him to do something, show me his underbelly. I need him to come at me, lunge, be horrible, do terrible things. I need to see a flash of temper in those eyes, a dark blur that moves fast and lands hard, a predator who wears the mask of normal.

"Jesus Christ," Patrick says, leaning his head back. "I talked to the cops twice already."

He doesn't sound horrible; he just sounds bored.

"You fucking—" I scratch at the door handle.

"Neely, you can't—" Tabitha's hands intercept mine, but I shove her away just as he locks the door.

"What the fuck?" he says, eyes still rooted on mine. But there's no shadow, no latent evil crawling up from the depths. I only see confusion there, and the slightest flicker of fear. It's not apprehension; not the worry of being caught, exposed; not the fear of the world seeing him for who he is. I know that shadow, have seen it streak across my face in the mirror. What he's scared of isn't punishment.

He's scared of me.

"Let's go," the blonde says. "Patrick, I don't think we should be here."

"No, *you* shouldn't!" I scream, shoving the window back down as he tries to roll it up.

"You shouldn't, you! Right there, you should be Mila! She should be alive, and she shouldn't be with him, she should be with *me*!"

"What the fuck?" Patrick asks, the only phrase left to him, his regular afternoon blown to pieces. Tabitha has backed off, hands over her mouth. The blonde pulls her phone up, points it toward me.

"Look, I see that you're really upset right now, okay?" she says, her voice soothing, like she's cornered a rabid animal, or trying to help a dog that's been hit on the road and isn't quite dead yet.

"It's horrible, what happened, I know," the girl says. "But I'm getting this on camera because you are acting irrationally, and I don't feel safe."

I glance at Patrick, the normalness of him. The absolute sum neutrality of all he has to offer.

"You're not safe," I tell her. "Anytime you are with him—"

"Like the time I spent with him on the night Mila disappeared?" the blonde shoots back, phone still recording. "Because we were together all night, and he did not leave."

"Sure did come, though," Patrick adds, shooting her a smile. There's a response on her lips, a play of muscles that infuriates me. They're flirting. Flirting while I talk about Mila, who should never have been with him; Mila, who never should have died; Mila, who takes in stray cats and even some lost people.

I look at the girl, taking in her red tank, the frill of lace at the top that lays smoothly against her tanned skin. "Did the compliments stop yet?"

"What?" she asks, eyebrows pulling together.

"Is it red with you?"

Her phone slips in her hand, her lips forming another question.

"Because with Mila it was yellow, and the compliments stopped, so she wore it more, and pretty soon it's all she's buying and all she's doing is trying to get it back to the way it was, when he first started in on her, and made her feel—"

"We're done here," Patrick says, starting the engine. The truck roars to life under my hands, and I make a grab for the steering wheel, but Tabitha is back in the fray, and this time there's conviction in it when she yanks me away. I spin off to the side and land on my knees as Patrick guns the engine, tires spinning, exhaust spewing.

"Fuck," I say, rolling up to a sitting position, flicking embedded gravel from my palms.

"Neely?" Tabitha asks, but she's at a safe distance, watching me.

I dust off my legs, brushing aside the blood that's starting to percolate from a scrape on one knee. Patrick's engine fades into the distance and the parking lot is eerily silent. There's a hand on my shoulder, Margaret, pressing down. Margaret, who always goes deeper, darker, farther.

And has been trying to tell me I did the same—but I went too far.

"Neely?" Tabitha asks again. She moves to step closer, hesitates, falls back again.

"It's okay," I tell her, coming to my feet. "I'm all right."

But I'm not all right, and I'm not okay, and nothing ever will be again.

Because I've always known there were monsters in the world.

And now I know: I'm one of them.

THIRTY-EIGHT

I'm a dead person.

The girl had watched me quietly as I got dressed for work, not even asking for water, as if she has suddenly realized I am not the kind of person who takes care of others. The man was also silent, making no assertions of amazing abilities, or predictions of my probable failure. What I am truly capable of has now become clear; he has nothing more to tell me. Sulla rested at the foot of the bed, curled into an orange ball, finally an indoor cat, no longer accusing me of anything, as I had accepted the blame. Margaret, with her dark eyes and needling observations sat next to me, keeping me company, as I wrestled with the knowledge of myself.

"What do I do?" I ask the ball of dust, but it knows nothing, never has. It sits on my bedside table, dirt that I have assigned meaning to.

Like myself.

The polo I am wearing is the wrong color, the green of the caverns replaced by the red of the zip lines, a golden slashing *Z* embroidered on my chest, covering the scratch, hiding the scab, the last bit of Mila and what we did together. Under my thumbnail, the red line of her blood has gone black, a token of something else that I did alone but can't remember.

"Psychotic break," I say to myself on the drive to my new workplace, filling the car with a noise, a sound.

Something.

Jessica meets me as I walk into the zip line station, wearing a smile that doesn't fade even when her eyes cut to my hair. It's greasy and slicked to my skull, sticking together in clumps and exposing white patches of my scalp from where I pulled it into a ponytail this morning. Jessica looks perfect, tan, muscular; her hair could have an Instagram account.

"Neely," she says. "I'm glad you could help us out today. Tabitha said things over at the caverns have been really hard."

It is. It's really hard when people you love die and you probably killed them. But I don't say that because somehow, for some reason, I'm still trying.

"Yeah," I say instead.

"Well, Erin and Nathan were looking forward to going back to the caves. Memory lane, you know. They met there. Annnndd . . ." She wiggles her fingers at me, a looping silver band on her pointer finger catching the light. "Don't tell anyone, but I think he's going to propose."

"Yeah, don't worry," I say. "I won't tell anyone."

My absolute lack of enthusiasm seems to drain her a little. Jessica falls silent, leading me to the deck out back where the zip line equipment hangs.

"Ever done this before?" Jessica asks.

"No," I say, following her, focusing on moving one foot, then the other, the bright sunshine hitting my pale skin so that it surely looks like Jessica is being shadowed by a flare, a blip on the screen, a ghost.

"Scared of heights?" she tries again, doing her best to draw me out. She's a brunette version of Mila, kind and glorious, caring about the rotten carp of a human being that's washed up at her feet.

"Sorry," Jessica says quickly, eyes bouncing off mine. "I didn't mean anything by that. A lot of people are."

She pulls a harness from a hook on the wall, the complicated array of metal and straps clinking, filling the air.

"A lot of people are what?" I ask, pulling my attention from the fine line of her neck as she arranges the harness on the deck in front of me.

"Scared of heights," Jessica says, standing back up. "I'm just saying that if you were, it's normal, and a lot of people are. It doesn't have to be because of . . . anything else."

My eyes stray to the bridge, the steel that marches across the valley, the tallest zip line running parallel to it.

"No," I tell her. "I'm not scared."

"Cool." She breathes a sigh of relief. "You don't need to be. These harnesses are foolproof. You literally can't fall out."

She shows me how to step in, then pulls the straps up and over my shoulders. Jessica is quiet as she adjusts the fit, then positions a helmet on my head, pushing my hair behind my ears and surreptitiously wiping them clean on her cargo shorts.

"You're all set," she says, giving my helmet a friendly tap. "The trolley rests on the line, and then you hook this into it, okay?"

She hands me a carabiner that's attached to my harness, and I look at it dumbly, amazed at this little piece of metal that will keep me from dying.

"Paxton is already at the platform," Jessica says, moving away from me. I follow as we cross the lot to the first zip, a tower about thirty

279

feet off the ground. "We'll get you up to the last line and make sure you're settled on the platform. Your entire job is to just take pictures of people coming in. You get to hang out in the sun all day."

Jessica throws her head back like this is a great thing, then glances over at me.

"Uh, you wore sunscreen, right?"

I nod, even though it's a lie. I can't really care about my skin, and don't expect anyone else to. I follow Jessica up the stairs to the first platform, where Paxton is waiting, casually perfect as he leans against a wooden pillar.

"Neely, hey," he says. "You ready to be a zip today?"

I consider telling him that I will never be anything other than a person who needs to be underground, but the truth is that I might as well be a zip. I might as well be out in the sunshine, suspended in midair, because underground can't keep the monsters away when the monster is me. I'll always be with myself, carry around the knowledge of who I am, what I have done. Anywhere I go, I'll carry a prison inside my head, serve as my own jailer.

"Sure," I say, the monosyllable almost washed away by the breeze.

"Okay, then," Paxton says, shooting Jessica a glance.

She's behind me, but I can feel her shrug, am aware of the *What's her deal?* question that is implied but unasked and remains unanswered. I know now what my deal is, but not what I'm supposed to do about it. I just know that up here, standing with two beautiful people overlooking a gorgeous view, I am the problem.

"I'll go over first," Paxton says, hooking into a trolley and jumping off the platform with no hesitation. He's gone in an instant, alighting on the opposite platform a hundred feet away and waving back to us.

"Okay, Neely," Jessica says. "Step up here, and I'll make sure you're hooked in." She takes the carabiner out of my hand, attaches it to the trolley, and puts the handlebar in front of me. "When you get out on the line you have to trust your gear, all right? You want to just hang from the handlebars like deadweight, don't try to pull yourself up."

"Paxton didn't," I can't help but point out. In fact, I'm pretty sure he was flexing every back and shoulder muscle he has, strictly for her benefit.

"Uh, well, that's because there's no counterweight for him," Jessica says, not meeting my eyes.

"Counterweight?" I ask.

"Yeah, I mean . . . basically"—she colors a little, blood rising to her cheeks—"the heavier a person is, the faster they zip. Some people need to have a counterweight thrown down the line when they're coming into the platform. It'll hit your trolley and slow you down, break your momentum, make you easier for him to catch."

I bark out a laugh. Nothing could make it easier to catch the metric shit ton of weight that is me, plus my baggage.

"So do it like this, okay?" Jessica says, moving in front of me and taking the handlebar, bending her knees so that her arms are straight, simply hanging. "When the counterweight hits the trolley—"

"The trolley will bounce off my head if I pull myself up," I finish for her, but I'm not terribly interested. My gaze is pulled to the bridge, drawn by the flash of morning sun off a windshield, someone going somewhere else.

Leaving.

"You ready?" Jessica asks.

"Sure," I say, pulling my attention back to her. She signals something to Paxton, their own language up here in the canopy, their playground my brother's place of death.

"He's ready for you," Jessica says.

I realize suddenly that she doesn't think I'll do it. That I am going to apologize, step down, slip out of the harness, crawl back to my car. She expects me to choke, to burn out, to fail. And part of me wants to, part of me wants to go home, to crawl under the sheets, talk to the pile of dust on my bedside table and look at Mila's old posts. But she's dead and so is Lance, and there is nothing for me here, so whatever.

"Fuck it," I say, and step off the platform.

It's slow at first, then I build speed, the trolley above my head singing a song of metal on metal as I cut through the air, leaves whipping past, carefully pruned branches reaching but unable to grab, knowing that I'm Neely, not Lance.

Knowing that I'm not for them.

I look to the bridge, all the air between me and it, all the oxygen and living things, the blue and the green and the bright call of life. Lance saw these things and joined them, living fully in the moments before he died. The bridge flies past, and I crane my neck, pulling myself up, trying to understand what drew Lance there, his final place.

I want something else.

I want—

My head snaps backward, the solid *thunk* of the counterweight hitting my trolley, which bounces off my face. A shock wave passes through my head, agitating my brain, knocking things loose. Arms are around my waist, and I'm on the floor of the platform, sucking wind, Paxton pulling at my helmet.

"Neely? Hey, you okay?"

He says words that I know, and I'm aware of the appropriate answers, but my vision is black stars, my neck a hot ladder of pain. An explosion has happened on my forehead, and it radiates outward, fingers digging deeply into my brain. Jessica lands expertly, her heels bouncing off the tree trunk that the second platform is built around.

"Did you tell her not to pull herself up?" Paxton asks, turning from me to her.

Jessica glances down at me, unsurprised. "Yep."

"I'm fine," I say, struggling to my feet. "That was my fault. I'm fine."

And only one of those things is true, because once again I have done the wrong thing.

"You sure?" Paxton asks. "That was a pretty solid hit."

"No, really," I say. "It doesn't matter."

Because it doesn't. Nothing does. Not the ringing in my ears or the dull pain that is now seeping through my teeth, the impact from the counterweight pressing from behind my eyes, exploring the sockets of my jaw.

"I'm completely fine," I say.

And I am, because for the first time, I recognize it as an absolute lie. I know that I am not fine, never have been, and accepting this means that others shouldn't have to. Grandma and Grandpa should not have to move around the black hole of myself in their home, Paxton and Jessica should not have to catch my stinking sack of skin, Tabitha should not have to throw me to the ground in a parking lot to stop me from hurting someone.

The only person that can stop me is me.

Cars have begun to fill the lot below the first platform, the morning tourists arriving for their first ride.

"I'm all right," I say again. "I can do this."

"Fair enough," Paxton says. "Just let me know if your vision gets fuzzy, or if there's any ringing in your ears."

"I will," I say, even though both are already happening.

We climb the rope ladders to the second line, traversing the valley, a silent procession as Paxton goes first, Jessica hooks me in, and follows behind. I hang like a dead thing, practicing, the wind singing in my ears, a steady roar filling them when it's not. My head balances oddly on my neck, and I can't figure out how to hold it, or what I've ever done with such an awkward thing before. The pain at the center of my skull throbs, reaching outward, sucking my vision inward, everything hollowed.

"Okay, Neely, last line. It's a long one," Jessica says, drawing my attention back to her as we stand on the final platform. We're seven hundred feet in the air, a quarter mile of line stretching to the opposite platform, the valley below us, the bridge parallel.

Watching.

Jessica says something else, but I'm looking down, at the trees below, feeling what Lance must have felt, a promise of wind and rushing, followed by nothing.

I grab the handlebar and step off, just as Jessica screams.

"Wait! You're not locked in!"

But it's too late and I'm flying, hands curled around the bar, my grip the only thing between me and donating my organs to whoever is hiking the trail below. Which really is kind of funny, so I'm laughing when the cord suddenly goes slack, my momentum broken.

"Hold on, Neely! I'm coming!"

Jessica is behind me, propelling herself hand over hand along the cord, her weight pulling it down, bringing me to a dead halt. I hang, suspended, seven hundred feet in the air. On the opposite platform, Paxton watches, hands over his mouth, frozen.

I let go with one hand, and wave.

The bar tilts to the other side, all my weight loaded there.

"Jesus Christ! Neely! What the fuck?!"

Jessica is next to me, her hands moving expertly as she loops a second carabiner off her own harness. She hangs, dangling freely, clipping herself to me. I grab my handlebar again with both hands as she pulls me back against her, arms clamping around my waist, her words, low and hard, in my ear.

"Listen to me, you stupid, crazy bitch," she says. "You're attached to me now, and these trolleys aren't made to hold more than one person. If you let go, if you fall even the length of this cord, it could snap, and I go with you. And I am not fucking dying for you."

"No," I say, turning my head against hers, wanting to speak, to let her hear me and know my intentions. But all that comes out is "No, no, no, no."

This isn't what I meant, not what I wanted. I wasn't trying to hurt myself, or Jessica, or anyone. I was trying to do what I was supposed to do, go to the other platform and take pictures of happy people doing things together in the sunlight, people who have families and boyfriends and girlfriends and children and moms and dads. People who know how to do this, how to move through a day and be a real person. I would document this for them, so they had something to hold and remember, something to tell them that there were good days once.

But I'm incapable, and I always do the wrong thing, don't shut the door or don't open it, let the words come out that are supposed to stay in, talk to monsters and hurt the living.

"I'm so sorry," I say, twisting my head, trying to tell Jessica, trying to let her know, trying to put all my thoughts into words, how she is like Mila and can be strong and right and beautiful, and how being like Mila and being near me is not a good mix, that I am dangerous and cannot be trusted, that I have made a mistake and now Jessica is here with me, fixing it, hauling us both hand over hand in midair, risking herself.

"Stop moving," Jessica says, her voice as tight as her arms, every muscle flickering as she hauls us forward.

We're halfway across when I spot Lance on the bridge, a soft body on the wrong side of the metal barrier. There's no hesitation, the decision already made. He falls, and his monsters go with him.

There are four.

I yell, reaching for him, abandoning my handlebar. Jessica grunts as my whole weight pulls down on her, every inch of me, skin and bones and muscle and sins, hanging from her harness. She wraps her legs around my waist, pulls me upward as I spin.

"I'm coming out!" Paxton yells, clipping onto a trolley.

"Don't!" Jessica screams, and there's a special kind of panic in her voice, the sound of caring for someone else, more than you care for yourself.

"I'm sorry," I say again, clamping my hands onto her harness, climbing her body.

"Just hold on and shut the fuck up," Jessica says through clenched teeth as I wrap my legs around her waist. I'm a parasite, clamped on to something more beautiful, more alive.

Feeding.

Jessica is dripping sweat, her palms bleeding as she drags us, inch by painful inch. Below in the valley, I see a hole in the canopy where Lance punched through.

"Almost there," Paxton yells. Jessica makes a final push, and I feel hands on my back, Paxton pulling me off Jessica as she collapses, feet barely on the platform as her body gives out. Paxton drags her forward, unclipping her carabiner as she crawls.

"Get her off me," Jessica says, slipping out of her harness, cutting all our connections. She stumbles off the platform onto the gravel path, lands on all fours, and pukes.

I get up, try to go to her, but Paxton pushes me back firmly.

"No fucking way," he says, pointing to the gift shop. "You go in there, and you tell them that you need a ride back down to the lot, and then you tell John that you need to go to the fucking hospital. I don't know what's wrong with you, but—"

"It's okay," I say, coming to my feet, cutting him off. "I do."

THIRTY-NINE

I do know what is wrong with me, and I know how to fix it.

But I have learned some lessons, and the things that should stay inside will this time. I will wire my mouth shut, hold my tongue, keep my secrets. I will not allow anyone else to be in danger because of me or be scared of me. I won't even hurt anyone's feelings. I will be still and quiet, until I can be no more.

The only thing that stops me is me.

The explosion in my forehead has branched out, a deep, pulsing pain that traces my bones, drips down my spine, radiates through my collarbone and out into my shoulders.

"Neely?"

Grandpa is in front of me, the zip line staff doing their best to pretend that neither one of us exists as they move through the back hallway, stepping around us. I pull my eyes to his, try to focus. But his features are slippery, and my gaze slides off, following a dust mote, someone's skin, floating free.

"I'm fine," I say. "I messed up, and I stepped off the platform before Jessica hooked me in. But I'm okay."

I am. That's the shitty part. Jessica's palms look like raw hamburger.

"They said you hit your head?"

"Yes," I say, nodding, my skull nearly continuing the tumble forward, landing in my lap. "But I'm okay to drive."

Grandpa looks doubtful, but I insist. "No, really. I'm fine. You can follow me the whole way home. I'll drive slow. If we leave my car, you and Grandma will just have to come back once she's off work, and you don't need to do more."

No one should do more because of me. I start my car and look over at the first tower, the kids following their parents up the stairs, helmets bobbing, carabiners in hand.

It's a beautiful day to be with the people you care about.

Grandpa pulls up behind me, patiently waiting as I back out, my movements an exaggeration of caution, checking to make sure I am in reverse, and then forward, and then reverse, and then forward, barely tapping the gas. I drive home slowly, no music, learning silence.

Grandpa follows me through the back door, calling after me as I follow my accustomed escape route to my room. "Neely, your grandma and I want to talk tonight, after dinner."

"Okay," I say, as my hands go to my face, pressing against my eyelids, the only things keeping the pressure in my skull from sending my eyes right out of their sockets.

"John said . . . ," Grandpa debates, swirling his keys on one finger.

"What did he say?" I ask, willing him to share something that doesn't matter, so that the conversation can be over, and I can move on. Move past. Move away.

"He said you should take next week off, and maybe consider if you want to return or not." His eyes drop away from mine, hiding things. "Apparently some things have happened at work that upset—"

"Right," I say. "No, I understand."

And I do, because I have done upsetting things. Tabitha having to physically restrain me from attacking Patrick was probably a little much for her to have to deal with on lunch break. Destiny having to smell me is way out of her wheelhouse. And also, I did choke out Josh.

"Maybe we were wrong," Grandpa says. "To let you get a job. We just thought—"

"No," I say quickly, stepping toward him, stopping short of reaching out. "You weren't wrong. I loved it."

And I did. I loved the caverns and the shadows, the drip of water and following in Margaret's footsteps. I loved tapping lights on and off, bringing a whole room into existence and snuffing it out with the touch of a finger. I loved the mist and I loved Mila, and only one of those things is still here.

Which is why I'm going back.

One more time.

But first I have some things to do.

I get all the cups from the kitchen and fill them with water, lining them around my bed.

I open the closet door, wide and inviting.

I write *shitbird* three times on the wall.

I crack the window, in case my dead cat wants in.

I put the dust in my pocket, to keep it safe.

My phone goes off; Tabitha calling. I am surprised enough to answer.

"Neely?" Her voice is cold, a thin thread of steel spun through it.

"Yes," I say.

"I just got off the phone with Destiny. The cops got Mila's phone records back."

"Okay," I say.

There's a silence that stretches, her waiting for me to speak, me willing her not to.

"Her last text was to her mom."

"Okay," I say.

"She said she was staying at your place."

"Yes," I say.

"That's . . ." Tabitha's breath leaves her, shock squeezing her lungs, fear twisting her gut. "That's all you're going to say? What the *fuck*, Neely? What *did you do*?"

"I don't actually know," I tell her. "But I believe it's called a psychotic break."

I hang up, glance down at my phone, reconsider.

Then I shoot her a text.

I'm sorry.

I cannot manage.

"Neely? Are you okay? I heard—"

Brian picks up on the first ring, my brother's only friend, the only person I am honest with.

"I think I know why Lance killed himself," I say.

"Wait, why would you—"

"It's not that he couldn't manage," I barrel forward, needing to get the words out, share my discovery with the one person who also shares my pain. "I know that's what his note said, but you were right. I read his Rock Bottom posts, and you were right."

"What was I right about?"

In my hand, the ball of dust shifts and reforms, rolling between my fingers. "He wasn't who I thought he was," I say, my voice cracking on *who*, an eternal question.

"He was angry," I admit, but I know it goes beyond that, touches on words I never thought would be associated with my brother.

"He was violent," I amend. "He wanted to hurt people, and he wanted to do things to girls."

"Yeah, I know." Brian's voice is quiet, the truth of my words reflected by the calm of his acceptance. "I just always hoped that he wouldn't. That he could stop himself."

The only thing that stops me is me.

"He did," I tell Brian.

There's a stretch of silence, then a deep sigh. "You really think that's what happened?"

"The last thing he said to me was—you can never truly know someone else. He tried to tell me. Tried to—"

"When was this?" Brian interrupts.

"Two days before," I explain. "He'd just came back from hanging out with you. He bumped into me in the hallway—"

"I remember," Brian says. "We'd gone fishing. We were actually on the bridge."

I think of Lance, standing next to his only friend, casting lines, clearing his conscience, making plans.

"So, if that's the reason why he did what he did . . ." I take a shaky breath, hoping that what I say next is the truth, for his sake—and mine. "Maybe he wasn't all bad. Maybe there was a part of him that was still decent."

The part that bottle-fed stray kittens, canceling out the part that wanted to control humans. At the very least, perhaps my brother achieved a sum of neutral.

"We can't ever know what he was thinking," Brian says. "That's not for us."

No, it's not. Like summertime picnics and Fourth of July parades, new snow on Christmas morning and a family gathered around the Thanksgiving table. That was not for us, either. Lance and I got blood and broken glass, our father cutting down trees to save the people inside.

"No," I agree with Brian. "We can't ever know. We can't know someone else, and sometimes we don't even know ourselves."

"Neely, are you okay?"

I don't know how to answer, because the truth should be hidden and my real self cannot be seen. I settle for what I told him in our first conversation, the beginning of my connection to the one person my brother showed himself to.

"Sometimes I am okay."

I hang up and switch off my phone so that he cannot call back, cannot text me, cannot reach out to the void inside of me.

So that I cannot tell him—those times are over.

FORTY

The shadows are long when I leave.

Grandpa is sleeping in his chair, Grandma not home yet. I back out of the driveway and head for the caverns. It's after-hours, everyone will be gone, doors locked, lights out. I drive in silence, teeth clenched, fingers tight on the wheel, each heartbeat pushing pain through my body. When I get out of the car, there's a familiar call, a throaty yell. T.S. emerges from around the visitors' center, spots me. Sulla trails behind him, not trusting me.

He's the smarter one.

"Hey, buddy," I say to T.S., going down on one knee.

He presses his nose into my hand, purring, and I push back, scratching along his jawline, his lip lifting, teeth showing as he rubs against the headlamp that dangles from my fingers. The gate clanks loudly behind me when I close it, T.S. rubbing against the metal bars, calling to me.

"No," I tell him. "You have to stay here."

He does, but I don't. I have only one thing to do, and then no more.

The door screeches open, and I inhale, breathing in the wet and the rock, the earth and the call of the darkness.

And then I pass through, under this red rock.

FORTY-ONE

The crime scene tape falls away like spiderwebs. Inconsequential, it tumbles to the cave floor as I make my way back to that place, that night, my light bouncing off walls, nothing in my ears but the trickle of water.

In the sacrificial table room, something skitters from under my foot, the yellow triangle of an evidence marker sliding into shadow. I look down, where some of Mila's blood still sits, not drying, forever liquid in this place where time is arrested. In the graffiti room, I haul myself onto the ledge, pushing hand over hand, following our path from that night, the final night, the only night that matters. Margaret's name looms over my shoulder as I push into the crawl space, pulling myself forward, rock below and beneath, pressure between my shoulder blades, something catching on my pelvis. I move forward, following the drag marks, knocking aside evidence markers, a path only Mila and I had followed, until others came, looking for answers.

Answers to why a girl has died and someone has killed her, answers to why you can never really know someone, and one human being cannot belong to another, and no one can be controlled, and how some of us still wish for that regardless.

I drop into the room where Margaret brought Anna, where forbidden things happened and then something much worse.

I fall headfirst, lamp landing in the dirt, my neck at an angle, my head an overripe fruit on the verge of bursting. My fist is under my stomach, my breath gone, dust and mist rising around me as I lift my head, my light landing on a pale face.

"Hey, kiddo," Margaret says.

FORTY-TWO

"You can't be here," I tell her, spitting.

"This is the only place I can be," she says, nodding to the wall, to her and Anna and a record of them, scratched into stone.

"Not right now," I say. "I have to—"

"What do you have to do?" Margaret asks, coming forward, pulling me to my feet.

"The only thing that stops me is me," I tell her. "I think I have to—"

But Margaret says it with me, our mouths moving in unison, our voices woven together, echoing off rock, an unholy choir, singing underground. My hand goes to my head, blocking the light, my fingers streaked across her face, her black eyes filling the space in between.

"You're me," I say, and she nods.

"You know what I know," I say, and she steps forward, pulling my hand down, the light blazing back at me in her pupils. "Maybe even what I forget."

"Do you want to remember?" Margaret asks.

I close my eyes, tears slipping down my cheeks, dropping, joining the blood on the floor, the mist in the air, smaller parts of myself to leave behind here in this room, before I go to the one beyond.

Before I go deeper, darker, farther.

"Yes," I say.

I open my eyes.

Margaret steps forward.

And kisses me.

FORTY-THREE

Mila steps back.

"Whoa, hey!" Her voice is high and alarmed but lined with an apology. "I didn't mean . . . I'm not . . . Sorry, Neely, I'm straight."

"I know," I say, moving toward her again, reaching out. "You've got a cobweb in your hair."

I pull it free, and it dangles from my fingers for a second before drifting to the ground. Mila stares at it dumbly, her headlamp following its path.

"Oh my God," she says, looking back at me. "I just came off as the most egotistical person in the history of the world, didn't I?"

"Not really, because I would kiss you," I tell her. "In fact, I really want to. But *you* don't want me to, and that makes it entirely unattractive."

"Wow," Mila says, shaking her head. "Neely, I think that's the most romantic thing anyone has ever said to me."

I laugh, glad I can offer her that. Glad to be here, with her, this girl I desperately want but will try not to need. This girl that I will graft my attraction for to the tree of friendship, and it will grow there, each of them strengthening the other until the bond is pure and healthy.

A sound comes from the crawl space, a call from the other room. The one with the pit.

"Did you hear that?" Mila asks, her head tilting to the side.

FORTY-FOUR

"You can do anything you want to do; you can be anything you want to be," the man says, his hands on my shoulders, the evening sun on his dark stubble, the checkerboard pattern of his flannel bright against his tanned skin.

The man who is my father, the man who is leaving.

The cinder block steps are cold, cutting through my thin shorts, my back against the trailer door, Mom's crying just leaking through.

In the grass, the children laugh, and my eyes move, searching.

The man sighs, puts his hand under my chin, lifts my eyes to his.

"Just don't fuck it up."

FORTY-FIVE

"Hello?"

Mila calls, and a voice answers her. But not a human one. It's a meow, high and plaintive, a note of panic echoing to us from the other room.

"Oh, shit!" Mila says, going to the crawl space, hauling herself up and calling into the void. "Kitty, kitty?" Then, true fear edging her voice. "T.S.?"

The cat responds again, more faintly this time.

"I shut the door," I say, nerves firing as I hope it's true. "I did. I shut the door."

FORTY-SIX

"You forgot to shut the door again, shitbird," Mom says, smacking Dad affectionately on the back of the head. His teeth clink against his spoon, milk-wet Cheerios falling back into the bowl.

"You're the shitbird," he says, sticking his fingers into milk and flicking it at her. She squeals and jumps, laughing as she drags a rag across the back of her neck.

"Shitbird," I say, giggling.

"Shitbird," Lance agrees.

And we all laugh.

FORTY-SEVEN

"Shit." Mila turns to me, the cat still calling out of the darkness.

"It's not him," I tell her, willing her to believe me. "It's not T.S. He was behind us, and I shut the door."

"Even if it's not T.S., I've got to go after it," Mila says, though I can't miss the fact that she didn't reassure me, didn't say of course I shut the door and did the right thing and didn't endanger anyone or anything. "There's all kinds of little forks and paths that a cat could fit into past that room. I don't want that on my conscience."

"Okay," I say, adjusting my headlight.

"No." Mila shakes her head. "You can't come. It's way too dangerous past this point. You've never done it before, you've been drinking, and you're high. If anything happens to you, it's my fault."

She's not wrong. My tongue is a dry dead thing in my mouth, my mind a pinwheel of images; Mila's face, Margaret's eyes.

The cat calls again, farther away.

Mila makes a decision, hauls herself into the crawl space that opens into the other room, the farther room, the last room.

"I'll be right back," she says.

And then she goes.

Deeper. Darker. Farther.

FORTY-EIGHT

"Lance?"

I turn my head, cheek sticky with blood, the seat belt tight against my chest.

He reaches for me, leaning as I lean, red fingers twining together.

I lick my lips, tongue dry, cracked skin on cracked skin, flies buzzing around Mom.

"I'm thirsty."

FORTY-NINE

There's a world where Mila comes back with a cat in her arms, angry and yowling.

There's a world where we crawl back together, leave the caves, let the cat loose to run across the lot, tail in the air, pissed at us.

There's a world where we laugh, and I take her home, say goodbye, and see her at work on Monday morning.

But the world I live in is the one where I keep talking after she's gone into the last cave, have a conversation with a version of Mila that is not there.

The world I live in is the one where I go, carrying all my delusions with me as I crawl away, leaving her behind.

The world I live in is the one where I cross the lot believing that I am holding her hand, that I am taking her home with me.

The world I live in is the one where I toss in my own bed, alone, hands on myself, wishing for something more.

The world I live in is the one where Mila dies in the next room, where someone chained her to a column and kept her there in the darkness.

The world I live in is the one where someone killed Mila.

But it wasn't me.

FIFTY

"Fuck," I say, eyes flying open.

"I didn't—"

But Margaret is gone, and I am alone.

Except . . . there is gravel falling from the entrance to this room, a light shining through, a head emerging from the crawl space.

Brian drops to the floor, stands, looks at me, light in my eyes, his hands on my shoulders.

"Neely," he says, grip tightening. "Neely, you crazy fucking bitch."

FIFTY-ONE

"What?"

I am an empty bag of skin, a small dumb thing. I am an eruption on my forehead, pain in my body. I am a collection of misspent thoughts and unwound wanderings.

But I am not a killer.

"Brian?" I say.

But he has no more words for me, simply turns my body to face the crawl space, the entrance to the other room. The last room.

"Go," he says.

And I do.

FIFTY-TWO

I drop into a crouch when I land, scattering an entire field of yellow triangles. They rattle off into the darkness, plastic footsteps ringing. My light follows one as it moves toward the lip of a giant hole in the floor, gaping, an open mouth. The triangle falls, clicks against the sides once, twice, and then nothing.

Brian drops beside me, dust kicking up around his feet as he spins, his light illuminating me, the pockmarked walls, one heavy, thick column meeting in the middle, a congealing puddle of blood beside it.

"What did you do?" I ask, voicing Margaret's question to me. "Jesus Christ, Brian. What did you do?"

"What did *I* do?" he asks, hand splayed across his chest, eyes wide with innocence. "You were the last person Mila was with before she died. She texted her mom, said she was going home with you. Well, technically *I* sent that text," Brian says, leaning in, his light in my eyes. "But it still doesn't look good for you, does it?"

"But she didn't," I say, shaking my head, a pendulum counting off different seconds of diverging truths. "She didn't come home with me." My hand goes to my chest, the scratches there perfectly spaced indentations of my own fingers.

"Nope," Brian agrees. "She was with me."

In here, in this room, where she came to save what she thought was lost.

"I was right," I say, my head lifting. "That wasn't T.S. It was you."

"Yeah, it was," he says. "And it wouldn't have had to happen at all if you two would have done what you were supposed to do."

"What?" I ask. "What were we supposed to do?"

"Not come down here in the first place," he says. "Not be fucking lightweights that get smashed and then have some weird-ass white-girl summer a mile underground. But you did what you did, so I did what I did, and now you're going to be the one that gets blamed for it, because you're a crazy person, and you do crazy shit, and you fuck everything up, and nobody likes you."

I flinch, push backward on my heels until my shoulder blades are against rock, cold stone and rivulets of cave water pressing back.

Nobody likes you.

"Mila liked me," I say.

"Well, that's one, and she's dead," Brian says. "So, you're at zero, and that's exactly how many people are coming to your funeral after they find you."

"Find me?"

"Yeah, down there," he says, casually tossing his head over his shoulder, toward the pit. "Where you threw yourself to your death because you couldn't take the guilt anymore."

I shudder as a trickle of water follows the path of my spine. There's a world where that happened, and it was almost this one.

Almost, but not quite.

"What did you do?" I ask again, my teeth coming together, the words grinding out of the spaces in between, finely milled, fit for this

309

time and this place, words for a boy who has done something to a girl. Something that should not have happened.

"What I had to," Brian says. "What I've *been* doing. Working my ass off, doing whatever I can, busting my knuckles and breaking my bones, fucking fighting for every goddamn penny, meanwhile everybody else has full tip jars because everyone else *is so* GODDAMN PRETTY."

He screams the last, the words filling the small space, traveling down into the pit, then back up, telling us that everyone else is goddamn pretty.

"Tabitha drives a BMW, Josh gets *all* the pussy, and Destiny shakes her titties for money that everyone is just throwing at her, because titties. Sure, sure, sure," he says, nodding, head jumping with every word. "I mean, I get it, yeah. Destiny's titties! I'd fucking pay to see them, because Lord knows I'm not getting them any other way, am I?"

"I don't—"

"Know? Of course you don't know," Brian sneers at me. "How could you know? You have no clue what it's like to be me, to fucking have to work for shit, not just ask. I break my goddamn back, and it all goes somewhere else."

His voice goes into a high register, his hands parroting the words.

"Brian, Jadine's gymnastic fees are due. Brian, we need groceries. Brian, your dad drank all his paycheck, and the gas bill needs paid. Brian, could you just DO IT ALL, PLEASE?"

His hands drop, the light blue of his eyes pale and dead, hopeless.

"I'm so sorry, Brian. I knew it was bad, but—"

"But not how bad, right? Not bad enough that when someone came to me with a way to make real money, I fucking jumped. I said yes faster than Destiny bending over for the camera, and it was smooth, oh man—" He snaps his fingers, eyes lighting up again. "For a while there, it was real nice."

"What was?" I ask.

"Heroin," he says. "It moves into the county, I store it down here, retrieve it when there's a buyer. It's not at anybody's house, it's not in anybody's car. It's somewhere no one ever comes, and nobody ever checks in—until now. Until fucking NOW, NEELY!"

He drops on all fours and crawls toward me, pressing me back farther. I cringe, putting distance between us, trying to melt into the wall, become rock, let the cave eat me so that Brian can't.

"Mila found your stash," I say quietly, realization sinking in. "But you didn't have to . . ." I shake my head, willing reality to be made clear to me. Asking for something that has never happened.

"We weren't going any farther," I tell him. "We weren't coming in here. We wouldn't have seen it. You didn't have to lure her." My breath catches as I choke on what might have been. "You didn't have to do that."

Brian's mouth twitches, a small smile blooming. "No, I didn't have to . . . but maybe I *wanted* to. Maybe I had other ideas, ones that are definitely illegal but had nothing to do with drug running."

I close my eyes against the headlamp, against his leer.

"But you didn't follow her," he says, shaking his head.

"I grabbed Mila when she landed and shut her up real fast, but it wouldn't have mattered if she screamed. You were a fucking loon at that point, talking to yourself, carrying on a whole conversation. You probably shouldn't smoke pot," he chides.

"You probably shouldn't, either," I say tightly.

"I did what I had to do," Brian says, shrugging at the inevitability of it all. "Shot Mila up to keep her quiet, followed you to make sure that you left." He shakes his head, light following the path of his gaze. "Do you know how hard that was? To wait?"

I think of Mila standing on the rock, her legs going all the way up, sunglasses dark in her light hair, lanyard dangling from her chest. I think of Mila, on my mind, all the time. Hoping I'm on hers.

"Yes," I say.

"You don't," Brian snarls back at me. "You don't know. I finally had her, all of her. There was nothing but her and me—" He snaps his fingers. "And a shit ton of heroin that I had to move brick by brick, crawling it out, moving it to another place. It took all night."

He sighs, head falling back, thinking about how hard he'd worked, what he'd sacrificed.

"I told her I'd be back, told her she'd have the chance to be very, very nice to me. And if she chose not to . . ." He shrugs. "I had ways to change her mind. Things I've been wanting to try for a while. Things that would take time and privacy."

He smiles again, teeth showing. "We had both."

His happiness slips away, sliding off his face like a mask, anger replacing it. "And then you show up, wanting to give flea treatment to a fucking cat. I had things to *do* that day, Neely! Things I'd been looking forward to for a *very* long time."

"You sick fuck," I say, breath catching in my chest, thinking of Mila, trapped. Mila with a boy telling her what would happen when he came back. Mila, who chewed her own thumb off so that a boy would never have power over her again. Mila, alone, in the dark.

"I could not believe it when she showed up on the table," Brian says. "Could. Not. Believe. It." He jabs his fingers into his palm with each word, accenting his incredulity.

Mila, who heard human voices, and moved toward the light, trailing blood behind her. Mila, who emerged from darkness only to fall into the arms of the person who would kill her after she tried so hard to live.

"You pushed her," I say dully. "You shoved her off the edge, didn't you? I thought you were trying to help her," I say, my voice small and weak, catching in my throat. "I thought you were a good person."

"I am," Brian says, truly baffled. "I didn't come back on Sunday. I went to church; I left her alone. I might have a need, but even I know that it's an unholy one."

I lift my head, no longer awestruck by the broken teeth of the cave, the frantic last fight inside of Mila that had shattered her, broken this, torn apart a sacred place and taken her somewhere even farther. I was ready to stay here, too. Down here, life is simple and the rules are clear—shut the door and don't touch pretty things.

I didn't follow the first one.

Brian didn't follow the second.

"An unholy need?" I repeat. "You're *hillwalker*. That wasn't Lance. It was you."

"Oh, Lance," Brian moans. "You and Lance are just as bad as everyone else. You realize that, right? Oh nooo . . ." He falls to his knees, hands clasped, eyes aloft. "Dear God, why did you take my mommy and daddy? Why did you make my life so horrible that I have to live with my grandma and grandpa, who love me and take care of me and give me everything I need and don't make me work and never ask questions and let me do whatever I want to do?

"Oh my *God*!" he shrieks, coming back to his feet, newly incensed, kicking dirt in my direction. "You both make me so fucking sick. You're literal crazy people, wandering around hearing things, and talking to shit that's not there, and you've *got a job*? And I'm working my ass off and being a sane person, and girls want to talk *to him*?"

My hand sneaks into my pocket, finds the dust there, what is left of a brother I didn't reach out to when I could, and whose memory I allowed to be tainted once he was gone.

"Lance wasn't like that," I say, rolling the dust in my hand, some of it jamming under my fingernail, meeting with Mila's dried blood, an alchemical mix that restarts my heart, fires my brain. "Lance wouldn't have hurt anyone."

"That's the fucking truth!" Brian agrees almost gleefully. "He wouldn't even consider it."

"Wouldn't even consider—"

"No!" Brian shouts, cutting me off. "I had some ideas. I tried. He was really into the one girl at Hobby Lobby, and I would've taken her friend, no problem. And maybe she would talk to him, but he wasn't going to get any off her, and I couldn't even get a goddamn phone number, so I was like, 'Hey, man, I've got some stuff in the back of the truck to convince them. Stuff like duct tape and handcuffs, and maybe if they don't do what they're supposed to do, we'll just *make* them do it.'

"And man, he did *not* like that," Brian says, eyes wide. "He got all upset and started his whole 'the world is broken and so is everyone in it, nothing matters and we're all lost, you can never truly know someone else, my only friend is a horrible human being and I had no clue,' blah, blah blah." Brian's hands flap, fingers puppeting my brother's words, mocking his morality.

314

"You can never truly know someone else," I repeat, thinking of the taut lines of Lance's face, the last piece of wisdom he passed on to me, leaving a dark and broken world behind after learning that his monsters weren't only in his head.

That he'd let one into his life.

"That didn't have to happen," I say. "He could have said something, told someone."

But he didn't, because we close doors and keep our heads down, don't talk about the hard things and pretend that the light exists independently, without the contrast of the dark.

"But it did happen," Brian says. "Lance happened. Mila happened. And now Neely will happen." He says our names, his trophies, ticking them off on his fingers. "But only when you're ready. Don't let me rush you."

"Ready for what?"

"To jump," he says, nodding toward the pit. "That's what you came here for, isn't it?"

I grab the side of the cave, find a notch for my fingers, pull myself up onto wobbly legs. I move forward, fingers trailing across the column, something that took a million years to form so that it could be present here, holding Mila in place, taking her control away.

"We're so soft," I say to Brian as I walk to the edge. "We are vulnerable things that break and come apart, splatter against the earth and the rain washes us away."

"You and your brother," he says, shaking his head. "Bunch of fucking freaks."

I stand on the edge of the pit, my toes peeking over, my light staring straight down, seeing nothing, promising an end. I may not have killed

Mila, but I am far from okay, and I know it. Despite all the denials, my monsters are real and may always be with me. If I do this right now, I will never have to decipher reality again, never have to fail Grandma and Grandpa, never have to wonder if someone else is thinking of me when they are the only thing I can think of.

It can end.

I might not have killed Mila, but she's still gone.

Brian comes to my side, his light joining mine, twin beams disappearing into darkness.

"Are you ready?" he asks.

"Yes," I say.

And then I push him.

FIFTY-THREE

THREE MONTHS LATER

The visitors' lounge is entirely beige and robin's-egg blue, a choice that someone must have made after googling interior decorating for the mentally ill. Tabitha is on the love seat but comes to her feet when I walk in.

"Hey," she says, waving as if she needs to catch my attention in a room where there are only three other people, another patient and her mom, plus the nurse.

"Hey," I say, coming to her side. We sit down together, and she glances around the room at the art, nonthreatening splatters of light green on white canvas.

"This isn't . . . so bad," she says. "I mean, you get to wear your own clothes and everything?"

"Yeah, it's a hospital, not a prison," I tell her, looking down at my jeans and hoodie.

"Right, of course it's not a prison," she says quickly, her eyes bouncing off mine.

We're quiet for a minute as she picks at a loose thread on the end of her jeans. "How are you doing?" I finally ask, and Tabitha barks out a laugh.

"Shouldn't I be asking you that?" she says.

"No," I say with a small shrug. "Because I'm okay."

"Really?" Tabitha asks, eyebrows raising. "I mean, you're . . . here."

"Yeah," I agree, gaze trailing around the room, assessing the blandness, the security of processing very few things, the promise that the people who are here actually exist. "But it's what I need right now. I don't have to pretend. I can just be sad and that's okay."

Tabitha sighs and leans back against the couch. "Okay, that actually sounds pretty amazing. What kinds of insurance do they take?"

I smile and run my hand across my thumbnail, at the wedge of dark blood and dirt still present there, working its way out. I promised myself I would leave this place once it's gone, once Mila and Lance are no longer with me.

"How are you?" I ask again, not letting Tabitha get away without answering.

"Uh . . ." She rests her head on the edge of the love seat, her dark hair tumbling as a tear gathers at the corner of her eye. "Pretty shitty, actually. I feel really bad about what I said, how I thought that you killed Mila."

"It's okay," I tell her. "I thought so, too."

"Wow," she says, lifting her head. "You are just, like, totally fucking calm now, aren't you?"

"Well, it's partly the meds," I admit.

I'd been terrified that I would react like Dad did and begin trying

318

to free people from trees. But the staff insisted that his situation was a rare one and that people react differently to medication.

"Plus, can you really get crazier?" Grandpa helpfully added.

Grandma slapped at his arm, and they shared a smile, one that showed under the tears like sunlight breaking through clouds.

"Yeah, I'm much better," I tell Tabitha. "I'm not trying to pull boys out of trucks."

"And I'm not throwing girls across parking lots," Tabitha adds.

"You're stronger than you look," I tell her, and we both laugh.

"But really, how am I? I am still 'processing,'" she says, putting air quotes around the last word. "That's what my therapist says."

"You're seeing someone?"

"Yeah," she says, wiping away the tear. "At first I was, like, why do I need to talk to somebody? I didn't even see Mila, and Brian was just, like, there one day, gone the next—sorry."

"No, it's okay," I tell her. "Him, I did kill."

"Right," Tabitha says slowly. "But is it horrible if I say I'm glad?"

"That's why I'm here," I tell her. "Trying to sort exactly that kind of shit out."

Whether I deserve to live, in the past, present, and future was always a question for me. With Brian's death on my conscience, the answer has become more pressing. So far, the answer is yes. So far, I have forgiven myself. Tomorrow might be harder, and the day after could be worse. But today, I am okay.

"Keep talking," I say, reaching out to tentatively touch Tabitha's hand. Her fingers mesh with mine, close around them.

"Well . . . I just feel like two people we know are dead, and one of them it turns out was really fucking horrible. And how is that even possible? Like, how did I not see that? How did I not know? And how could he be that way? How does a person do that?"

"I don't know," I say honestly, and give her hand a squeeze. "Keep talking."

And she does.

And I listen.

FIFTY-FOUR

Mila is in a different part of the cemetery than Lance. The only place the two most important people in my life are close together is under my fingernail.

It's raining, but Grandma and Grandpa were okay with bringing me here for my weekly hour out of the hospital. They have been okay with a lot of things that I was not expecting, like my admission to talking to people who aren't there, and the blunt statement that I am gay.

"Okay," Grandma said, her eyebrows raising up to her hairline, one of them struggling to make the path back down as she considered the situation. "That's okay."

"I know it's okay," I told her, to which she had glanced around my hospital room and asked if I had enough clean underwear or if she should bring more from home.

Grandpa holds the umbrella over Grandma as I walk forward, stepping out into the rain. The drops hit me, wet and cold. They will drip from my skin and onto the ground, tunnel down to Mila, then past her, going somewhere deeper, darker, farther.

"Hey," I say to her, expecting no answer. It has been an adjustment, having no one under the bed, or in the closet. No voices that answer and no applause, no need to repeat other people's words, tacking *shitbird* onto the end.

Someone has brought mums to decorate Mila's grave for the fall. They are brilliantly yellow, and I flinch, wishing they were anything else. But wishing is not action, and thoughts are not behaviors, and feelings are not facts, and I am learning.

"T.S. is staying with Grandma and Grandpa," I tell Mila. "Without you there, he kept wandering away at work, and John was worried about him. The rest of the staff thought maybe I might want him. So he's got my old room all to himself. For now."

For now. Until I can come home. Until I am better.

"Soon," I add.

But not too soon, because even though I didn't kill Mila, I wasn't good for her, either. If she had lived, I might have been able to be a friend and only that, love from a distance, keep my desires at bay. But also I might have lain alone in a bed, scratching myself, checking my phone, looking for her anywhere I could find her, thinking of her first thing in the morning, and last thing at night, saying her name and wanting only her smell. Seeing only her. Talking only about her.

I am talking about her now. And often.

So that I won't let that happen again to another girl.

So that I won't let that happen again to me.

"Soon, but not yet," I say.

To Mom I say that I am doing all right but not well. Grandma does not tell her that I am growing up wonderfully and she would be proud. She just cries, and so does Grandpa.

To Lance I say that I could have done better and I have regrets. I tell him that I will leave my door open once I am home.

The last grave is one that the caretaker had to help us find, one that is almost bare, only the slightest indentations on the stone let me know that this is where Margaret Sander rests. In the caves, underground, her name lives stark and bold, unread, in the dark. Here, in the light, she has faded into anonymity.

Grandma and Grandpa hang back as I spend the most time at this grave, with this perfect stranger, telling her everything that I have done, the things that I have wanted and the things that I have broken, the things that I have left behind and the ones that I am heading toward.

Then I turn, and I leave, walking in the rain, tears falling on the ground.

Not deeper in, but further out of myself.

Not darker, but crawling for the light.

Not farther, where no one can reach me.

RESOURCES

There are many resources available for those struggling with suicide, suicidal ideation, and/or mental health issues. Below is a short list of some of the well-recognized resources that can offer help.

988 CRISIS HOTLINE: 988LIFELINE.ORG

The 988 Suicide & Crisis Lifeline is a national network of local crisis centers that provides free and confidential emotional support to people in suicidal crisis or emotional distress 24 hours a day, 7 days a week in the United States. We're committed to improving crisis services and advancing suicide prevention by empowering individuals, advancing professional best practices, and building awareness.

CRISIS TEXT LINE: CRISISTEXTLINE.ORG

Text HOME to 741741 from anywhere in the United States, anytime. Crisis Text Line is here for any crisis. A live, trained crisis counselor receives the text and responds, all from our secure online platform. The volunteer crisis counselor will help you move from a hot moment to a cool moment.

NATIONAL MENTAL HEALTH HOTLINE:
MENTALHEALTHHOTLINE.ORG

It's easy to get overwhelmed when you or someone you love is in distress, and talking to friends or relatives may be difficult. Reaching out saves lives, however, and the mental health hotline provides the ear of a compassionate professional who knows how to deal with a mental health crisis. Sometimes, a brief conversation is all it takes to put things in perspective and move forward. The Mental Health Hotline at 866-903-3787 can answer your questions confidentially and free of charge.

SAMHSA'S NATIONAL HELPLINE:
SAMHSA.GOV/FIND-HELP/NATIONAL-HELPLINE

SAMHSA's National Helpline is a free, confidential, 24/7, 365-day-a-year treatment referral and information service (in English and Spanish) for individuals and families facing mental and/or substance use disorders.

THE TREVOR PROJECT: THETREVORPROJECT.ORG

The Trevor Project is the leading national organization providing crisis intervention and suicide prevention services to lesbian, gay, bisexual, transgender, and questioning (LGBTQ) young people ages 13–24.

ACKNOWLEDGMENTS

This is my thirteenth novel, and it was a rough one to execute. Thanks to my family and friends who supported me during what was my own personal long stretch of bad days while writing this novel.

As always, great thanks goes to my agent, Adriann Ranta Zurhellen, who read a query from an aspiring author a decade ago and thought she seemed like an okay writer. My editor, Ben Rosenthal, has been a pivotal point of support for me throughout my career. This is our ninth book together, and I'm still combing for the comments in my edit letters for the moments when I make him laugh.

The team at Katherine Tegen Books has always come through for me, from the art department to marketing, to school and library. It's the best imprint to be a part of, and I count myself incredibly lucky to have been with them for so long.

Lastly, greatest thanks, respect, and support to all the educators, librarians, and booksellers operating on the front lines during the current onslaught of book banning. They take the brunt of the charge, and books like mine are available to read because of the personal and professional risks that they take.

Solidarity, my friends.

Mindy